Hard Winter
The Novel

Hard Winter
The Novel

by
Neil Davies

Omnium Gatherum
Los Angeles

For Cathy, Jonathan and Rhianne

CHAPTER 1

My name is Norman Leonard and at one time I lived in Liverpool, North West England, with my wife Chrissy. We were among the stubborn few that stayed. The speed of the advancing ice had taken everyone by surprise and the edge of the glacier had already reached the ruins of the Forth Road Bridge, the old one, not the narrow one-lane nightmare they threw up some years back when a heavy ice storm finally snapped the suspension cables. Before long, the glacier would rumble its ponderous path down into England and pretty soon Cumbria would become as uninhabitable as Scotland had been for the last five years.

On the morning of the 18th December 2118, however, I thought we still had time to talk, to plan for our future. I was wrong. Funny how that date is forever burned into my memory. 18 December, Eighteen-Twelve, like the Overture. The year Two-One-One-Eight. Sounds more dramatic that way don't you think? More apocalyptic. That's a good word for it. Apocalyptic.

I wasn't the first to be proved wrong by the ice. Way back in 2062 the nuclear winter after the oil trouble had hurried things along, forcing governments and scientists worldwide to alter their forecasts, their strategies. They've been getting it wrong ever since. Even now, more than fifty years later, I've heard the snowfall in the Sahara is still radioactive.

Chrissy and I had made a nest near the River Mersey out of bits of garbage scavenged from looted buildings, close to the Liver Building. The massive Liver Birds hung off their rooftop perch, precariously dangling over the street below. For a brief time we lived in the building itself, but then the gangs moved in, selling drugs in return for possessions. Cash was worthless in our post-exodus city.

Our nest, a deserted, below pavement level coffee shop called, if I read the broken sign correctly, Café Parisienne, was not as warm or secure as our deserted office in the Liver Building had been, but we were neither strong enough nor stupid enough to argue when the gangs moved in.

8:30 in the morning. Wrapped in layers of split and damaged jackets rescued from clothes shops that looters hadn't stripped bare, I dragged my legs through knee-high snow.

We'd been lucky to find enough clothing to keep us both reasonably protected from the bitter weather. When most of the population of the North of England began their migration south, back in 2110, they took whatever they could with them, whether it was theirs or not. That's the nature of the beast, the nature of man, selfish and self-serving. I believed it to be a strength, not a weakness, a necessary trait to survive in the new, icy world.

I stood on the old ferry dock and watched the icy sludge slide by. Patches of white ice slipped through, but mostly it was grey slush, sluggish and heavy looking. The air was sharp and clear, one of the few benefits of the evacuation and reducing temperature, the centuries-old odour of industry and modern life frozen and discarded, leaving a crispness previously only found among the peaks of mountain ranges. On the far bank stood the ruins of Birkenhead, where the riots had been particularly bad and the fires that followed were allowed to rage out of control. It had taken weeks for the conflagration to finally die, leaving behind soot-blackened husks of buildings, grotesque sculptures of melted glass and metal and more dead than anyone ever cared to count.

I was still looking at the skeletal silhouette on the opposite bank when I heard a sound, a roar. It was distant, barely audible above the daily blizzard that was building around me, lifting the snow from the ground, stinging my face, but it turned something in my stomach. There was a rawness to it, a primitive power that stripped away my sophisticated modern façade and stirred deep race memories. It scared me. Perhaps it was nothing, just the wind finding a gap to squeeze through, falling ice from the edge of the not so distant glacier? But somehow, I knew these were poor rationalisations and I found that, unwittingly, I now thought of it as a Roar, capitalised, giving it an importance I did not understand but that, nevertheless, felt right.

For a short while I stood there, straining to hear through the growing howl of the wind, the hiss of the snow building into higher and higher drifts against the nearby buildings, the dull rumble of the heavy water in the river. I didn't hear the sound again and I tried to convince myself that it had, after all, been nothing unusual or unnatural. It was just the over-active imagination of a middle-aged man who'd lived too long with sharp fear and dull resignation.

I dragged myself back up Water Street, where there was no longer any distinction between pavement and road. Not that it mattered. The only cars left were those abandoned and frozen beneath the snow, burial mounds of human engineering undulating between rapidly decaying buildings.

The clumsy exit of an addict from the Liver Building as he slipped on snow packed into ice by hundreds of his fellow users startled me. I edged nervously into the deep doorway of the Cunard Building, hoping he hadn't seen me. While I didn't blame people for turning to drugs, that didn't mean I liked or trusted them.

I waited until he rounded the corner and disappeared

out of sight before moving. I'm sure that addicts, like the few others who had stayed in the city, were far too involved in their own problems, their own survival, to worry about anyone else but, nevertheless, they worried me. I knew it didn't make sense. After all, there were much worse things in the world than someone high on drugs.

Chrissy was boiling snow in a pan when I got back to our nest. The fire of scavenged wood blazed brightly, ironically in an emptied-out central heating boiler we'd found in the back room of the café. The crackling wood, the drifting sparks, the smell of wood-smoke was comforting, welcoming and warm. Well, never *truly* warm, but it seemed that way to me. The draughts rolling down the steps and through more holes and gaps than I cared to count ensured it was always on the edge of freezing, although they did also provide ventilation for the smoke. Every cloud, as they say.

I'd cleared the steps before heading to the river that morning, but already they were covered with snow and I trod cautiously as I descended. Out of habit I flicked the light switch on and, even after so long without electricity, was momentarily surprised when the café remained dark.

In reality the cutting of the power hadn't really made that much of a difference. There had been no TV or radio for some time. The streetlamps had broken long before, and once the bulb in your own light blew where would you get a replacement? Any that hadn't been looted had been crushed under foot in the rush to leave. If I'd known more about electricity, about DIY, about anything really, I might have been able to do something, make something, but I worked as a clerk in a solicitor's office and paid other people to do my manual work. I preferred to be ignorant rather than make an effort. I have a lot of regrets about my life before the freeze. I guess we all do.

"Any more ice in the river this morning?"

Chrissy looked up and smiled as she spoke and, as always, I felt immensely grateful that she was with me. In so many ways she was my opposite, seeing the good in people where I only saw the bad, always finding something to smile about. Her cheerfulness lifted my natural scowl and eased the worry lines on my forehead. Sometimes I felt that Chrissy was all that kept me from becoming one of the many suicides we had seen as the cold tightened its grip on the city.

"Maybe a little more, but nothing to worry about. There's still time before we have to move. What's for breakfast?"

Chrissy lifted the stick she used for stirring from the pan. Limp, unidentified leaves dripped from the end, dug out from the snow further along the river. Trial and error, and several days of stomach cramps and sickness, meant we were good at recognising edible from poisonous but neither of us could give a name to the plants we ate.

"Last night's soup."

"At least it's hot."

I walked to her and put my arm briefly around her waist, barely able to reach though she had never been fat. The reason was simple and practical. We both dressed in several layers of clothes, some our own, most left behind by others. Chrissy's outer coat, a big fur-lined monstrosity (morals be damned, it was too cold), I'd stripped off the frozen body of an old woman I found while digging through a drift looking for wood. I never told Chrissy that, of course. She thought I'd found it in an abandoned shop and I wasn't about to tell her otherwise.

With all those layers of clothes, we looked like two sumo wrestlers, but I still thought Chrissy was the most beautiful woman I'd ever seen. It took more than shapeless clothes to hide that. Not that there'd been any sex since the cold really settled in. We'd had a healthy enough sex life before, but freezing temperatures, constant fear and a reluctance to allow any skin beyond the bare essentials to feel the sting of the icy air were very effective anaphrodisiacs. We loved each other. Sex just wasn't an issue anymore.

We hadn't thrown off everything from our life before the freeze began. After all, we weren't savages. It was true that we had no bath or shower, but we scrubbed our hands and faces as best we could with hot melted snow each morning and night. No doubt we smelled, both we and our unchanging clothes, but I can't say we noticed it.

"I was looking over at Birkenhead," I said, easing myself down onto an old rug we'd dragged from the remains of a market stall. "It's sad to see so little left of the place."

"They should never have rioted. If only they hadn't been so impatient."

I sighed. This was one of the few subjects where Chrissy and I disagreed. Most of the major towns and cities had riots, not just Birkenhead, but Chrissy, true to her nature, believed people had been too hasty, that they should have trusted our government more.

"They would have sent help if people had waited. They wouldn't have left people stranded."

"But Chrissy, they sent army units to evacuate the people they deemed important: local politicians, judges, policemen, scientists. The rest of us were left to face the cold."

"They advised people to leave. Of course, they took the people they needed to keep the government going, otherwise there'd be anarchy."

"There *is* anarchy! They abandoned us, cut off the power a week after the evacuation was announced, stopped supply trucks getting through because they considered it a waste of resources. They left people to die."

"The government wouldn't just leave us..."

"We don't have a government anymore, at least not any kind of democratic one. All we've got is a small group of people hiding away somewhere who are determined to survive and flourish while the rest of us freeze and starve. No wonder people rioted."

"I'm sorry Norman but I just don't believe that. The

government is doing the best it can and, as soon as it's possible, they'll send help for us. People were being unreasonable. Expecting more than was possible. There should never have been any riots."

"Perhaps you're right," I conceded, unwilling to prolong the argument. It was something we would never agree on. Chrissy was far too nice and generous a person to believe the worst of others. "Maybe they'll send help as soon as it's possible."

"Of course they will. Everyone just needs to be patient."

I smiled. There wasn't much else I could do in the face of such optimistic faith in others.

Fortunately, and despite her trusting nature, Chrissy was not naive. When the riots had hit Liverpool, we hid ourselves away, avoiding the mobs, the looters as best we could, delaying our own evacuation to avoid the crush of the crowds. We heard by word of mouth how thousands died during that time, so I believe we made the right choice.

I decided not to tell Chrissy about The Roar. I was probably making more out of it than necessary anyway. It was just my imagination and I didn't want her worrying about something that was probably nothing. What difference would it make if I told her?

"How long are we going to stay here?" she asked, moving the conversation deftly away from unpleasant memories.

"We're safe; we have food," I glanced at the boiling pot, "sort of. We don't freeze. I don't think we should risk travelling just yet."

"But sooner or later the glacier will reach us. We can't stay then."

"It's a big risk going out there, not knowing where our next shelter or food will come from."

"We've seen groups of people heading out the city before now. We could join with one of them. It'd be safer with a few of us."

"No. Chrissy, you know my feelings on that. How could we trust them? How do we know they wouldn't kill us in the night? I've heard rumours that people have turned to cannibalism."

"Not everyone's evil, Norman. We're not the only good people left."

I said nothing, not willing to risk our lives on the goodness or otherwise of strangers. If I was honest with myself, I wasn't so sure I wouldn't do exactly the same to any strangers who joined us. 'Dog eat dog' was probably more literally true now than it had ever been.

I couldn't help wishing Chrissy was more realistic about the likely nature of other survivors.

CHAPTER 2

We heard the sound first, a great roaring, thundering express train of a sound, deafening and painful.

"What the hell is that?" Chrissy called, an edge of panic creeping into her soft voice.

I'd been shovelling the freshly fallen snow away from our doorway and stood, shovel poised above the thick drift, staring towards the river.

"I don't know." I had to shout to hear myself above the noise, growing louder and deeper with each second. I felt panic clench in my chest.

Dropping the shovel, I grabbed Chrissy's hand.

"Oh my God!"

A great rising, rushing wall of slush and ice poured over the banks of the Mersey, rising above the tops of all but the highest buildings. It seemed unreal, the creation of a CGI artist in an office somewhere in Hollywood, too solid to be made of the same stuff I watched moving past me every morning, too tall to be the flat, lazy water that filled the river.

We stared, open mouthed, as it hit the Liver Building, the impact shaking the ground beneath our feet. Above the roar of the water, we heard windows smash, the wood of the great doors cracking, torn from the brick surrounding them. Crashing over the rooftop, the wave lifted the Liver Birds from their perch and tossed them on the angry, spitting surface of the water. We stood, unable to move, our feet frozen by fear as the river emptied into the surrounding streets, crossing The Strand in seconds, blocks of ice gouging a path, sludge and debris and water rumbling between buildings that shook and splintered in its wake.

By the time we ran, both of us shouting, screaming, still holding hands, we were already splashing through the edge of the approaching disaster. Within seconds, the swirling waters snatched our feet from under us, and Chrissy's fingers were dragged from mine.

"Chrissy!"

I clawed against the flow of rushing water, desperately trying to drag myself forward, spitting out mouthfuls of the river, swallowing more, reaching in hope for the hand that was no longer there. Through stinging, blurred eyes, I watched the bundle of clothes bouncing away from me, impossibly distant, ruthlessly tossed and battered by the fury of the flood. It barely seemed possible. That couldn't be my Chrissy, lost among the littering of wreckage from the waterfront. She was my life. We were meant to be together forever, not ripped apart by an impossible wave. Any minute now, she would grab my hand and we'd swim to safety. She *had* to!

I cried out, screaming my despair, my loss, into the smothering roar of the water still flooding the city. In that moment, that outpouring of anger and grief, I accepted the impossible, that Chrissy had truly gone, torn out of my life by the uncaring, brutal power of the river. I felt my will to live drain from me. There no longer seemed any reason to fight.

The wall loomed ahead of me. I knew the current was driving me towards it, intent on destroying me as it had Chrissy. I closed my eyes, accepting the approach of death because I had nothing left to live for. The constant roar of the river grew muffled, fading behind the sound of my own blood rushing through my body. Time seemed irrelevant, an inconvenience that carried me forward with casual malice. I expected no white light, no tunnel, no loved ones waiting for me. Death was the end, and without Chrissy that was all I desired. An end.

There was crushing impact, intense pain, then nothing.

CHAPTER 3

I guess I was lucky I didn't drown, or smother in the thick, black, icy mud that the river left behind in its slow withdrawal back within its banks.

I didn't feel lucky.

When I regained consciousness, my head and ribs winning the battle with the rest of my body for sharp, almost unbearable pain, my first thought was Chrissy. Chrissy, pulled away from me by the merciless power of the water. Chrissy, lost somewhere, maybe injured, calling for me and I wasn't there for her. Chrissy, beautiful, wonderful Chrissy, quite probably lying in the mud, dead!

My scream of anguish, of pain and loss, echoed through the empty Liverpool streets. There was no shame or embarrassment in that shout, that bellow of emotion. I had lost the woman I loved. Nothing I'd ever felt compared to the agony, the gut-wrenching loss of that moment.

I cried. I sat there in the middle of a street I didn't recognise, not knowing how far the wave had carried me, and cried.

How could I go on? Why should I go on?

Knowing that Chrissy would be there alongside me when I woke was often the only thought that made the black, freezing nights bearable. When I stood on the ferry dock seemingly alone, I always knew she was waiting for me back at the café. Now, for the first time in my life, I was truly alone. What could possibly make such loneliness worth suffering? What was my life worth without Chrissy?

I feared the answer was 'nothing'.

I've no idea what time it was, nor do I know how long I was helpless with grief, racked with sobbing, but darkness had fallen, when I finally regained enough control to start thinking with some semblance of clarity.

I said earlier that I guess I was lucky. I didn't realise at the time just how lucky I was. The floodwater, despite its power, had left me more or less fully clothed. I'd lost a layer or two, perhaps, both gloves and my woolly hat, but the majority of my body was relatively warm, if wet. Nevertheless, I had problems.

As I lay unconscious in the mud, and for most of the time I'd sat there awake and crying, my right hand had remained buried, covered with thick, icy sludge. I couldn't feel my fingers. I felt physically sick when I looked and saw the ends had turned black, the skin beginning to peel, hard slivers curling away from the pink pulp beneath.

Frostbite!

I didn't know a lot about frostbite, but the little I knew knotted my stomach. If I hadn't been so worn out, so exhausted, I think I would have panicked, but that required energy I just did not have.

I needed to find somewhere to rest, to sleep if possible. Sharp stabbing pains from my ribs dragged an involuntary shout from me as I pushed myself to my feet. I staggered, dizzy, my head pounding, and struggled towards the nearest buildings, holding my frostbitten hand at the wrist as if that would somehow stop the condition from spreading.

A McDonalds finally gave me the shelter I needed. The interior of the fast-food restaurant was little more than wreckage, thick with mud, looking and smelling evil enough to keep me out. But the broken glass of the doorway and the cracked frame provided some cover from the night wind that grew stronger as the last light of the sun bled into the cold, wet, shining sludge of the streets.

I gave little thought to what might have caused the

wave. Perhaps parts of the glacier cracked and fell into the water, causing an effect like throwing a pebble into a pond? Perhaps it was an accumulation of factors, of weather and freeze and god knows what else. Perhaps there was no natural cause at all. It didn't really seem important. What was important was the devastation it had brought to the city and to my life.

Sleep was fitful and unsatisfying as I tried to find some warmth, some comfort, curled up inside what remained of the restaurant entrance. At some point in the middle of the bitter night, my right arm began to ache, dull at first then growing sharp and all but unbearable. I was sweating, despite the wind-blown snow rising in drifts at my back. My face burned. My lips were dry and cracking as I opened my mouth, a low moan pushing past my swollen tongue. Although my arm stabbed pain through me, my whole body ached, every muscle, every joint. Only the years of surviving the freeze and a now instinctive fear of hypothermia stopped me from ripping my coats off, desperate to cool my boiling skin. I had enough sense left to know I was sick, very sick.

The frostbite. It had to be. What else could cause this pain, this illness? I had no doubt. My frostbitten fingers were spreading their blackness through my body. It was almost tangible, a solid ball of dark decay rolling up my arm, across my shoulders. Eventually it would reach my heart, and I would die.

Unless I stopped it first.

Driven by panic, by pain and fever, I pushed at the interior door, trying to force it against the mud that was quickly solidifying behind it. I had to get inside. Inside, I would find what I needed. I heaved my whole weight against the glass. A crack snapped and lengthened. The door edged slightly inwards. Eyes blurred with sweat, right arm and shoulder throbbing, chest labouring, I threw myself once more against the door. Pain shot through me, panicking me even further.

The frame shifted, but not enough. Then the crack in the glass spread, grew, multiplied. The pane of glass shattered.

I fell inwards, crying out as shards of glass, jutting teeth-like from the frame, ripped at my layers of clothing. One less layer and the glass would have cut me. The icy mud, although hardening, gave enough under my weight to cushion the fall, saving me from adding broken arms and legs to my catalogue of injuries. Nevertheless, the agony that shot from my ribs, my chest, tore a growl of pain from me quite unlike anything I had heard from my lips before. The sound was animal, desperate, pitiful. I had almost certainly broken some ribs when the flood had slammed me into the wall, but for now they would have to look after themselves.

Dragging myself to my feet with the help of tipped-over tables, I staggered into the dark mess, tripping over chair legs that projected at all angles from the mud. The foul mix of swamp and decaying food made me gag. I barely held back the vomit that rose in my throat. At least with the extreme cold there were no flies buzzing about.

I tried to dig my way around the counter, but too much mud had piled against the walls, and I wasn't about to attempt to climb over. The broken remains of drink dispensers and cash registers looked to be painful obstacles. Fortunately, the passage of the flood through the main restaurant area had punched large holes into the wood panelling at the front of the counter. Gouging more wounds into my outer layer of clothing, I was able to slowly, painfully crawl through.

Feeling light-headed and curiously detached, I ransacked the kitchen, racing against what I was certain was approaching unconsciousness and death. I found what I needed half buried in the mud coating the sink bowl. A knife. Long, sharp, serrated. I've no idea what it would originally have been used to cut, but it was perfect for my needs.

There are moments when you can't give yourself time to think, to reconsider or question your actions. I had known what I needed to do when I broke in. If I hesitated now, I would probably chicken out.

I slammed my right hand down onto the kitchen counter, blackened fingers splayed, the knife clutched tightly in my left fist. Both the counter and the blade were thick with mud.

I lay the serrated blade across the base of my fingers, closed my eyes, and began to saw.

Perhaps I was too cold, too numb, too in shock to truly feel it, but the pain, sharp and burning as it was, was not as strong as I'd feared. It was barely more intense than the ache it was trying to remove.

Blood spurted, spluttered from the ragged wounds as I pulled and pushed, too afraid to stop. I cried. I screamed. As the metal teeth scratched across the bone I almost lost my conviction, but I gripped the knife tighter, pulled and pushed harder and the teeth dug into the bone and then through it.

The blade reached the kitchen counter with an oddly satisfying chunk, reminding me of Chrissy chopping carrots in our own kitchen before the freeze.

Sobbing from memories more than pain, I stared down at the black, dead things that had once been my fingers, floating in the dark, swirling mixture of blood and mud. I saw my thumb, black and decaying, and lifted the knife once more.

Just one more to do.

I retained enough common sense to make unhygienic but effective use of the icy mud to help stop the bleeding and then bandaged my hand with towel from a roll high enough on the wall to have avoided the floodwater.

A heavy food preparation unit remained upright and, despite being half buried, was only slightly cracked and a little unstable. Quickly I swept the debris off the surface and climbed up. At least I was out of the mud. I might be able to sleep without waking up face down and unable to breathe.

Lying on my side, curled up into an infantile, foetal ball, I closed heavy eyelids and tried to imagine the pain in my body receding. I slept or perhaps passed out would be a more accurate description.

At some point in the night I heard, or dreamed I heard, The Roar. It sounded closer.

CHAPTER 4

I slept a lot for the next two days, or at least I think it was two days. Difficult to keep track of time when you're in and out of fever, racked with pain apparently from every inch of your body and generally delirious.

The first time I remember waking I heard shuffling, someone moving through the restaurant. My sight was blurred, impossible to focus, but I saw a figure approach me, wrapped in clothes that were familiar, wonderfully, ecstatically familiar.

The hood fell back. The hat pulled off. Even with my tear-filled eyes, I knew who it was. Chrissy! Magically alive and miraculously here with me, the two of us together once more.

"Chrissy!"

My voice broke, my raw throat straining to push out the words I needed to say.

"Chrissy, I'm so sorry for leaving you. I couldn't reach you. I tried, I really tried."

Coughing racked my body, bloody phlegm spat out, crimson against the dark mud.

"I love you so much Chrissy. I need you. I didn't know how I would survive without you."

She said nothing, simply stood looking down at me. I began to fear she might hate me for failing to hold on to her in the flood.

"Chrissy? Can you forgive me? We're together again now. Nothing will separate us ever again."

Another coughing fit, dry heaving. My throat burning;

my mouth tasting bloody.

I reached my mutilated hand towards her and tried once more to focus. But the blurring was worse. Her face and body smeared across my vision, darkening, dissolving.

"Chrissy."

I managed to cry out once more, a feeble, pitiful sound, as she became nothing but broken kitchen equipment and dark shadows.

She was gone. Worse, she had never been there. She never *would* be there again.

I suffered the momentary joy and terrible loss several more times until even the vaguest hope died. Chrissy was never coming back. I had lost her forever.

As the fever began to break, I was able to draw on memories to replace the cruel visions.

Some of the time I remembered the good things; riding the ferry from Liverpool over to Woodside, driving into Wales to stroll along the pier at Llandudno, watching a show at the Liverpool Stadium, shopping, stopping for coffee, talking, laughing. Making love in hotel rooms because, somehow, that always seemed more romantic than at home. Asking her to marry me after just one week of knowing her, because I was *that* sure. But always, before long, more recent memories would shoulder their way in, forcing me to face a reality I would rather forget.

I had nightmares about watching that bundle of clothes dragged mercilessly along by the raging current, and in the nightmares I could see Chrissy's face, her mouth open, screaming, her eyes glaring at me with shock and, yes, hatred. Hatred that I was not swimming after her, not rescuing her. Then her screams would turn to abuse, spat my way with red-faced vitriol. Most times the nightmare would end there, with my wife, my loving, caring, intelligent wife reduced to a swearing, cursing, hate-filled animal. But that second night, with a wet sun smearing watery light behind the Radio City tower and the night gradually giving way to day, the nightmare ended with a huge, dark shadow darting beneath the surface of the water, a shadow that rose in an explosion of slush and ice behind Chrissy. Although I was looking straight at it, the shape was indistinct, like something on the periphery of vision. Brief, fleeting, a mountain of darkness framed by splashing floodwater, a glint of impossibly huge and sharp teeth, and then it crashed down onto Chrissy, seemed to suck water after it in a whirlpool of death, and was gone.

I sat, wide-eyed, staring out the smeared, broken glass frontage of McDonalds towards the River Mersey. I couldn't see it, couldn't hear it, but I knew it was there. That was enough to plant a solid seed of fear in my soul.

CHAPTER 5

An elderly couple, in their seventies at least, walked by the front of the restaurant. Actually, it was more of a stroll than a walk, for all the world as if they were out for a Sunday afternoon wander around the city. The sight was so incongruous, so ridiculous, that I laughed, and that laughter seemed to break the melancholy that had settled over me since the impromptu surgery on my hand and the cruel visions of Chrissy.

They were quite probably insane, wandering around like that, and I really didn't want to get caught up in whatever fantasy world they had created around themselves. I might feel obliged to stay and help them in some way, and with Chrissy gone, the only person I wanted to look after was me.

Selfish, yes, but sensible too. When there was the two of us, we helped look after each other. Now there was just me, I only *had* me, and I decided I wanted to live. As hard as that would be without Chrissy, seeing something as normal as an elderly couple taking a stroll made me realise that I was not ready to give up just yet. Perhaps it was some base animal instinct for survival or just another facet of my character that others might find self-centred, perhaps even arrogant. I *deserved* to live. I was *going* to live. Yes, it might have been animal instinct, unworthy of the so-called higher social morality some humans aspired to, but that's what we were. Animals. There was no longer any place for the airs and graces, the social niceties, in our brutal, frozen world. Only the animals would survive, and

I would be among them.

After scavenging what I could from the kitchen, which was very little, I carefully stepped out onto the street, making sure there was no one else around, elderly couple or otherwise. In its bandage my hand throbbed, but I had grown used to it over the last few days, had even begun to get used to using my left hand for everything, so I paid it little attention as I headed away from the river.

My ribs still stabbed pain through me, and my feet, cold and blistered, throbbed. I drew a gasp with almost every step, but I needed to get away from the river. I wasn't thinking logically and had no destination in mind, but the nightmare still haunted my waking thoughts, and the dark shape that had been so hard to see in the dream felt all too possible a threat even in daylight. Did I really believe there was some kind of sea monster in the River Mersey? I didn't honestly know, but I *did* know that I wasn't going to stay and find out.

Snow settled and drifted over the mud, mud that had a hardened crust on the surface that if stepped on too hard would give way. Progress was slow and tiring. It wasn't long before my legs felt almost too heavy to lift. Accumulated mud and snow had, indeed, weighed them down, but it was my muscles that were giving way. I could no longer lift my feet out of the holes in the snow but rather had to drag them until I was almost crawling on the packed surface. Exhaustion broke my resolve to stay clear of any other survivors.

I heard them before I saw them, an impossibly jolly, busy sound of people talking, laughing. Starved and exhausted I dragged myself toward the noise and found, to my despair, that I had hopelessly lost my sense of direction in the snow-hidden streets.

Before me lay the road sloping down to the Kingsway tunnel. It ran under the River Mersey to the Wirral Peninsula. Instead of moving away from the river, I had somehow circled around back towards it.

Around the mouth of the tunnel and, as far as I could see, inside the dark unlit tunnel itself, makeshift tents, lean-tos and other self-constructed shelters spread across the road, warm crackling fires dotted between them. Most of all, there were people, nearly all of them dressed similarly to myself, in layers of no-doubt borrowed or stolen coats. Nearer the fires, some had braved the cold, removed all but the thinnest of overcoats and warmed gloveless hands before the flames. There were some older people there, and I wondered if the two I had seen outside McDonalds had strayed from this camp. I saw a few teenagers, but most were undoubtedly in their middle years. It had become a typical frozen city demographic as those older and younger family members who did not evacuate died under the extreme climate that had settled over the country.

But it was not the range of ages that surprised me, rather the simple fact that there were so many people of *any* age. My own experience was that those who remained in the city did so in solitude or with one or two close friends and partners. This was something new to me. Survivors had gathered here and made a camp, settled in against the deepening winter as though it would one day pass. As though they believed that summer would come again.

They were stupid, ignorant, possibly dangerous people but I was tired, hungry and could go no further. I collapsed at the edge of the camp and, as unconsciousness smothered me, saw people hurrying towards me.

CHAPTER 6

"We liberated most of the bedding from city centre furniture shops, gave it a good clean and shared it out. Of course, it's difficult to *keep* things clean, but we try."

Harry spoke like that. *Liberated.* Not the word I'd have chosen, but then Harry was an educated man, more educated than me certainly. In the past I'd disliked people who paraded their education, perhaps I felt in some way inferior, but the way Harry spoke was so natural, so unaffected, that it was impossible to take offence. Harry was one of those instantly likeable people, and there aren't many of those around.

"I'd have thought the shops would have all been looted."

"Many had been," nodded Harry. "But most of the looters hadn't bothered to break into the storerooms. They just took what was on display. We appropriated some from the local pubs, clubs and offices as well, but I personally find it a little distasteful, knowing people have used it before, probably not even washed it before leaving. But we all have to make sacrifices in our brave new world."

I didn't personally consider sleeping on used bedding and sitting on used furniture much of a sacrifice, but I said nothing.

Harry had volunteered to look after me, following my collapse at the edge of the camp, and the tent we now shared was his home. To say it was 'cosy' overestimated its size. Grubby green canvas, held aloft by worryingly narrow poles at front and back, bowed over our heads and at our backs, weighed down by the daily snow that gathered as quickly as it was cleared. It was the sort of tent children put up in the back garden, but I wasn't complaining. It gave some shelter from the daily blizzards, and the sacking on the floor and two thick duvets made for a comfort I'd not felt for some time. The near constant press of canvas at my back or on the top of my head was a small price to pay for the relative comfort and security it accorded, however temporary.

"You all seem quite settled here. No plans to move on?"

"This is our new home, our place in the sun, so to speak. Why would we move? Oh, eventually I think we'll expand, but this is a good base to start from and to wait it out."

Wait it out. Wait what out? Did they think all this was just going to disappear one day and everything would return to normal?

They were foolish to do anything but move south, away from the encroaching glacier and whatever else came with it, but I kept my mouth shut. They were happy to give me shelter, food and drink and I was not about to jeopardize that by threatening the comfort zone they had created about themselves.

"Did I tell you I was a history tutor over at Birkenhead Sixth Form College?"

I smiled, for once feeling generous enough towards my fellow man to show patience.

"You had mentioned it, yes."

"That was back before they closed everything down of course. Before the weather deteriorated."

He lifted a hand to his thick-rimmed glasses, wiping the one lens that remained, squinting out from behind them to the point where I wondered why he bothered wearing them at all.

"Were you over there when the riots began?"

"No. I'd left by then."

That was as much as Harry would ever say about the riots. He busied himself folding the corner of the duvet he sat on, folding and unfolding repeatedly, nervously.

The riots were not the only subject Harry refused to talk about. Any attempt to engage him in conversation about the state of the country, what the government was doing, or not doing as the case may be, or the many dangers existing in the wider world beyond the camp failed. He would talk about the camp, the weather and anything to do with his old job as a tutor and that was all.

I liked Harry, it was hard not to given the unconditional kindness he had shown me, but his limited conversation made him incredibly *dull* company. Then, two or three days into my stay, with my head still pounding and my hand aching, Harry took me totally by surprise.

Without any preamble, he put down the water-damaged old paperback he often read, carefully marking his place with a scrap of paper, and said, "Jenny got lung cancer in her thirties. We never understood that. Neither of us had ever smoked, but we had to accept the diagnosis, however strange and unfair it seemed."

It was so unlike Harry to talk of such a thing that it took me a moment to think it through.

"Jenny. Your wife?"

Harry smiled, his eyes closing, memories no doubt rushing through his mind.

"Yes, my wife." He sighed and opened his eyes, the dim candlelight catching on the first tears trickling down his cheek. "She was a strong woman. Hung on for almost three years before it got too much. She died in her sleep, peacefully. I guess I should be grateful for that. I *am* grateful she died before the freeze happened."

His voice, already quiet, dropped to a whisper and he stared down at his interlaced fingers as if in prayer.

"I wouldn't have liked her to suffer this."

I didn't know what to say to that, it made no sense. Surely, he wished his wife were here with him. To keep him company, to share his life, such as it was. God knows I wished Chrissy were still with *me*.

I chose to ignore it, avoiding any possible confrontation,

any disagreement with this man who was helping nurse me back to something like full strength. After all, he had re-dressed my right hand without making any comment about the roughly amputated fingers. The least I could do was allow him his own personal craziness without challenge. Harry's sudden unexpected openness about his wife broke some unseen barrier in my own mind. Without truly being aware of what I was saying, or why, I began to tell him about Chrissy, about our life together before and after the freeze.

"She was clever, you know. Not like me. I mean, I didn't know her at school, we went to different ones, but she told me later how she was in the top group in nearly all her subjects. The only one she struggled in was languages. I was never much good at languages myself. But then, I wasn't much good at anything else either."

I studied the floor, my feet, my hands, the bandaged right cradled in the left, vaguely aware that I was rambling with little sense of coherence.

"Our first meeting was in a pub, The Crown, down on the dock road in Bootle. Back then there were still container ships and ferries coming in daily, and The Crown, like most of the pubs round there, was full of lads from the ships with cash in their pockets, looking for some fun with the local girls. I remember she was wearing this white blouse and blue jeans. I genuinely couldn't take my eyes off her. I walked her home, didn't even get a goodnight kiss, but I remember being so happy. Silly really."

I looked up at Harry, expecting him to be laughing or just ignoring me. Instead, his eyes were full of compassion and his smile understanding, encouraging me to continue.

"It was probably only a couple of weeks later that the first ice-breaker put into port and we started hearing stories about freak icebergs drifting dangerously close to the shipping lanes. Funny how looking back you can see things starting to change.

"We got married a year or so later. By then she was

working at a local school as a classroom helper. It was way below her abilities, but jobs were hard to come by and, anyway, she loved being around kids. Never wanted any herself, and neither did I, for that matter, but she loved being around other people's. With both of us working, we managed to get a mortgage on a terraced house out in Fazakerley, and that's pretty much it."

My voice creaked and strained with grief, with emotions I had rarely displayed to anyone other than Chrissy.

I hesitated then, faltering over the next important piece of my story, how my life had been destroyed. Harry sat patiently, quietly, giving me the time I needed. I'm sure he understood just how difficult this was for me.

I cried when I told him about the wave, about losing grip of Chrissy's hand, about how helpless I was as the only person I had ever truly cared about was torn from me, ripped not only from my hands but from my life. I still wondered if I was capable of surviving without her.

Harry laid a hand on my shoulder, a simple gesture of caring that I appreciated more than I could say as fresh sobs shook my body. I'd never allowed myself to lose so much control in front of another person before and it felt both exhausting and strangely liberating.

CHAPTER 7

After several days, I felt able to walk about the camp a little.

The people were friendly and trusting, much more trusting than I would have been in their position. Not only had they allowed me to share one of their tents but someone had given me a woollen glove for my unbandaged hand, salmon pink in colour but I was in no position to complain. They smiled at me as I walked among them and no one showed any concern at a stranger wandering their camp.

"Are you feeling better now?"

The question came from an old woman who sat at one of the many small fires. She looked up briefly from her knitting as she spoke and smiled. Her weather-worn face creased with the movement, crow's feet at her eyes stretching into laughter lines.

"Yes, erm..." I stuttered over the words, unprepared for any actual conversation. "Yes, much better, thank you."

I noted the colour of the wool and raised my gloved hand.

"Did you make this?"

She didn't even glance upwards. "Yes, I thought you might need it."

"Thank you." I felt I should say more, but even showing that much gratitude to a stranger was uncomfortable for me. It was not something I was proud of but kindness and generosity had been in short supply since the freeze.

I hesitated before moving on, unsure whether more was expected of me, but as she continued knitting, I turned and walked further into the camp, towards the twin mouths of the Mersey Tunnel.

At the entrance leading under the river to the Wirral there were several men constructing a wooden barrier, a thick wall with one small doorway. The structure was a patchwork of old floorboards, disused doors, planks torn from staircases and packing cases, any wood they had been able to scavenge. It was ugly but seemed solid.

I interrupted a man sawing a plank to size. Like everyone else in the camp he seemed happy to smile and talk to me, even though he had to stop his work to do so.

"It's impressive," I said, feeling a compliment was a good way to open the conversation. "What's it for exactly?"

If the directness of my question offended him, he didn't show it. He simply brushed a thick fringe of hair out of his eyes and looked with pride at the nearly completed wall.

"If the weather gets too bad, or we get another flood, we can shelter in the tunnel. Once the door is closed behind us, we'll be safe."

I opened my mouth to speak but found there was nothing I could say in the face of such simple optimism. Had they not seen the power of the last flood? Did they have no concept of the forces they faced? I could not imagine that a wooden barrier, however thick, however well-constructed, would hold up for long. And once the water broke through into the darkness of the tunnel, no one had a hope of getting out alive.

"I'll let you get back to work then."

"No problem. Stop by again any time."

The sound of his sawing mingled with others who sawed and hammered as I stepped over the dented but still standing crash barrier that divided the two roadways. Their effort was futile, a waste, but who was I to say anything? This was their chosen path and they obviously felt it to be right. Why should I try to persuade them otherwise? I had no intention of staying in the camp that long anyway.

The other mouth of the tunnel, where traffic would roar

through into Liverpool, had no barrier. Instead, bags and boxes of supplies were piled up inside, going back at least twenty feet. They would not be protected against another flood, but they were sheltered from the worst of the blizzards that blew ferociously most days.

As though the mere thought of it had acted as some kind of telepathic catalyst, the snow chose that moment to start falling. By the time I oriented myself and headed back towards Harry's tent, the wind was rising, and I knew another blizzard was on its way.

The rest of the camp, tents, ramshackle structures, clotheslines heavy with wet clothes, fires surrounded by people cooking or just warming themselves straddling the lanes of the approach roads, reminded me of old television news reports from refugee camps around the world. Yet there was no sense of panic, and little sense of deprivation. These people had settled into a pattern of survival and had become comfortable with it. I felt that a large part of that pattern was the denial of the reality facing them, but there was no doubt that, at the moment at least, they were as content as anyone could be. Even the increasing strength of the wind and the heavy snow did not seem to dampen their general good nature and optimistic outlook. I was the only one hurrying to reach shelter.

As I reached the tent, I noticed, with some surprise, a group of perhaps five or so men and women heading up the long, curving road away from the tunnel. I hadn't expected to see anyone leaving the camp. Harry was reading as I pushed my way through the canvas doorway and I wasted no time asking him about the group.

"They'll be a collection team," he said, carefully marking his place in the book before putting it to one side. "Most of us are part of one team or another. Some go out collecting wood for the fires; others scavenge for food. At the camp itself there are teams for food preparation, cleaning and tidying, storage, construction."

Despite my cynicism, I could not help but be impressed.

"You're very organised. Must have taken some doing."

Harry smiled. "We had help getting started."

"Who from?" I was intrigued.

"I've a couple of friends coming over soon. Wait until they get here and then we'll tell you."

I didn't see the point in waiting, but if Harry wanted to play it that way, I could go along with it. I guess it wasn't often any of them got a chance to tell their story to a stranger.

Harry's friends, Martin and Simon, arrived as darkness fell, and the blizzard thankfully eased. The four of us sat around a small fire Harry had built near our tent. We cradled broken mugs of thin, unnamed soup in cold fists like four friends out camping, as though the freeze and the flood had never happened. It was a strangely comforting feeling and I felt guilty at experiencing it without Chrissy.

Martin was a tall, broad man, ex merchant navy, Harry had told me earlier, full of tales of foreign ports and wild adventures with local police and prostitutes. Harry said not many people believed him, but they were happy to listen and laugh along with him. Simon, also tall but slim, came from a local government background. In his own words he was 'low down in the civil service and not destined to rise very far'. Harry told me that what he failed to bring in wild stories of his past, he more than compensated for with a dry wit. Both were open and friendly and good company around a campfire on a cold evening.

"Harry told us about your wife," said Martin soon after we had settled, his voice soft and at odds with his large, bullish frame. "We're very sorry for your loss. You must be finding it so hard."

"Yes," agreed Simon, his voice deep but quiet. "If there's anything we can do to help. Both Martin and myself lost our wives some time ago, like Harry, so we know it's difficult, but you *can* survive it."

I managed to mumble "thank you" as I struggled to hold back the tears. Not for the first time since arriving at the camp, I felt both confused and grateful for people's kindness. It was an uncomfortable mix of emotions and I needed to steer the conversation away from any mention of Chrissy.

"So," I forced a cheeriness into my voice I didn't feel. "Harry says you're going to tell me how you all got so organised."

"Well, most of the early organisation was done by a few women from a local Women's Institute group," said Harry, taking a sip of his soup.

The Women's Institute? I thought he was joking and had to stifle a laugh as I saw the serious look on the faces of Martin and Simon, both of them nodding in agreement. Could he really mean the same group of old and middle-aged women who congregated in church halls all over the country to drink tea, eat cakes, watch slide shows and gossip? I had never had cause before to look beyond this stereotypical image and it was not something that sat comfortably with me. The W.I. would forever be associated with small parish churches, village fetes, coffee mornings and occasional annoying but well-meant interference in local affairs. It was difficult to move away from that ingrained and apparently misinformed opinion.

"This didn't just come together by accident," said Martin. "A lot of hard work went into getting this camp set up."

Harry and Simon nodded. As I looked at the numerous, glowing pockets of warmth spotted about the cold night, painting flickering colour over pale but happy faces, I began to understand what Martin meant and to admire the women at the heart of it all. It could have been no small task to gather disparate survivors together and get them working to a common goal, sharing with each other, putting aside their selfish needs for the sake of the greater good. I wasn't sure I would have been persuaded, but obviously many were.

"They did a good job." I felt they expected me to say something.

"We wouldn't be here if it wasn't for them," said Simon,

his voice softened by a tone that was almost reverential. The others once again nodded in agreement.

To my relief, the conversation moved on to less serious matters after that. We spoke of our past lives, of the daily routines that had developed within the camp to keep it running, and I told them a little about the life Chrissy and I had led before the flood. It was never easy to talk about Chrissy, but they made it as painless as it could be. The co-operation and care for other people demonstrated within the camp as a whole did make me feel a little guilty, I admit, but although my determination to ensure my own survival at any cost was shaken slightly, it did not break. What these people were doing was good and impressive, but it was, in the end, worthless. The glacier would continue on its path. The cold would deepen. Perhaps another wave would roll down the river, and this camp and the people in it would perish.

And then there was that *other*, that nameless something that more and more preyed on my mind. Whether it was the sea monster of my nightmare or something else entirely, I knew there was more than the ice heading our way.

Martin and Simon were regular visitors as the days hurried past, and their continual good humour plus the rest Harry ensured I got was rapidly rebuilding my strength. Before long, I would be ready to leave. It would not be easy to walk away from the camp and the few, but good, friendships I had discovered there, but I knew that I must.

I told no one about The Roar, but I heard it on the eighth night. It was definitely closer this time.

CHAPTER 8

About ten days into my stay Harry asked if I'd like to accompany him, Simon and Martin on a 'little foraging expedition'. It had never occurred to me before then that the three friends would be one of the groups going out from the camp, but perhaps I should have guessed it. Their disparate backgrounds had caused me to wonder at their friendship, but what quicker way to forge bonds between people than to share the same risks and dangers?

I suffered only a moment's hesitation at the prospect of deepening my involvement in the camp, and in the lives of these three friends, before agreeing. My various aches and pains had lessened to just about bearable, and I was ready to do something other than wander idly from tent to tent interrupting other people in their daily tasks.

So, no more than an hour later and wrapped in as many layers of clothing as we could comfortably move in, the college lecturer, civil servant, merchant seaman and solicitor's clerk headed out from the tunnel and trudged up the snow covered road back into Liverpool.

"You know, I always forget how steep this road is," said Harry, turning to me and smiling encouragingly as I struggled to keep up.

"It's not so much the steepness," replied Simon, striding ahead of us. "It's the length. Goes on forever and never lets up."

I said nothing, concentrating on walking and trying to ignore the numerous muscular pains that reminded me how unfit I was.

As we trudged round the long bend, I could see where the tunnel road merged with Scotland Road, one of the major routes through the city. During the evacuation, this road had been gridlocked. Now, like every other pathway through the city, it lay snowbound and deserted, the only vehicles remaining long abandoned and buried beneath heavy drifts. Everywhere I had seen, both before and since the flood, was the same. Frozen, barren, broken and dead.

These thoughts were not helping my already morose mood, and I consciously dragged my attention from the city to my three companions on this expedition.

Both Simon and Martin carried homemade spears. Simon's looked like an old broom handle with a knife strapped to the end. Martin's effort was more organic, whittled from a tree branch, stripped of leaves and smaller branches with a piece of sharpened chipped stone for a blade. I had seen Harry sheath a knife and slide it into his topmost coat pocket. Only I was unarmed. I'm not at all certain I would have been able to use a weapon anyway, with no fingers on my right hand and my left aching with sympathetic pain.

"Expecting trouble?" I asked Harry as we cut off from the road and half crawled up a steep embankment, the drifting snow giving traction that the underlying ice would have denied us.

"Not expecting, no," he replied, breathing as heavily as I was. Both of us struggled to keep up the pace of the other, fitter, two. "One group reported seeing a pack of wild dogs though, so it's best to be safe."

"Dogs? I didn't think there were any animals left in the city."

"No, I've not seen any myself either. I always presumed that any left behind in the evacuations would have starved or frozen to death. But Mary, one of the wood gatherers, is adamant about what her group saw last time out." He paused, adjusting his glasses as they slipped down his nose. "There's no point arguing with them of course. Whatever they *actually* saw, they insist it was dogs, and who knows, maybe they're right?

"Maybe."

"Although," said Harry, chuckling quietly to himself, "I heard a rumour that someone spotted a big cat roaming around a short while ago. You know, tiger, puma, that sort of thing."

"Has there ever been a time when someone *hasn't* insisted they've seen a big cat prowling through the English countryside?"

"There's always a place for the cryptozoologist."

"The what?" Most of the words Harry threw into a conversation I could just about follow, but he had me on that one.

"It's a person who studies non-existent or, perhaps I should say, undiscovered animals, as well as animals outside their natural environment."

"Thank you Professor."

"Sorry." He smiled sheepishly. "Old habits die hard."

"Come on you two!"

The shout came from Martin, already at the top of the embankment with Simon. Harry and I fell silent as we concentrated on pushing ourselves up those last few yards.

I can't speak for Harry, but every muscle in my legs ached and complained at the unfamiliar exercise and I dragged, rather than lifted, my feet for the last few yards, swearing under my breath as the snow began to fall and the rising wind whipped it into a stinging blizzard.

Once over the top we slipped and slithered our way down the lesser incline and over a half-buried, half-collapsed fence into a ghost town. Empty shells of houses stood either side, roofs collapsed under the weight of snow, doors and windows smashed open by looters or, quite possibly, earlier foraging groups from the tunnel camp. The structures provided some small shelter from the weather, but the crumbling desolation gathered shifting shadows and imagined movement on the periphery of vision. Any moment I expected people to emerge from their houses and continue their daily routine as if nothing had ever happened. That most, if not all, were probably long dead did nothing to dispel the irrational conviction and it left me nervous, jumpy and nauseous, my stomach twisting and cramping with fear. This was something I had never experienced among the deserted buildings around the ferry terminal and surrounding streets. People had worked in those buildings, but people had *lived* in these.

The street seemed familiar. No visible road signs remained, nor any visible road for that matter. Nevertheless, I *knew* this place.

The broken end of a white sign jutted from the snow. The first few black letters on the sign, B E V, and the old telephone exchange on my right, confirmed it. Bevington Street.

Chrissy's parents had lived down this road. I still remembered the nerves, the terror, when she'd taken me home to meet them for the first time, and how nice and easygoing they were. Traits their daughter inherited.

The memories hit me hard. Clear images of Chrissy and her parents flashed before my eyes, reminding me, as if I could forget, of the loss I was still struggling to accept. I felt frozen to the spot, wanting to turn and run but unable to. Tears blurred my eyes, trapping wind-blown snowflakes and trickling them over my cheeks. I didn't need to be reminded. My memories were painfully clear and all-to-often forefront in my mind.

"You okay?"

Harry had spotted my distress and stopped, looking concerned.

"My in-laws lived here," I said. "Just wasn't quite ready for it."

Harry nodded, his expression of concern softening to compassion.

"Did they get out before the freeze?"

"They died long before it got that bad," I said. "It's probably just as well. They were old. I doubt they would have survived long."

"You okay to carry on?"

"Sure. You go ahead. I'll catch you up in a moment."

I let Harry get a little way ahead of me before moving again, not wanting him to see the struggle I faced in simply putting one foot in front of the other. No longer did I feel just nauseous, my chest was tightening, a cold fist of dread squeezing, crushing. I knew what lay further down the road and I was not sure how capable I was of facing it.

It was little more than a ruin now. Some sections still stood but it was mostly crumbling walls, empty windows, scattered rubble, the skeletal remains of a building that was once the focal point of the local community. It rose up before us out of the mist of the blizzard. Chrissy's old school.

It was a place that had held strong, happy memories for Chrissy, and, because of that, for me. She had talked of it often and even taken me to see it when we visited her parents. It had already closed by then, but the buildings were still intact, the windows in place. It looked as though it could open up again at a moment's notice if needed. We sneaked in one time, wandering the corridors, stepping into classrooms. Chrissy regaled me with tales of her time there, her friends, the teachers, everything. It made me wish I had gone to the same school and had known her back then. To be honest, I wished I had known her every moment she had been alive. I wish I hadn't wasted one minute of my life without her. And now she was gone, and I was alone.

I couldn't walk any further. I fell to my knees, sinking in the snow halfway up my thighs and sobbed uncontrollably.

I really thought I was stronger than that. I thought I had passed through that first overwhelming sense of grief, but it obviously lay dormant just beneath the surface, needing only the slightest excuse to burst forth and destroy me once again. It was embarrassing, a weakness, but I could do nothing to prevent it.

The others gathered around me as, in broken words

forced out between sobs, I explained the significance of the ruin before us and of my memories. I was ashamed of losing control, but if they felt anything other than sympathy, they did not show it. Instead, they offered words of kindness and understanding. They had each lost their wives and had suffered their own grief. They knew the power of memories.

I had to get away from this place, from anything to do with Chrissy, if I was going to survive. I would never, *could* never, forget her, but I could not afford to be constantly faced with brutal reminders of my life with her. Accepting that she was gone was hard, perhaps impossible, but it would be easier away from the Mersey, away from Liverpool, away from the home we had shared.

"You don't need to come inside Norman," said Martin, his large hand on my shoulder. "We won't be long. We just need to look for anything that may have been left behind."

"Of course." I nodded, trying to smile. "I'm sorry. I'll be okay in a moment."

"Will you be all right out here on your own?" asked Harry.

I looked back up the street, at the deserted homes, the snow-covered gardens, and then back to Harry.

"I think I'd rather come with you."

"Are you sure?"

I nodded, knowing that this was one time when I would feel safer with other people rather than on my own. Ghosts inhabited both the houses behind me and the school in front, but perhaps they would bother me less if I were in company.

At first glance, the long, straight entrance corridor and glass-fronted school office were as I remembered them, but then the filter of memory slipped away and reality forced its ugly truth on me. The overhead light fittings had long since been looted and exposed wiring hung pendulous from the ceiling, forming thin, twisted stalactites. Snow, blown in through the broken double doors, drifted against the walls for almost half the length of the corridor and the glass of the office was shattered. All that remained were jagged shards buried in the frame.

Towards the far end, where there had once been a brightly coloured display wall through a set of locked double doors, the roof had collapsed under the weight of the snow. We clambered over broken, jagged masonry, twisted fronds of steel bars and sharp ice to reach the interior of the school building. There was no longer an upper floor. It had long ago fallen into the ground floor and been covered by snow. Simply walking was treacherous.

"Mind you don't twist your ankle," advised Harry. "It's a long walk back to camp and I doubt we could carry you all the way."

My 'thanks' was heavy with sarcasm but I don't think Harry noticed, concentrating, as he was, on his own slow progress.

Martin and Simon, a little ahead of us, probed the ground with their spears pushing aside rubble. Occasionally, they crouched to pick unidentifiable pieces up before discarding them once again.

"This is hopeless," called Martin, turning back towards Harry and me. "We're not going to find anything here."

Strangely I felt responsible, embarrassed. I had a connection to this place and somehow it seemed like my fault that nothing worth scavenging was left in the ruins. I was about to apologise when Simon held up a hand, silencing any response.

"I can hear something up ahead. Listen."

We listened.

I wasn't certain but I thought I heard quiet shuffling and a low rumbling sound, almost a growl. It was faint, but it turned my stomach, reminding me how nauseous I already felt.

"Dogs," said Harry. "I guess Mary was right. It sounds like dogs."

"Let's just back out of here," said Martin. "I don't think wild dogs are going to be all that friendly."

I knew he was right. If there were dogs surviving in the

snow and ice they would be hungry and angry, centuries of domestication discarded, useless in their new world.

As I had been the last in, I would be the first out. I wasn't sorry about that, not until I clumsily scrambled back over the fallen ceiling into the entrance corridor and found my way blocked by four dogs.

These dogs were like none I had ever seen before. They were white, stained with patches of dirt and what looked like dried blood. They stood about three feet high at the shoulder, well-fed and muscular. They were hunters and successful ones too. They weren't starving, but that didn't mean they weren't hungry.

I could hear the others slipping on fallen rubble behind me as I stood, frozen in place.

The dogs bared their teeth and growled. Not the faint growl I had heard before but a loud, rumbling, vicious growl.

I heard Martin curse behind me.

"Oh shit. Wolves!"

"Wolves?" I said, incredulously. "White wolves? You've got to be joking."

"Arctic Wolves," said Martin. "Saw quite a few when I was working up in Alaska many years back."

"What are wolves doing here in England?" asked Harry, sounding every bit as stunned as I was.

"Look around," said Simon. "Not hard to figure out really. England *is* the arctic now as far as they're concerned. And from what we heard before the radios packed up, there's enough frozen sea out there for them to get here without too much difficulty."

I jumped as, behind us, I heard more growling, more movement. The wolves were closing in. They surrounded us.

"I didn't think wolves attacked humans," I said, a note of fearful pleading in my voice. "Isn't that just storybook stuff? A myth?"

"Maybe before things changed," said Martin. "But I

guess these days they take whatever food they can find."

"I make it three behind us, another four in front." Simon gripped his homemade spear in tight fists. "I don't think they're going to let us walk out."

I saw Harry unsheathe his knife. It was obvious he was scared but he was ready to fight. I wanted to hide in a corner somewhere, and let the others battle it out with the wolves. My whole body trembled with fear. My legs felt weak, my mouth dry. This was no ancient species memory of man's struggle against his age-old rival in the food chain. This was mind-numbing fear of strong, vicious animals whose only wish was to kill and eat me.

"Norman."

I jumped at the sound of my name, momentarily disoriented.

"Norman," Harry repeated. "It might be best if you get behind..."

He never finished his sentence.

The wolves attacked, powering into a co-ordinated sprint towards us, saliva spitting from their open jaws, teeth bared, ready to bite and tear.

I let out a cry of alarm and scrambled backwards, tripping, falling hard onto rubble. It hurt even through the layers of coats I wore. Behind me, I could hear other wolves attacking Martin and Simon. I heard the men's grunts and shouts of effort as they stabbed with their spears.

A blur of white fur launched at Harry. I saw him falling, the knife blade flashing in what little light from the far doorway pierced the gloom. The blade dulled, and it took me a moment to realise it was blood spurting from the wolf that stained it.

I struggled to stand, feeling guilt that my single intention was to run away. What could I do against one of these wolves? I had no weapon. I wasn't a fighter. I didn't even have two good hands!

I was almost on my feet when something heavy slammed into me, knocking me backwards once more. Hot stinking breath made me gag and then something locked onto my arm, its grip powerful, unshakeable. The wolf bit down, teeth piercing all but the last layer of clothing. I screamed. I pushed, struggled, panicked! I could feel its back legs scrambling for purchase on my lower body. Its front claws scraped my face gouging bloody lines across my cheeks. The jaws tightened. The teeth penetrated the last layer and dug painfully into my arm.

As I struggled, I looked around desperately for help.

Harry, having pushed aside the dead body of the first wolf, slashed wildly at the remaining two.

Martin, his spear buried deep in the eye socket of one wolf, wrestled another barehanded.

Simon, my last hope, caught my eye, saw my helpless pleading, and turned from the wolf he had been keeping at bay.

His spear thrust was true, puncturing the wolf on top of me in its side. The blow lifted it from me with raw physical power. The wolf's jaws ripped my coat but not my arm. Simon drove the spear further in, twisting it. He pulled it out to thrust it once more.

I looked towards him, full of gratitude. The wolf that Simon had turned from to save me, leapt onto his back, knocking him into the ice and rubble. Before he even had time to cry out, those vicious jaws locked around his neck, biting, tearing, ripping chunks of flesh from the man who had saved my life moments before. Arterial blood spurted, staining the white fur of the wolf, and the snow drifting into the corridor. With a victorious growl, the wolf buried its muzzle into the gore that had been Simon's throat, chewing down meat, muscle and gristle. Simon's body jerked. His fingers twitched, and his legs kicked, but I guessed he was already dead. No one could survive that mauling.

The two wolves attacking Harry suddenly backed off, weaving quickly around him. They joined their companion at Simon's body, fighting each other for the best feeding position.

There was a snap and a whimper and, for the first time since the attack on Simon, I pulled my eyes away from the grisly sight and saw Martin throw aside the body of the wolf he had been fighting. The animal's neck was bent at a strange angle, no doubt broken. He made to move towards Simon and the three wolves feeding there but a shout from Harry stopped him.

"No! We can't help him now. We need to escape while we can."

"But I can't just leave him." Sobs broke Martin's voice. "We can't let these bastards eat him!"

"We have no choice." Harry was on his feet, the bloody knife still held tight in his hand. "If we don't take this opportunity, the wolves will attack again, and we might not be so lucky next time."

"Lucky?" Martin's voice was almost a scream. "Is Simon lucky? How can you say lucky?"

"Three of us are still alive," said Harry, his voice quieter now. I could see the struggle on his face but I think he was right, trying to calm Martin down. "Let's go before more of us are killed."

Martin turned his eyes on me, and I shuddered. There was a look of contempt there, a disgust and, yes, perhaps even hatred. He knew that Simon had lost his life saving mine and there was no doubt he held me responsible. I didn't need his look to make me feel guilty. I was every bit as disgusted at my cowardice, my uselessness and inability to look after myself as he undoubtedly was. I knew I had caused Simon's death, but I also knew there was nothing I could do to change it.

As Harry finally coaxed Martin along the corridor towards the exit, I pushed myself to my feet and, with one last look at the three wolves tearing lumps of bloody meat from the man who had saved my life, I hurried after them, ashamed but alive.

CHAPTER 9

"Are you sure I can't persuade you to stay? You know, your hand's still not properly healed, and we could always use another person. Surely you'd be better with us than on your own?"

I studied Harry for some sign of insincerity, tried to imagine what personal gain he could get from my staying. It was so hard to think that anyone could be kind and generous without some hidden agenda, particularly since Simon's death.

"I don't think Martin would be sorry to see me go."

Harry sighed. "We are all grieving for Simon, but Martin more than most. They were great friends."

"He blames me for Simon's death."

"We all look for someone to blame at times like these."

"He's not the only one. I've seen him talking to others, pointing me out. He's turning the whole camp against me."

I'd already noticed the difference. People talked less, many avoiding me altogether. Eyes full of anger and hatred bored into my back as I walked by. No one had to say the words for me to know what they were thinking. Simon was one of them, and he died saving me, an outsider, because I was too much of a coward to fight for myself.

"Not everyone can be a fighter, Norman. Things will calm down soon enough. People will forgive."

"Forgive? So you blame me too!"

Harry raised his hands defensively, shaking his head. "I didn't..."

"You didn't have to." I felt betrayed, empty inside, but it

wasn't in me to blame Harry or anyone else for the way they felt. After all, I *knew* I was to blame. My own guilt and self-disgust hurt much more than any words others could say.

"You're still more than welcome to stay. I'd like you to."

Harry's personal plea touched me. Had the whole camp been like Harry, I might have been tempted. But I had never intended to stay for long and the mood towards me in the camp simply strengthened my resolve.

"I need to get away from the river, from Liverpool, to move south. You should too. It's not safe to stay here."

I heard a long exhale from Harry and his shoulders visibly relaxed. I think he was grateful for the change of subject.

"It'll be a long time before the glacier reaches us, if it does ever come down this far. It has to stop some time. Who's to say it won't do so before it gets to us?"

I shook my head, unable to decide whether it was blind optimism, an inability to face the unpalatable truth or some quasi-religious belief that fate or God or whatever they believed in would not allow them to die. Whatever the reason, Harry was simply stating the belief I'd heard from many people around the camp since I'd been there. It frightened me.

"It's not just the glacier, there's something else too." For a moment, I considered telling him about The Roar, but what could I say? I'd heard a noise and it scared me? I had a strong feeling that something was coming, something worse than the glacier, but I had no proof, nothing I could use to convince Harry or anyone else.

That night I dreamed of Chrissy. I stood safe and dry on the edge of a raging flood watching as Chrissy twisted and turned in its unrelenting grasp, her face one moment clear, the next swamped by a wave. She screamed my name, and reached for me with her hands, but I just stood and stared, not moving, not even attempting to reach her, an ineffectual, useless excuse for a husband.

A dark shape darted beneath the surface of the roiling

water, visible even through the silt-heavy murkiness of the river. I knew it was heading for Chrissy but I did nothing. I didn't even shout a warning to her.

I heard The Roar rising in the distance, climbing and climbing in volume until the buildings around me shook, the ground beneath my feet cracked, and a great gout of water exploded around Chrissy. She was swallowed by jaws rising from beneath her, the jaws of a giant white wolf, a collar of twisted cord around its neck, a leash of rope, stretching to the fist of an indistinct figure on the far bank, a figure whose whole form dripped blood.

The next morning, over a breakfast of tasteless, nameless cereal mixed in warm water, Harry placed his hand on my shoulder, giving it a comforting squeeze.

"I've been thinking about what you said last night and I'm sorry, I should have realised it earlier. The memories must be so painful for you so close, to your home. Of course you must go if you feel you have to." He smiled and reached under his makeshift bed, pulling out a small package. "I asked around and got some food and water for your journey. It's not much but..."

"I'm surprised you got anything, or didn't you tell them it was for me?"

The words were bitter but, in truth, I didn't know how to respond and bitterness came easiest to me. Why would any of these people, who I felt viewed me with contempt, perhaps even hatred, show generosity towards me? By my inaction, I had killed one of their own. That they would continue to show me any kindness, was beyond my understanding.

Harry shook his head. The look of pity in his eyes was almost more than I could bear.

"Of course I told them it was for you, Norman. They're hurting over Simon's death and, yes, some may blame you to some degree, but that doesn't make them cruel or heartless."

"I'm sorry," I mumbled, embarrassed by my difficulty in accepting kindness at face value. "Thank you."

The sun had barely dragged itself above the horizon when I finally declared myself packed and ready to leave. Harry shook my good hand in an awkward left-handed shake and smiled.

Neither of us spoke. Between last night and breakfast earlier, we had said all we needed to say.

He exited the tent with me and I took one last look around the camp. Already people were hard at work, cooking, sewing, knitting, and building. Some glanced towards me but no one spoke. It was the quietest I had ever heard the camp and it was unnerving knowing I was the reason. They might not have wished me direct harm, but they did want to see me leave.

I hesitated as Martin approached, his shoulders hunched, tense, his face blank, unreadable. Harry made a move to step forward between us but I held up an arm to stop him. Martin felt the loss of Simon most of all, and I felt he deserved a direct apology from me, unnatural though that feeling was. I waited until he stopped and stood almost toe-to-toe with me. His eyes were dark, his brow furrowed.

"I'm sorry..."

I barely saw his shoulder move before his fist slammed into the side of my face. A blast of pain momentarily blinded me as jaw, teeth and cheekbone shuddered under the impact. I stumbled sideways, my legs losing rigidity as I fell to the ground.

As my sight slowly returned, flickering with the pounding in my head, I could make out Harry and two other camp members restraining Martin. He glared at me, all blankness gone from his face now, replaced by fury. I could taste blood in my mouth and the whole side of my face throbbed. Surprisingly, I felt no animosity towards him. Had I been able to move my jaw enough to talk, I would still have said sorry. His actions I could understand, certainly more than the unfathomable generosity of the rest of the camp.

No one helped me as I climbed unsteadily to my feet. I guess that was more than their limited generosity would allow. Harry held out a hand to support me as I walked by the still clenched fists of Martin, but I waved it away. I did not want to compromise him in front of the camp. This was my walk of shame, my punishment for the death of Simon, and in some strange self-flagellating way it felt good as I trudged up the road away from the tunnel.

I looked back once before reaching the bend in the road that would take me out of sight of the camp, and saw only one person still watching me— Harry. Even Martin had turned away, and I knew that everyone but Harry would do their best to exorcise me from their memory. I didn't mind that. I had no intention of ever seeing them again anyway, but I was glad that Harry had stayed to watch me go. I never had a brother, but I suspect that what I felt for Harry was the kind of love brothers share. Strange how in such a short time a complete stranger can have an impact on your life. Humans are social animals and, even though I had avoided it most of my life, so was I. I never thought I'd miss anyone except Chrissy, but, as I reached the main road and the wind grew stronger, stinging, icy blasts tearing at my already swelling face, I had to accept that I didn't always know myself as well as I thought I did.

CHAPTER 10

It was growing dark and I found some shelter in the remains of a greenhouse that was still just about standing in someone's front garden. I made a space for myself among the broken flowerpots and shrivelled tomato plants, thankful that the glass that remained had kept most of the snow outside.

I was still shuffling around trying to get comfortable when I thought I heard a low growl. I stopped moving, kept silent, and listened. Definitely a growl, no mistaking it this time.

Wolves!

Already trembling with fear, with unwanted memories of Simon's death and the vicious jaws dripping saliva and blood flooding my mind, I risked lifting my head enough to see out of the greenhouse. The approaching night had bleached the colour from the garden, but I could still clearly see the low wall and the broken gate. The houses on the far side of the road were little more than silhouettes against the darkening grey of the sky. The moonlight was negligible, hidden behind heavy storm clouds. I had difficulty remembering back when nights were lit by streetlamps, houselights, and shop front displays. Sometimes it seemed the nights had been black forever and that a cloudless sky was nothing more than an ancient myth.

I saw a movement, white against the grey, at the garden gate. A wolf, a low growl coming from the back of its throat, sniffed the ground.

I dropped back down quickly and, I hoped, quietly.

Could the wolf follow my trail through the snow? I closed my eyes, trying to stop the shivering fear that shook my whole body. Surely, the animal would hear my heart thumping heavily in my chest. The snuffling and growling drew closer, now just outside the greenhouse. My stomach spasmed, a cramping pain that almost made me cry out, forcing me to literally bite my tongue. I tasted blood in my mouth.

Paws crunched on broken glass. I smelled damp fur and rotten breath. The wolf was so close that barely a pane of glass separated us. Surely, it would see me and attack.

I opened my eyes, and found myself staring through frost-webbed glass at bared teeth, and dirty white fur matted around the slobbering jaws. I knew I was about to die, yet my brain focused on the one anomaly with the wolf. Around its neck was a collar of twisted cord. My nightmare!

The wolf yelped, making my whole body jump in surprise, and it jerked backwards. I saw the rope tied to the collar grow taut. The wolf yelped again as it was dragged away from the greenhouse towards a tall figure standing in the gateway. Sounds, other than the wolf, reached through my fear: I heard the crunching of feet in the snow, and the angry commands of the wolf's master as he dragged it from the garden. If I hadn't been so terrified, so deaf and blind to anything but my approaching death, I would no doubt have heard them sooner.

Norsemen, that's what I called them, and my instinct for self-preservation, or cowardice if you prefer, told me to avoid them. My rescue from the wolf was accidental, I'm certain. If they knew I was hiding in the shed, they would have killed me.

I risked lifting my head and saw the figures marching by the other side of the garden wall. Marching in silence. I honestly think they would have been less frightening if they'd been shouting, or singing, or talking, or... anything. There was a threat contained in that silence, just as the low growl of the wolf had been far more terrifying than the barking of a dog would have been. They had no need to warn others of their approach, no need to strike terror into the hearts of opponents with a war cry. Their presence was enough.

They wore furs. Not fur coats but furs, animal furs and skins. I don't know enough zoology to say what animals they had killed for their clothes, but the colours and patterns were varied. Some were striped, and some had irregular patches reminding me of the cows and horses Chrissy and I had seen on daytrips to the countryside before the freeze. Every one was armed. They carried axes, knives, long poles with crudely fastened blades at the end, baseball bats, cricket bats, wooden clubs shaped from tree limbs, hammers, chains, a machete. Some of the weapons looked professional, others hand-made, still others scavenged. I saw no rifles or pistols or any kind of firearm. I guess that, even if they had once owned any, the ammunition would be hard to find. Some had rope clenched in their fists and it was obvious the wolf I had narrowly avoided was only one of several travelling with them.

I counted thirty Norsemen before I got scared I they would see me and scrambled back out of sight.

If this murderous looking group continued as they were, they would likely come across the tunnel camp before too long. Perhaps that was their target? If the wolves they had with them were the same that attacked me, Harry, Martin and, of course, Simon then perhaps those wolves were leading them. The camp had precious few weapons, and even fewer people to wield them. Although greater in numbers, the people in the camp would stand no chance if the Norsemen decided to attack.

I'm ashamed to say that, for a long time, I lay there shivering, and not just from the cold. I did nothing while my mind twisted itself into Gordian knots of conflict.

Those people had taken me in, fed me, looked after me until I was ready to leave, even after I caused Simon's death. Martin's punch was justified and no reason to leave them to die.

I rose, pushing myself up on one arm, determined to warn the camp, but years of caution, of avoiding conflict of any kind, stopped me.

By going back, by trying to outflank the Norsemen and warn the others of the approaching threat, I would be putting myself in considerable danger. I was no hero.

But that argument was growing weaker. I knew how much I owed the people of the camp. Could I really leave Harry to face the Norsemen without some chance of defending himself? I didn't need to stay, to be in any way heroic, I simply had to warn them and get out of there. Surely, even I could do that much for people who had saved my life.

Self-preservation is a powerful instinct, but guilt and that underlying social animal I've mentioned before are strong counter-forces. Checking that the street was now deserted, I hurried off in an awkward limping run back towards the tunnel.

I didn't dare follow the main road back, not being certain how far ahead of me the Norsemen and their wolves were. Instead, I took a circuitous route, keeping as parallel to the main road as possible but cutting through housing estates using pathways and cycle lanes. I relied on my memories of the area from back when I was dating Chrissy and we would walk for miles just to be alone together. But I'd forgotten how thick snow creates a uniformity of the land, covering landmarks, obscuring signs, and hiding the familiar beneath its hauntingly beautiful, pale, undulating sameness. Time and again, I found myself disoriented, surrounded by a featureless landscape. I feared I was lost and with that fear came panic. How could I get to the camp in time to warn them when I was unsure of my direction? How could I be sure I would not simply walk into the Norsemen and be torn apart by the wolves? Continuing took a resolve I did not realise I had. The belief that if I did not move I would freeze and die anyway, helped to push me on. I tried to trust what instinct I had that my direction was true.

In time, and to my relief, taller structures stretched out of the clinging snow. When I recognized University buildings and the flyover, I knew I was almost at the tunnel. I was no longer afraid of being lost but simply afraid.

The closer I got to the tunnel, with dark shadows edging in and visibility, through snow and descending night getting worse by the second, I became unnerved that there had been no sign of the Norsemen. Perhaps they had veered off and would go nowhere near the camp? Or perhaps I had taken so long deciding on my course of action and finding my way through the snow that they were further ahead of me than I thought?

A shrill scream stabbed through the silence, shocking me out of my introspection. Behind it came other sounds, shouting, clattering, more screams, and I knew I had delayed too long.

I almost turned to leave, to skulk away. After all, what could I do now? But the sounds, the voices of people I had lived with, the screams of those who had saved my life, would not be exorcised from my mind. I could not ignore what was happening to them. Had they taught me nothing through their kindness and generosity? What if Simon had continued defending himself rather than saving me? A few short weeks ago there would have been no question. I would have valued my own life above everything else. But something was beginning to stir in me, subtle changes in outlook, in my perception of my place in society. However, this was not the time for such considerations. This was a time to *do* not *think*. I pushed on towards the tunnel, tears running icy tracks down my cheeks at the unending bombardment of violent sound. I don't claim my action made sense, but it was just somehow *right*.

I scrambled to a vantage point above the road leading down to the tunnel. For once heedless of the snow around me, I edged forward on my belly on the same embankment

I had so recently climbed with Harry, Martin and Simon. Squinting through the ever-strengthening blizzard, I looked down on bloody chaos.

In the flickering, shifting light of the campfires, the Norsemen and their wolves, now freed from their leashes, attacked. Most of the camp were unarmed and could offer no defence as clubs, blades, fists and feet crashed, slashed and pounded through them. Blood spattered from broken skulls and slashed bellies. Two wolves dragged down a running man tearing chunks of flesh from him as he screamed and struggled. Norsemen lifted an old woman from her feet and threw her into a fire. She cried out for help. By the time she stopped moving, her flesh bubbling, fat spitting, her attacker was snapping the neck of another helpless victim.

The hypnotic brutality of the scene would not allow me to turn away. I watched, sickened, terrified, as people who had helped me were slaughtered. What could I do? To attempt any sort of rescue would be suicide, and yet watching them die while I did nothing but hide was voyeuristic, cowardly and shameful. I hated myself, wishing I had the courage to die bravely trying to save the lives of those who had saved mine, knowing I did not even have the courage to turn and run for fear of being seen. I was transfixed, trapped as much by my own weakness as by the vicious marauders below.

My attention was drawn, morbidly, to one knot of fighting at the edge of the camp. Someone was fighting back with weapons made for hunting not battle. Three Norsemen had cornered a tall, broad figure unmistakable even from this distance. Martin.

He fought bravely. The Norsemen suffered their only apparent casualty as his homemade spear thrust into the throat of one of those around him. But the blade stuck and the other two were on him instantly, pounding him to the ground. One of them butchered him with a machete. Its blade caught the light from a nearby fire. The red of the flames and the red of Martin's blood merged into one.

I cried, unable and unwilling to stop the tears that flooded my eyes. First Simon and now Martin. Where was Harry? Had he managed to escape or was he already dead? My shoulders heaved with sobbing, as much in shame as sorrow.

In the fading light of fires sputtering with the bodies of the dead, I watched the survivors herded into the centre of the camp by Norsemen. They barely restrained the wolves, now back on their leashes. I counted seven of the younger women separated from the main group of perhaps twenty or so people. Someone raised a voice in protest. A Norseman swung a baseball bat splintering the knee of the man who had cried out. He fell to the ground, glasses dislodged from his face, and lay black against the blood stained snow.

Harry!

That was the closest I came to moving, to rushing down there in anger, but I would not risk my life, even for one of the few people I had ever genuinely called friend.

The barrier in the mouth of one tunnel, that great thick wall of wood that was meant to hold back floods, was broken. Great gashes were hacked into it, and the door was ripped from its hinges. Some had taken shelter there, but once the Norsemen were through no escape was possible. None were left alive.

At the opening of the tunnel, the Norsemen dragged out boxes of supplies, smashed them open. All that work, all that organisation, destroyed in a few minutes of fury.

The women who had been separated from the others were roughly stripped of their clothes, forced down into the freezing snow and raped. Their screams shattered the last small amount of self-respect I had left. I finally forced my body to start shuffling backwards, away from the camp, as they unleashed the wolves on the other captives. The last thing I saw before I tore my eyes away was a wolf's jaws closing on Harry's throat as he lay, defenceless, in the snow.

CHAPTER 11

When dawn pushed its weak light into the sky the next morning, I was as far from the Mersey Tunnel as I could be. I had walked all night. It had been impossible to even consider stopping, let alone sleeping, with the memory of the slaughter so fresh in my mind. Not to mention the fear that the Norsemen may return the way they had come.

Did I feel guilty? Shit, yes. If I hadn't delayed, if I'd gone to warn the camp as soon as I saw the Norsemen, maybe it would have been different. Maybe, warned in advance, Harry, Martin and the others, would have been able to defend themselves or run away. Or maybe they would have stayed to welcome the newcomers in the same trusting way they'd welcomed me. Maybe I would have ended up dead if I'd gotten to them before the Norsemen arrived.

Maybe.

It's a big word, that *maybe*, and one that would not leave me alone the whole night. As I walked, the bleak, spectral white of the snow against the black of the sky presented a mirror of the hopeless wasteland inside me. Mostly I tried to convince myself I'd done what I could and it was good that I was not among the dead. Sometimes I had a hard time believing myself.

The next day, with a watery sun still low in the sky and wind and snow rising to blind and hinder my progress, I literally stumbled into the remains of a small camp. I tripped over the wheel of a discarded bicycle buried by the snow. One broken spoke pierced the white crust and caught briefly on the bandage round my right hand. That

I didn't scream in agony, was due solely to the numbness of my damaged hand. The extreme cold was allowing me to forget the ravaged stumps of fingers and the probable infection within.

Unfortunately, neither the cold nor the clothing wrapped around my nose and mouth could completely mask the smell of death and decay. The smell was pungent like rotting meat and sewage left out in the sun back when 'summer' had some meaning.

Over time, scavenging for food, doing whatever was necessary to survive, both Chrissy and I had become hardened to death, to the frozen corpses we would find. It was always disturbing, no matter how many bodies we'd seen to come across the dead before the snow and ice had done its job. The smell would hang in the air and would stay with us for hours, sometimes days, afterwards. Both Chrissy and I agreed that we would never get used to the smell.

The bodies in this camp were not frozen. The smell was sickly and putrid. As I looked closer at the remains, sudden dizziness overcame me, the rotten odour seeming to fill my head, spinning the world. It took a moment for my vision to settle, and then what I saw turned my stomach. Someone had hacked at the bones with axes, ripped and torn flesh with knives, and severed limbs. They'd dragged internal organs through the snow. The trail showed crimson through a thin layer of newly fallen flakes. As hardened as I had become to finding the dead, I was not prepared for the butchery inflicted on these poor people. My legs almost buckled beneath me as I realised, with terrible certainty, that the same fate awaited the bodies of my friends back at the tunnel.

When I approached the black remains of the central fire, my stomach finally clenched and spasmed. I barely had time to drag the clothing from my face before I vomited. My throat burned. Tears stung my eyes, as I coughed and spluttered.

Bones lay all around. Many were half buried by new

snow. Most had scraps of flesh still trailing from them. A fire-blackened foot, ripped from the leg at the ankle, had bite-size chunks of flesh torn away. The protruding bone, gnawed, rested on its heel, toes pointing skyward. More body parts were scattered about, and they were all in similar condition as the foot. By the fire, on a makeshift roasting spit, a human thigh was skewered on a stick. It was cooked and then discarded only half-eaten. Wolves did not cook their food. Only humans.

I ran blindly, just wanting to get as far away from the gruesome scene as I could. I fell several times. Once, I landed heavily on my thankfully numb bandaged hand. Each time I scrabbled to my feet in panic. I was terrified that the Norsemen might return to finish their feasting, might fall on me, tear me apart and eat me. I thought I heard the growling and snuffling of wolves as they followed my scent. I pushed myself harder not waiting to see if it was my imagination or reality. I felt light-headed, unsteady, and I thought I might pass out. I shouted, cursed, bullied myself into consciousness. I let the ache in my muscles, the pain in my head keep me moving forward away from the bodies, away from the wolves, imaginary or not.

I tried not to think about what might be happening at that very moment at the tunnel camp. Tried not to imagine Harry turning slowly on a spit over a raging fire. The mind is cruel that way. It's capable of building the most detailed images of the very things you don't want to see.

I've no idea how far or for how long I ran, always through backstreets, alleyways, and gardens. The daily blizzard blew at my back as though encouraging me on my way, pushing me, *herding* me in a direction of its choosing.

I've no doubt now, looking back, that herding is the right word.

I used to believe in science, that wind was simply the movement of air between areas of different pressure. Now I believe it's a sentient and cruel force.

Driven by fear, blinded by snow, herded by wind, I

stumbled and staggered on ice-block feet until the snow underfoot gave way to slush, the hard soil to boggy marshland. I stopped, and peered through the wind-driven snow. I cried out in despair and fell to my knees less than twenty yards from the banks of the River Mersey.

I had no idea where I was, other than back at the cursed river. I don't even know if I was upstream or downstream of Liverpool city centre. There were the empty hulks of industrial buildings nearby, chimneys and towers. The icy sludge of the water, flowing even slower than I remembered, ran against a natural bank rather than the man-made jetties and pathways I was familiar with. The wind no longer pushed at my back having succeeded in its cruel task, and even the snow seemed to ease.

At that moment, I felt I was damned to be forever shackled to the river. Even the elements would ensure I could not escape. I screamed my despair and frustration to the sky. There seemed nothing else I could do.

CHAPTER 12

The Roar woke me.

Pale sunlight flared off the surrounding mud, although I had no way of knowing whether it was the same day or the next. The Roar still echoed off the walls of the abandoned factories as I struggled to move stiff, frozen muscles.

The sound was close, closer than ever before. And loud. Deafening. The sort of volume that made me cover my ears as a child standing on Liverpool docks with my dad as a departing ship blew its whistle. My dad called it a klaxon or, sometimes, a foghorn, but to me it was a whistle. Memories of old films with steam-driven ships filled my imagination. The Roar was even louder. My ears rang long after the last echo had died.

There was no doubting the direction this time. To my left, further along the river.

I edged cautiously forward feet sinking to the ankles in mud and water as I moved closer to the bank of the river. I stopped as two sheets of ice floated past each more than ten feet in diameter and six inches thick above water level. Who knew how much was beneath? There had never been ice flows that size, that thickness, on the river before. Another followed close behind, and then another even larger. It rose to a craggy peak some eight feet in the air, a mini iceberg on the River Mersey.

Had the glacier moved that fast, that close? It seemed impossible.

The Roar came again, even louder, rattling the nearby chimneys, dislodging loose bricks that clattered to the ground or bounced in random arcs from rooftops. I staggered back, almost falling, as rubble splashed close by. Mud splattered my clothes, my exposed face. Still The Roar continued and my ears no longer just rang, they hurt. I was terrified and excited, adrenalin pumping, heart fluttering behind aching ribs. For the first time I noticed there was no *single* Roar, but several, layered. One started behind the other, wave after wave, building to a crescendo that drove me to my knees and shook the ground beneath my feet before it fell away.

In the ringing silence that followed, the sudden cessation of The Roar, another sound grew. It was a deep rumbling, more an unsettling sensation in the bowels than something heard. It was lower than thunder, like an explosion slowed to half-speed. I felt the ground around me tremble once more. The mud shimmered. Flat sunlight fell on its surface broken by ripples and undulations that followed no obvious pattern. The river grew restless. Lapping wavelets grew into larger waves that broke on the bank and flooded around my feet. As the memory of that deadly earlier wave flooded over me, I fought the panic that threatened to consume me

Over the rumble, I began to hear other sounds. Falling masonry, smashing glass, the confused noise of demolition. Stepping off the bank into the river, the icy water covering my knees, I stared along the river, squinting, trying to focus through snow and the serpent-like tendrils of an eerie mist that undulated between the banks some two hundred yards from me. Grey, ghost-like silhouettes of buildings, barely visible against the snow-laden clouds, pushed upwards out of the mist. The distinctive towers of the Liver Building were prominent among them. After all I had been through, I was still so close to my old home and the inescapable memories of Chrissy. The weight of despair seemed to physically push me down into the river, and I struggled to stay upright. Would I never be able to escape? Was I cursed to wander in circles, always coming back to my memories and the tragedy they held?

As I turned away to leave, other shapes formed behind the buildings drawing my attention back. Huge shapes shifted behind the buildings coalescing out of the cloud-filled sky. Icebergs? But these shapes did not drift or flow with the river as icebergs would. They lumbered, rolled, *walked* out of the fog of distance like men. But they were taller than the tallest city centre building, broader than the ferry terminal. They were impossible creatures from nightmarish fairy tales that I could only stare at, open-mouthed with incredulity.

I forgot all about the cold, not noticing as the water level began to rise, and the surface grew even more restless. What I was watching could not be. It was surely a mirage or evidence that my mind had finally snapped. But it was hard to argue against the rumble of their progress, the shaking of the riverbed beneath my feet or the apparent sheer *solidness* of their bodies as they fell upon the Liver Building. Hands the size of bulldozers reached down, scooping, grabbing, shovelling fistfuls of something into broad, snarling mouths. I thought about all those people who would, no doubt, have returned after the flood subsided, drug addicts and dealers perhaps, but still people, running and screaming as those monster hands fell on them from above. Even at this distance, I thought I saw the flailing of arms and legs, and heard the screams of terror and agony as bodies were tossed into those gaping jaws.

Standing there in the river, frozen by fear, only one word came to mind to describe the creatures destroying the city, eating the people, however melodramatic and childish it might sound. *Monsters*.

I counted three of them, three monsters, before one turned his eyes to the sky and began The Roar. The other two quickly hung their heads back and joined the awful noise. This was the sound I had heard. The call of these creatures, these monsters.

The water had almost reached my waist and was rising

rapidly. It shocked me out of my immobilizing fear. The monsters were moving down the river towards me, and they were moving fast.

Blocks of ice rushed ahead of them, lifted on six-foot waves as huge legs waded through the water. I struggled to the bank, half-swimming, half-scrambling, ignoring the screaming pain of ice-cold muscles, the pounding of my head. I had stood watching too long. I had squandered my opportunity to escape. The monsters must have seen me. They were coming here for one reason only; to crush me, eat me!

The harder I tried to run, the slower I seemed to go. It was no longer water I waded through but treacle, sucking at my legs with every step, draining what little strength I had. My stomach spasmed, but there was nothing left to vomit. My bowels and bladder screamed for release but, in a futile and subconscious attempt to retain some dignity, I held on. Escape seemed impossible, but despite my body's attempt to surrender, my mind retained enough stubbornness to keep pushing.

A wave burst over me, heavy with ice and slush, knocking me face down into the snow and mud. A block of ice broke over my shoulders, gouging a furrow in my cheek. Before I could recover, another wave rolled over me, lifting me from the mud, tossing me forward like a bundle of inconsequential rags. A heavy weight settled on my back, pushing my face into the water. I panicked, flailing desperately, twisting, bucking, trying to dislodge whatever pressed down on me before my breath gave out. I gulped the icy water into my lungs. The weight shifted, slid, and I was free. I pushed upwards, gasped for air, and turned to look at what had almost drowned me.

The body of a man floated at my side, eyes open, jaw locked in a rictus of fear. A gruesome tangle of skin, muscle and anonymous viscera trailed from his left shoulder where the arm had been torn off. A serpent of blue-grey intestines writhed from a gaping wound in his stomach. I turned away, wishing I hadn't looked, knowing the image would never leave me.

Coats sodden, shoes almost falling off, I pushed back onto my feet and ran, only vaguely aware that I was shouting and screaming. There were more bodies in the river pushed downstream from the city. I urged my body to try harder, to escape. I shoved torsos, arms, legs, even, on one occasion, a head aside, trying not to remember they had once been people like me.

I could feel heavy footsteps shaking the ground, hear the great slosh of water, imagine those giant monsters drawing closer and closer. I was sure they were reaching out with their fingers grasping at my back.

I screamed louder, tried to urge tight muscles to greater exertion.

Don't look back. *Don't look back.* It became my mantra. Don't look back. You don't want to know how close they are, just keep running!

I cried. I screamed. I ran.

Another wave rolled over me breaking against the wall of the factory a hundred yards to my left. For a heartstopping moment as the wave lifted me from my feet and carried me, head under water and breath held by instinct, I thought I would drown or be smashed against the fast approaching wall. But the wave broke. The water receded, and I was dumped hard on the ground. I gasped for air, greedily sucking it in. I trembled with the knowledge that a few moments more and it would have been water I sucked in not air.

An open doorway into the factory was close and I considered hiding there, cowering in the darkness. But I remembered the sounds of demolition, the monsters striding about the buildings of Liverpool, and I knew the factory would not be a safe hiding place.

Looking up as I pushed myself to my feet once more, I saw the next wave approaching and the heavy block of ice surfing at its crest.

I threw myself flat against the ground, willing my body to sink into the earth, closing my eyes, pulling in one last deep breath before pressing my lips tight. I knew I was about to die. Hopelessness overcame any thoughts of flight. I could do no more. I could *run* no more. I thought of Chrissy and wondered if this was how she felt as the water carried her away.

The wave slammed into me, tugging at my clothes, my arms, my legs, my head. It tried to lift me from the ground, to spin me in its maelstrom, to crush me with its ice and break my bones against the brick of the factory. My body shifted, slid, and I prayed for more weight, more mass to hold myself to the ground. Slivers of ice cut at the exposed areas of my face. The wave ripped my shoes from my feet and whirled them away. It tugged at my trousers, dragging them down around my thighs and I remembered television images of naked flood victims and wondering why they were never wearing clothes when the flood hit. I didn't want to be found naked. I didn't want the indignity of being stripped by the wave and exposed in death. Is that pathetic? To worry about modesty when faced with death? I can't possibly explain it. But at that moment, how I *looked* when I died was more important than *if* I died!

The wave broke and the ice hit the ground less than three feet beyond me. I felt the tug of the water receding, but it was slight. The water had nowhere to go. The rising level of the river had all but reached the factory.

I swam. My head broke the surface. I gasped for air and a cry of fear exploded from deep within me.

Puzzled by the lack of wind and the absence of falling snow, I looked back over my shoulder Looming above, sheltering me from wind and snow, was one of the monsters. Its head was down, and its great red eyes stared straight at me.

CHAPTER 13

We stared at each other. Me paralysed with fear; the monster with its heavy mono-brow furrowed in concentration. Was this thing intelligent enough to know what I was? I had no way of knowing. There was no humanity in those eyes even though physically we shared some similarities.

It had two arms, two legs and one head. I couldn't say whether it had feet, paws or claws as they lay hidden beneath the flooded Mersey, but judging by the great hands that swung back and forth high above my head, they would be feet much like ours. Thick, dirty-white hair, coarse and knotted, covered its body. The belly of the thing was bloated and heavy, and beneath it swung huge misshapen male genitalia. Funny how the fairy stories never mention that in their tales of monsters because, let me tell you, it frightened me!

Its head, still pointing resolutely towards me, sat on a short, thick neck. That same, coarse, dirty-white hair bristled on its chin, hung from its wide, cavernous nostrils and sprouted from its large plate-like ears. Every so often the mouth stretched open, and jagged, black-yellow teeth ground into view. It may have been my imagination, but I swear I saw tattered remnants of clothing stuck between those teeth. I thought of the people who had lived and done business from the Liver building.

A great arm thrust down towards me, fingers splayed to grab. I screamed, closed my eyes, felt the impact with the water and waited to be lifted. I tried not to remember those teeth. As the arm pulled back and I rolled and spun with the sudden movement of water, I realised I still floated in the river. I opened my eyes, shocked by my good fortune. The monster held one of the floating corpses in its hand, and I found it impossible to look away as it tossed the limp, ragged body into its mouth. The teeth closed, crunching on the bones. Blood spurted from between its lips, spattering in heavy crimson raindrops onto my upturned face.

I was just another piece of crap floating in the Mersey. It was pure luck that the creature had chosen the nearby body and not me. Maybe it could not easily tell the difference between a living human and the surrounding flotsam and jetsam? I had no way of knowing how these creatures perceived the world about them. All I can say is that, either through disinterest or ignorance, it raised its head as it swallowed the last morsel of its food and paid no more attention to me.

I thought of swimming, slowly, gently, but was scared that even that would be enough to allow it to focus on me. The flooded river was shallow where I floated, and I could touch the bottom with my feet, but it gave me no comfort. I dared not swim, wade or do anything other than drift with the natural movement of the water. Although I had avoided the immediate death these monsters brought, I was trapped and would likely die of hypothermia or lose consciousness and drown before they moved on.

For the first time in my life, I felt truly lonely. Always comfortable with my own company, I had never been one to feel the need for other people. When Chrissy came along, she was the one person I really wanted to be around. I missed her, but even in that dreadful feeling of loss, of grief, I had not felt the need for other human beings. Now, however, floating, helpless beneath the splayed legs of a giant monster, facing death either at its hands or in the cold, wet grip of the River Mersey, I felt the need for others.

I thought of Chrissy and struggled to hold back a sob for fear of alerting the creature to my presence. I wanted her with me, yet the thought of my wife being trapped as

I was, of being cold and frightened and facing a horrible death, was something I could not contemplate. For the first time, I began to understand why Harry had been glad his wife died before the freeze.

Harry. Yes, I thought of Harry too. The nearest I'd had to a friend for such a long time, even though we had known each other so briefly. If Harry had been there we could talk quietly, encourage each other to stay awake, stay alive. Then I imagined Harry struggling in the hands of the Norsemen, alive while strapped to a pole and cooked above the open fire, screaming as his flesh bubbled and burned.

I shook the thought from my head, wondering whether I should have entered the fray back at the tunnel after all. At least I would already be dead. Perhaps death at the end of a spear or through the twist of a knife would not be as bad as death at the hands of these monsters? As long as I was dead before they cooked me.

I jerked back from the edge of a dark, dreadful nightmare, spitting water.

The monster above me shifted restlessly, turned to look at its companions over by the far bank and lifted its head towards the pale, snow-filled clouds.

The Roar shook more bricks loose from the factory walls, tumbling masonry splashing into the river dangerously close to me. My ears ached with pressure and a sudden warm wetness down my jaw line told me they were bleeding. I could feel my eyeballs vibrating in their sockets, my teeth loosening in my gums. The Roar invaded my body, squeezed my internal organs, loosened my bowels, made me nauseous and faint as the other creatures joined the call.

I tried to turn and swim, to escape while there was enough noise and confusion to cover my movement, but my muscles were heavy, reluctant to obey my urgent demands on them. More bricks fell. One hit my side. Another glanced off my head, gouging a bloody furrow from the top of my skull down to the hollow of my cheek. I twisted in the water, floating, out of control, barely conscious. My foot caught on a block of ice as it drifted by. It swung me around until I lay alongside it. With my last, brief burst of energy, desperate fear of passing out and drowning providing a much needed injection of adrenalin, I swung an arm onto the ice-flow, pulled myself half out of the water and spread my arms and upper body on the cold, but solid, surface.

The Roar reached for new intensity and a thick, heavy blackness descended on me.

CHAPTER 14

Once again, I was cursed with good luck.

The sheet of ice I clung to in my unconsciousness floated downstream away from the monsters, away from the city. I would have drifted out to sea if I hadn't been spotted and pulled from the river.

Whispers, incomprehensible sibilance, weaved into my thoughts long before I felt able to open my eyes. Voices, wind, the hiss of snow underfoot, a crescendo of noise that first confused then panicked me. Norsemen! Who else could it be?

I opened my eyes, screaming, "Don't kill me," as I lashed out with arms and legs. The first white blindness of light faded into vague shadows, outlines, people. I tried to push them away, to kick at them, but my arms and legs were weak, useless. Hands pressed down on me, holding me, pinning me to the ground. I screamed some more, not words just animal sounds of fear. There was no hope. I had seen what they did to Harry and the others at the tunnel camp. I knew I was to be butchered and eaten.

And the monsters. What of the monsters? Even if by some miracle I escaped the Norsemen, the monsters would get me. Perhaps they'd get the Norsemen too?

That thought seemed suddenly funny to me, very funny, funny beyond all reason, and I began to laugh.

"The monsters will get you."

A part of me was surprised at how manic, how crazy my voice sounded, but even that seemed funny to me.

"You can kill me and eat me but the monsters will eat you!"

I no longer struggled. What was the point? What little strength I had left had dissipated with the uncontrollable laughter. I had nothing left to fight with.

"Calm down."

They were the first coherent words to penetrate my resignation, spoken softly, close to my ear by a shadow I could now discern as a man.

"We're not going to harm you. You're safe."

Safe? That made no sense but, with my laughter exhausted and all avenues of escape long since discarded, I tried to examine the word with some semblance of sanity. No axe had fallen on me. No knife skewered me. Not even a fist or voice had been raised in anger against me now that I thought of it. If these were Norsemen, they were surprisingly non-violent. For the first time since regaining consciousness, I allowed myself to consider that I might have been mistaken. I was still scared, still unable to move, but perhaps death was not as imminent as I believed. My head began to spin. My stomach spasmed, and nausea overwhelmed all other sensations. I vomited. The cold taste of river sludge filled my mouth. Water ran from my nostrils.

Most of those holding me stepped back. As my nausea subsided, my eyes finally focused allowing me a view of wooden poles holding up heavy cloth. The floral pattern suggested curtains. Some kind of makeshift tent or lean-to.

One man drew nearer, bent over me and smiled.

"My name's Stephen. Welcome to our group."

I could feel dizziness spiralling up again from deep within my head. I wanted to say something, to reply, to get some answers before I blacked out again.

"Are you going to eat me?"

I saw the man laugh before the darkness dragged me down once more.

The second time I woke the world shook and rattled and I felt the sting of the daily blizzard on my face. I felt constrained. For a moment panic almost took control again before I realised I wasn't tied down, simply wrapped in blankets.

I was moving, lying on some kind of stretcher made from tree-limbs and old planks of wood and tied with bits of string, wire, anything that could be twisted and tied. The stretcher was hitched up to the back of an old horse. I could smell it before I stretched my neck far enough to see the tail and rear-end, and I felt every rock, every pot-hole, as it pulled me along. The two outside tree-limbs dragged winding railway lines through the snow. With each jolt, my right arm and feet shot searing bolts of pain through my body.

"You're awake."

The voice surprised me. I hadn't even realised there was someone walking alongside me. In fact, there were several people keeping pace with me, but this one person, the person who spoke, kept close. She looked down at me and her eyes smiled.

She was young, maybe early twenties, and her voice was soft with a hint of amusement behind it, even in these conditions. I couldn't see much more about her as she was wrapped in a heavy overcoat two-sizes too big for her, wore a scarf around her lower face and a thick woolly hat pulled down over her ears.

"Where am..." My voice cracked. My throat was dry, and my lips were chapped and painful.

The girl leaned closer, held a plastic water bottle to my lips and poured a slow trickle into my mouth. Water never tasted so cold and soothing. I coughed and she pulled the bottle away.

"My name's Sally. We couldn't wait until you woke up. We had to keep moving. Stephen said we needed to get away from the river and move inland, south."

Stephen. I vaguely remembered the man from earlier. The leader of this group? Perhaps. At least they were moving, not trying to lay down roots like Harry...

My stomach tightened as I remembered my shame

at not helping, not having the courage to hurry and warn Harry and the others. They were dead because of me, because of my selfishness, my cowardice.

It took several minutes for my stomach to unknot and the feelings of guilt to ease. During that time, the girl, Sally, said nothing. She simply walked alongside me. Sometimes she looked at me. Occasionally she looked back into the blizzard.

"I'm sorry," I said, shamefully aware that my grief was as much for myself as it was for the others, for the way my actions made me feel, for what they said about me.

"That's okay. It gets to us all sometimes, even Stephen. Everyone's been through such a lot." She closed her eyes for a moment as though holding back tears.

"Could I have some more water please?"

She held the bottle to my lips once more and the steady, welcome trickle eased the dryness in my throat.

"Can I ask where we are?"

Does that seem a strange way to phrase the question? Perhaps I should have just said 'where am I,' which was certainly my first approach, but that seemed too much of a demand and I felt I owed Sally more respect than that. I was grateful to these people whoever they were. They had not attacked me, or eaten me. They seemed to be trying to take care of me, and they were moving. That, most of all. Moving, away from the River Mersey, away from the monsters, the Norsemen, the memories, I was grateful for that.

"To be honest, I don't know. I'm certain we crossed into Cheshire the same day we pulled you from the Mersey, but I don't know if we've got as far as Shropshire yet. There aren't exactly a lot of signs around anymore. We're moving south, that much I *can* tell you. We're trying to keep ahead of the ice and those... things it seems to be bringing with it."

"Things? You mean the monsters? You've seen them?"

I felt excited, exhilarated almost, that someone other than me had seen those creatures and lived. It was the final proof I needed that I wasn't completely crazy.

"Yes, monsters. We've seen them, at least some of us have, but only from a distance. I wouldn't want to get any closer."

I said nothing, trying to suppress the horrible images of that thing standing above me, bellowing out The Roar.

"I used to live in Bowness, in the Lake District. Do you know it?"

"On Lake Windermere? We visited a couple of times before the freeze." I stumbled a little over the memory of better times, but Sally did not seem to notice.

"That's right, Windermere. You know, if you'd asked me back then, I would never have expected the lake to overflow. It had frozen around the edges so it was wide enough and thick enough for people to skate on, but the water still moved through the middle and the outflow through the River Leven was clear. There was no reason for the water level to rise." She paused, her eyes defocused with that middle-distance stare so many people get when recalling their past. "In fact, most of the smaller rivers running into it had frozen over. Only a few of the bigger ones, Brathay, Trout Beck and so on, still had flowing water. If anything I expected the lake to start draining until it was shallow enough for the whole thing to freeze."

"But it did? Overflow I mean"

"Yes, eventually. I suppose I should have seen the signs, but... well, I'd not long split up with my boyfriend and I used to spend quite a few evenings walking down to the lake edge. I was doing the whole romantic, poor, lonely me thing. I heard the ice cracking a few times, but I didn't think much of it. I guess that could have been the start of the water rising."

"You can't blame yourself for not guessing what was coming because of a little ice cracking."

"I know but, well, maybe it's because my parents were Catholic. I'm very good at the guilt thing."

I almost spoke up about my own guilt at failing Chrissy

but held back. I wasn't ready to face more of the raw emotion such an admission would no doubt bring out of me.

"I was only a librarian anyway. I mean, I read about a lot of things and knew a fair number of facts, but I didn't really *do* anything. My ex-boyfriend used to get at me about it. He was an outdoors type, you know, lots of walking, climbing, and exercise. A lot of the old people said he was foolish to climb in those conditions but, to be honest, neither of us really knew anything *but* those conditions. We were too young to really remember anything before the freeze so I guess we just accepted it."

"Did you climb too?"

"Me?" She laughed. "No, not me. Sally Halkin, librarian, future spinster of this parish most likely. That was me. I could tell you lots of facts *about* climbing, but I never had the nerve to do any myself. Not back then."

I'd never been much for physical activity myself, at least nothing beyond walking, so I sympathised with her. I also understood what she meant by 'not back then.' Conditions forced all of us almost daily into situations we had never previously imagined. I, for one, had never encountered near death at the hands of a monster before. An extreme example, perhaps, but not one I was going to forget easily.

The tree branch forming the right-hand side of the stretcher chose that moment to drop into a hole before bouncing out again. It jerked me and pain shot through most of my body. I cried out, clenched my teeth, screwed my eyes shut and hissed at the sudden agony.

"You okay?" Sally placed a hand on my shoulder and that small human contact was soothing, more than I would have imagined.

"Nothing a few hundred prescription strength painkillers wouldn't fix," I said, opening my eyes and looking into her worried face. "I'm fine. Can't complain about a few bumps, all things considered."

"Are you sure? I could ask if we can stop for a while if you want."

I shook my head and forced a smile. The last thing I wanted was to stop moving.

"Really, I'm okay."

Her eyes still held some doubt, but she straightened up again and seemed content to accept my assurances for now. Grateful that I had not caused any delay in our travels, I prompted her to continue her story.

"So, what made you leave? You say you never did anything, and yet you got out, survived."

There was a moment's pause as she gathered her thoughts.

"I honestly don't know why. Maybe some kind of sixth sense thing? I just know the lake started making me uneasy. It might have been the ice cracking, or perhaps subconsciously I realised that the one or two boats still anchored there, just beyond the ice, were riding higher than usual? I don't know, but something got me restless. I still don't think I would have actually left if Stephen and the others hadn't turned up in town one day."

She smiled and I couldn't help notice how that one action brought a sparkle, a life, to her eyes.

"Caused quite a commotion, all these strangers appearing over the hills and filling the town. I think some of the older residents hid in their homes as if they were afraid it was some kind of invasion, but the rest of us couldn't wait to meet and talk to them. We wanted to find out what was happening outside. Other than backwards and forwards along the road to Windermere, or the occasional boat ride to Lakeside and Ambleside, we didn't stray far from our homes. It was something of an occasion to meet people who weren't from the Lake District."

I could imagine the effect such a varied influx of people would have on what had, by the sound of it, become a rather insular community. To someone like Sally who so obviously yearned for knowledge, the stagnation of the town around her must have been incredibly frustrating.

"I'm guessing they managed to persuade you to join up

with them?"

"There was no persuading. I *wanted* to leave. Something just clicked inside me. All that unease around the lake, splitting up with Brian, my ex, and just generally being fed up with my life... Stephen's group gave me a way out of all that and I had to make my mind up fast. They weren't stopping. That was obvious. They wanted to keep moving, keep going south, away from the glacier. By the time they were on the road I was with them."

A snort of laughter, edged with sarcasm and bitterness, escaped her.

"It's not like I needed to pack a lot. I was living in Mr. and Mrs. Shelley's spare bedroom that they had the nerve to call a one-room flat and charge me rent for. A librarian's wages, before they stopped altogether, never allowed much in the way of luxuries. So, a few things thrown into a messenger bag and I was away."

"I bet you surprised a few people."

She laughed a genuine laugh this time, a pleasant, soft laugh that I wished I could hear more of.

"To be honest, I think the only person more surprised than me was Brian. I mean, he pretty much dumped me because I never did anything, and here I was running off with a load of strangers. I wasn't the only one, mind. There were a few others like me who were fed up with being stuck, and wanted to get out, but no one I really knew, except by sight perhaps."

We fell into silence and for a while the only sounds were the soft mumblings of quiet conversations among the people walking alongside us, the rattle of my stretcher and the soft crunching of the horse's hooves in the thick snow. I knew I could no longer hold back the question I needed to ask.

"So, when did you see the monsters?"

"The monsters, yes." Her voice quietened and I had to strain to hear.

"We'd climbed up one of the hillsides. I couldn't tell you which one. The snow made them all look the same, and it had filled-in most of the valleys between. Sometimes it was impossible to tell if you were walking with solid rock beneath you or a drop of hundreds of feet to a valley floor. I was right at the top when I decided to look back, certain I'd get a good panoramic view of the town. I'd lived there my whole life, after all, so one last goodbye seemed an okay thing to do. What I saw instead was the lake overflowing, breaking the ice at its edges and pouring out into the town. It flowed into the streets and submerged buildings."

She hesitated as though gathering her strength to remember what must have been a traumatic sight.

"I was too far away to see people, but I could imagine without seeing. There was no way they could have escaped. And then, wading across the lake, those creatures. I could see *them* well enough! I think they came from Trout Beck you know, that's where one of the original glaciers that made the lake in the first place came from. I think they came down from Trout Beck pushing the water ahead of them in some way. They flooded my town and killed the people I'd grown up with. Killed Brian and Mr. and Mrs. Shelley."

"There was nothing you could have done to help them," I said, seeing her eyes fill with tears and understanding the feeling of hopelessness she would have experienced. "At least you're alive. That's how you need to think of it. You're alive and that's all that matters."

It was hypocritical of me, to say the least. I knew it was good advice, just not any I could take myself. How was I meant to be happy that I was alive when I had failed to save Chrissy? Better I was dead and Chrissy lying on this stretcher. Fortunately, Sally was a stronger person than me, but the grief she was feeling was still evident.

I looked away. It's not right to stare at people as they suffer private grief.

The stretcher bumped into and out of another deep pothole. The agony from my arm and feet ripped a scream from me.

Sally leaned closer, her grief forgotten in her concern. "We have a doctor and a couple of nurses in the group. As soon as we find somewhere to stay for the night, they'll take a look at your hand. You were in a bad way when we found you but there was only time for a quick examination back then. Don't worry. We'll look after you."

We hit another hole beneath the snow. I suffered another burst of hot agony and passed out.

CHAPTER 15

Doctor Armitraj seemed competent and efficient, if a little lacking in bedside manner. Shortly after the group had set up a rough camp for the night, making tents and shelters from old curtains, bed sheets, even large coats, anything that would give some respite from the cold and the wind, he entered the lean-to they had constructed above me. He was as dishevelled as any of us but carried an old leather doctor's bag that, along with his straight-backed confident stride, leant him the seriousness and importance his role demanded.

"Hello," he said without looking at me.

It was entirely possible he was addressing Sally and not me at all.

With fast, almost rushed movements, he sat himself alongside me and proceeded to examine the damage thoroughly, showing little patience for my occasional gasps of pain. When he finally spoke, his words were as hurried as his actions. More than anything, he reminded me of a hyperactive child I had been at school with. The teachers never liked him. I can understand why.

"I can see someone has tried to help," he said brusquely and I thought of Harry doing his best to limit the damage I had inflicted on myself. "Unfortunately, they didn't do a very good job. The infection from your fingers and thumb has spread throughout the hand and wrist. You have extreme frostbite of the toes. No doubt from spending too much time standing in icy water and mud."

He made it sound like I had done it deliberately. Yes, I

had cut off my fingers and thumb, but I thought I had been doing the right thing. As to standing for too long in water and mud... I hadn't exactly had a choice! I looked to Sally, who had stayed nearby, and received a supporting smile that lifted my spirits.

I had no idea whether the doctor assigned her as my carer or whether she'd volunteered. Either way, I was glad for her presence. She was kind and seemed to care. I felt that was more than I deserved, but I wasn't going to turn it away.

"I'm a little concerned about the head injury," continued the Doctor. "What caused it?"

I winced as he prodded the still tender wound on my skull.

"A brick."

"It could have caused a lesion on the brain. We don't have the equipment to test for that. All we can do is wait."

I felt it was too late to worry about something that might or might not cause complications a few years on. I wasn't sure we had that long.

"What about the hand and feet Doctor?" asked Sally, placing a comforting hand on my shoulder, a gesture I was already growing inordinately fond of.

"We don't really have much choice in terms of treatment. We have to stop any further spread."

He thought for a moment and then looked up at Sally.

"May as well just get it done. No point in delay. Could you get my nurses for me?"

I wasn't sure I fully understood what the Doctor was planning to do, but it took some time for me to work up the courage to ask. By then, Sally had returned with two girls not much older than she was. I presumed they were the nurses.

"What's the plan Doctor?" I tried to sound strong, even light-hearted, but failed completely. My voice shook too much to be believable.

"We need to amputate, I'm afraid." Doctor Armitraj

said it matter-of-factly as though he was telling me to take two aspirin a day.

"Amputate?"

"Yes, we really have no choice."

I was stunned, scared, and barely noticed one of the nurses handing him a tall bottle. I could scarcely believe it when I finally noticed the label.

"Vodka?" He was going to drink before operating?

Doctor Armitraj smiled, the first time I'd seen him do that, and nodded.

"Unfortunately we have no other way of sterilising the instruments and, for that matter, no anaesthetic. We ran out some time ago. This will help you."

No anaesthetic? No sterilisation? He had to be joking.

"Listen," I said, not even trying to hide the shake of fear in my voice. "I'm not sure about this. Is it really necessary?"

"Mr. Leonard." Doctor Armitraj spoke slowly, methodically. "I am not in the habit of performing unnecessary surgical procedures at the best of times, let alone in these conditions. While there is certainly some risk in amputation, your chances of survival if we do nothing are significantly worse. Obviously the choice is yours, but you should take my advice and let me amputate."

The choice was mine? I wasn't sure I wanted it. In the silence that followed the doctor's explanation of the situation I simply stared, first at the makeshift roof and then at each of the people standing by me. Their faces were set in professional blandness giving no hint of their inner thoughts. All except Sally who smiled uncertainly at me.

"What do you think?" I asked her. It was an unfair question, and I regretted it the moment I finished speaking. I was just too afraid to take all the responsibility of the decision on myself.

Sally hesitated a moment, that uncertain but supportive smile never slipping, and then spoke in a voice so quiet I had to strain to hear her.

"While you're alive there's always hope."

They were not the most original words I had heard, but I could not deny their significance. I had no idea what I might be hoping for, but I still felt I owed it to the memory of Chrissy, and of Harry too, to survive, to see this journey through to whatever destination it might finally reach. Others had died while I lived. To give up now would make a mockery of their deaths and render them even more meaningless than they already were.

My decision was made.

"Let's just get it done."

Preparations were carried out with a speed and efficiency that, even in my half dazed, fear-clouded state, was impressive under the rough circumstances. I could do nothing but lie there, taking occasional gulps from the vodka bottle as they offered it to me, and wait. The alcohol certainly numbed my mouth. I had no idea whether it would be effective anywhere else on my body.

Using the same bottle, Doctor Armitraj did his best to sterilise the blades of the unsettlingly large knife and small hand saw he had removed from his bag. I did my best not to look, but some malignant, magnetic force emitted from those tools pulled my eyes back. The knife gleamed and looked reasonably surgical, but, try as I might, I could not see the saw as anything other than one you would buy from a D.I.Y. store. The jagged teeth seemed to grin at me as though it knew my doubts, or perhaps that was just the vodka beginning to work.

Doctor Armitraj thrust a short piece of thick wood at me.

"Place this between your teeth. It will save you biting through your tongue."

It was indicative of the state of my mind that I did not flinch at this offer. I simply opened my mouth and bit down.

The doctor nodded to the two nurses and they moved. One stood behind my head, and the other at my feet. In strange, unspoken synchronisation, they placed their hands on me. One pushed down on my shoulders; the other my legs. I genuinely believed I could not be more afraid than I already was, but somehow more fear slithered in at that point.

I felt Sally's small, cold hand take mine at that point and I gripped it tightly.

I was shaking and sweating and, as Doctor Armitraj leaned over me, the knife gripped in his gloved fist, I found one final question running through my mind. Eyes open or closed?

Fear made my decision for me and I shut my eyes as I felt the cold of the blade on my arm just above the elbow. A moment of white-hot pain screamed through me as the doctor pulled the blade across my skin. He sliced through the layers of fat and muscle, and scraped across the bone as I bit hard on the wood in my mouth. The world seemed to spin in the darkness inside my head. My eyelids fluttered beyond my control. They opened enough for me to see the doctor replace the knife with the saw. I suffered more burning agony as the metal teeth bit into the bone. The rough grating sound forced an early memory of my father making bookshelves in the garage into my mind. I could hold onto consciousness no more. I felt it slip from me with something close to gratitude.

CHAPTER 16

Sally told me the surgery went well when I finally regained consciousness. I was hungover, in pain and grateful that she was still at my side. Doctor Armitraj and the nurses had left several hours before after staying with me long enough to ensure I was stable. The bandages on my arm and feet felt heavy, clumsy and alien to my body, but I guessed I would get used to them, probably just at the point when they could finally come off. I managed a small smile at Sally. I wanted to say thank you, but speech seemed beyond my abilities at that moment. Only pathetically weak sounds escaped as I opened my mouth.

She brushed a hand over my forehead, seemingly oblivious to the film of cold sweat. Exhausted, I closed my eyes and fell asleep.

The next few days fell into a routine. They dragged me along on the stretcher. Sally spent most of her time walking alongside me. Different women and children took turns riding the horse that pulled me. Each night Doctor Armitraj or one of the two nurses checked my arm and feet and asked me banal questions, presumably to look for worsening brain activity.

I lost track of the days, but after a while I was able to walk a little. Someone in the group made crutches out of a couple of tree-limbs and I swung along on those quite nicely. The pace was slow, because of the weather conditions and the need to make sure the slowest didn't fall behind, but it suited me perfectly. I felt guilty when I saw people placing bags and boxes onto the stretcher once I was walking.

The stretcher obviously hadn't been made for me as I'd originally thought. It was to carry provisions, to ease the strain on those walking. While I lay there, they'd had to carry everything. If they'd complained, it hadn't been to me.

Once I realized this, I tried to walk as much as I could. There were times when I had to lay back down on the stretcher, but whenever possible I endured the pain and discomfort. It only seemed fair.

Although I was back on my feet, I was in no mood for sightseeing. I spent most of my time with my head down concentrating on just moving. However, I could not completely ignore the desolation and icy blandness wrought on the landscape by the long winter. With most of the destruction hidden under the snow, it was easy to forget that much of this blindingly white, icy desert that stretched on all sides of us had once been bustling towns and villages. Occasional outbursts of stone and brick broke the monotony. Tops of ruined castle towers, church steeples, and sometimes the frozen uppermost branches of the tallest trees interrupted the otherwise featureless panorama. The constant snow, even heavier and deeper out in the country than it had been back in Liverpool, had covered all that was unique about the different counties of England. It left behind a sterile uniformity that was un-interesting and hostile.

Over a few days, the visits from the Doctor and nurses grew more infrequent. One evening, a man pushed, smil-ing, into the lean-to and sat alongside me.

"My name's Stephen," he said. "It's nice to finally talk to you, Norman."

Stephen. So this was the man I had heard about, the leader of this group. He was a young man, certainly younger than me, and had the looks and physique of a natural athlete. No doubt, his brown hair had once been immaculately styled, but now it was long and lank. His chin sported thick stubble. He must have made the effort to scrape at it with a knife each morning to prevent it lengthening into a beard. When I was with Chrissy, I did the same. Now I didn't see the point.

"I've heard a lot about you," I said, returning his smile. "Seems you've done a good job pulling everyone together."

I meant it as a compliment yet he seemed strangely unsure how to take it. He would not be drawn on the subject of his leadership. Instead, he held up a pair of boots. His smile broadened.

"We were talking the other day about how difficult it would be, you know, walking now your toes have been amputated, so me and some of the others have managed to reinforce the toe area in these with wooden blocks. Bit like really macho ballet slippers," he said. "We searched around and luckily found some spare ones about your size. They won't be a perfect fit but..."

I smiled, a little embarrassed by the thoughtfulness and work put into the makeshift orthopaedic boots.

"I've nothing to give in return..." I began, but Stephen waved me into silence.

"They're a gift Norman. We don't expect anything in return. Now, try them on."

They were a reasonable fit. Certainly, better than I could have expected given the circumstances, and while the wooden blocks didn't quite fit snugly against my toe-less feet, they did make walking easier as I demonstrated by limping back and forth a few times. I even managed to walk without the crutches.

"Thank you," I murmured, still uncomfortable with having a reason to thank anyone.

Stephen smiled and nodded. I began to feel the pleasure that comes with being welcomed into someone's family. I wasn't even close to feeling *part* of that family, but being treated as a welcome guest was more than enough.

Stephen became a regular visitor after that. Most of our conversations were not about anything of great importance, but one evening I decided to tell him of my experiences and give more detail about the monsters and the Norsemen. I knew he had wanted me to talk about this for some time but was too polite, and too concerned for my feelings, to ask.

"The Norsemen look disorganised, dishevelled even," I said, trying to remain impassionate about the memories to avoid breaking down again. "But don't be fooled. I don't really know anything about armies and all that, but they attacked the tunnel camp like they knew what they were doing. I don't think they'd be stopped easily."

"And you say they have wolves with them?"

I closed my eyes for a moment, remembering the confrontation in Chrissy's old school and how Martin had identified the creatures.

"Arctic wolves, yes. There are packs out there on their own, but the Norsemen have some as kind of pets I guess, on leads. The packs are hungry, scavenging for food and dangerous because of that, but the ones the Norsemen have are like attack dogs. Trained to be vicious."

He seemed lost in thought for a moment, then spoke.

"Sally says you think these Norsemen might be eating some of their victims? Are you sure the things you saw weren't just cut off for the wolves?"

I shuddered at the memory of the deserted camp I'd stumbled into.

"I'm sure. They'd been cooking body parts. You don't bother to cook them if you're just throwing them to your pets."

Stephen nodded, apparently accepting my logic.

"And the monsters. Sounds like the same things some of us saw destroying Bowness a while back. But you say you heard them as well? Talking?"

"No, not talking. They shout at the sky, calling out maybe to each other, I don't know. I call it The Roar because... well, because that's what it is. I can't think of any other way to describe it. But they all do it together. It's deafening and frightening."

We fell silent for a short while after that and I decided I had talked enough. Perhaps I could encourage him to be forthcoming.

"How did you come to be heading south, leading this group? You know about me, it's only fair I learn something about you too."

He smiled, nodded and began.

"I lived in Carlisle, not too far from the castle actually. You could see it from the top floor if the snow eased up a little. My parents died pretty early on from the cold. They were in their 80s, and just too old and too frail to withstand it I guess."

"I'm sorry."

"Seems forever ago now. Not something I think about much to be honest, not anymore. I stayed in the house on my own until it became obvious that the glacier wasn't going to stop. By the time I left, the Eden, Caldew and Petteril had all burst their banks. Even though I was some way from the rivers, the streets were beginning to flood. If we had anything like your wave I didn't see it, but like I said, I was quite some way from the rivers."

"Did a lot of you head out together?" I wanted to get the conversation away from talk of rivers and waves. Too many painful memories.

"No, not at all. I actually started out on my own. Just packed a few things and headed off, going south, nowhere more specific than that. South, away from the glacier. Other people just sort of appeared, and joined me as I went by. Some of them had heard stories. A few had seen things, or thought they'd seen things, from a distance, but no one had the up-close experiences you had. We'd worked out that there was something else pushing ahead of the glacier, but until you came along we had nothing definite, just rumours and things seen from a distance."

"I'm not sure whether that makes me a welcome addition or not."

"It makes people face the reality, and that can only be good."

A middle-aged woman stepping through the entrance behind Stephen interrupted us at that point. She pulled down the scarf from over her mouth before she spoke.

"Sorry Stephen but we need to know if we're going to be camping here for the night or moving on for a while."

"We've got, what, about two hours before dark?"

She nodded. "Pretty much. There's a lull in the storm at the moment and some people wonder if we should take advantage of that to get settled in."

"And what do you think, Mary?"

Mary hesitated for the briefest of moments before voicing her opinion.

"I think it's a sensible idea but, you know me, the faster and further south we go, the more we put distance between ourselves and whatever those things are back there the better. By the look of the sky we've got another forty minutes, maybe an hour, before the storm really picks up again."

Stephen nodded his understanding and turned to me.

"It's difficult judging these things, you know. Obviously we're trying to get south as fast as we can, especially with the extra information you've been able to give us, but these are long days and people need to rest as much as possible."

He was lost in thought for a moment and then turned back to Mary who still stood in the doorway.

"Tell everyone to get ready to move out. We'll travel for another hour at the most, shorter if we find an ideal spot for the night or if the storm starts picking up sooner than expected. I'll be out in a minute."

Mary nodded, pulled the scarf back over her mouth and hurried out to pass the word.

"So how did you become the leader of this group then?" I asked. It seemed a logical question after the display of leadership I'd just witnessed.

He laughed, looking a little embarrassed.

"It's not something I call myself. Others call me that. I'm not sure why, but as more people joined I seemed to find myself pushed to the front. I was always the one welcoming people, and explaining things. I was never shy of public speaking, university debating society and so on. But once they'd started calling me their leader, I couldn't really do otherwise."

"Well, you've managed to keep everyone together and moving south. That's no small achievement."

"I honestly believe we all stand much more of a chance if we stick together. If people feel part of a community then they'll support the others and know, in return, that those others will support them. It's important. It's always been important, but now even more so. We're all we've got against whatever's coming after us."

Against a whole lifetime of belief, he was starting to convince me.

Not all our conversations were so serious. Many times he would stop by simply to talk about the latest gossip or memories of his early years in Carlisle. Whatever the topic, it was always a welcome and pleasant distraction from my own memories and self-pity.

Others would also visit during those early days, just to say hello, to introduce themselves, or to pass some minutes in general and pleasant chatter. Most of their stories were similar and involved running from the glacier or flooding. The rumours of something else out there scared everyone. It became obvious very quickly that Stephen's description of his own contribution was modest to say the least. His leadership had been instrumental in gathering the group together and continued to be vital to its success.

Mary, who, after her earlier interruption took it upon herself to become a regular visitor, told me her view of Stephen early on, and it seemed typical of the group as a whole.

"I didn't know the people I was travelling with," she said

after inviting herself in and sitting opposite me. "I don't think any of us did at that time. We just fell in together 'cause we were all running away in the same direction. Needless to say there were arguments. Couple of the men, Jack and Clive if I remember right, both fancied themselves the alpha male of the group." She laughed, shaking her head at the memory. "Macho bullshit! When we joined up with Stephen's group, he put an end to that sort of posturing. A quiet word from Stephen stopped more arguments than any violence ever did."

She almost became wistful at this point, her admiration for Stephen bordering on adulation. It made me a little uncomfortable.

"Don't know what he said to them, but he just has that natural quality, you know? Leadership. He brought everyone together, got everyone believing there was a reason to keep going. Gave us all... what's the word..."

"Optimism?" I offered.

"Yes, optimism, and a feeling of community. Like we all belonged together. Without that, I don't think we'd still be moving forward or surviving."

She fell silent after that, but her words stayed with me. That feeling of community she mentioned, the way the whole group worked together for the common good, was nothing short of remarkable in the current harsh and often barbaric times. Not so long ago, it might have been seen as communist or, perhaps, a liberal democracy, but those political labels were obsolete in our world. That, at least, was one good thing to come out of the freeze.

In moments when I was alone, I found the easy kindness of people like Mary, their obvious genuine concern, would draw tears from my eyes. I was vulnerable, in pain, weak and maybe that accounted for some of my emotion, but I don't believe it explained all of it. Decades of cynicism cannot begin to be stripped away without some discomfort.

Among all my visitors, Sally continued to be my near-constant companion, my carer I suppose.

One evening just like many others, she sat beside me and unwrapped the scarf from her face. She took off her woolly hat, and like she always did, she untied and retied her dark hair into a ponytail with a frayed piece of string.

"I guess I always wanted to be a librarian. Well, either that or have a job in a museum. I always loved books and history, archaeology, and myths and mythology always fascinated me. It was the toss of a coin really, that and what jobs came up first that I became a librarian."

"Ever see anything like the monsters in any of those books?"

She hesitated, as if unsure whether to continue. I had the impression she was about to tell me something very few others had heard.

"Well, at first I thought they might be *Gigantopithecus*, but they didn't seem ape-like enough, so I thought maybe *Gigantanthropus* but even that doesn't quite fit..."

I held up a hand, smiling.

"I'm sorry, you'll have to simplify this a bit for me. Gigantowhatever? Beyond me I'm afraid."

She returned the smile, looking very pretty and charmingly embarrassed that her knowledge was greater than mine.

"*Gigantopithecus*. Giant Apes. They've been finding fossilised remains since way back in the Twentieth Century, and there's been arguments about them ever since. Most scientists go with the giant ape theory, but there's a significant number who believe the fossils are not of giant apes but giant men, *Gigantanthropus*. The so called *True Giants* that some mythologies speak of."

"But you don't think these things are either of those?"

"Well," she hesitated again, her fingers playing with loose strands of hair, picking apart split ends, a strangely appealing mannerism that I had started to become familiar with. "I'm not sure many scientists would agree with me, but to my mind they more closely resemble old drawings of Icelandic Trolls. Although they're much bigger than any

I've ever read about. In most cases the trolls are described as being human sized whereas these... well, you know."

I smiled encouragingly and nodded, barely able to suppress my excitement. Not only was she another witness, evidence that I was not completely crazy, but she had some idea what the hell they were. I don't know why, call it instinct if you will, but I believed her. Even though my only previous encounter with trolls had been the kind that hide under bridges and eat unwary goats, I *knew* she was right.

"And these people you told us about," she continued, warming to her subject as her confidence grew, "these cannibals, these Norsemen. I think you named them well. You know, it wouldn't be our first invasion by Norsemen. Right where I lived, Lake Windermere, got its name from an old Norse lake, Vinandr. Someone stuck *mere* on the end which is old English for lake, and you got Vinandr's Mere. Over the years it became Windermere." She shuddered. "I think they frighten me more than the monsters."

Icelandic trolls. Norse raiders. Ridiculous as it sounded, it made some sort of sense to me. As though the heavy, ponderous shifting of the glaciers had pushed these creatures out of the nightmares of the superstitious and driven them into our reality. They were doing as we were doing. Keeping ahead of the ice.

Sally reached inside her coat and pulled out a misshapen piece of metal, narrowed to a point at one end with the other wrapped in cord that looked like vine. A knife. I flinched away from it.

"Sorry," Sally quickly returned it to her coat. "I just wanted to show you. I made it myself, with a little help to shape the metal. I wanted to say that, however scary these Norsemen might be, we won't go down without a fight. I have my knife. Most of the others have some kind of weapon too: bats, pieces of wood with nails in them, other kinds of knives, spears even. Dennis and Mike, who helped me with the knife, are ex-soldiers, and there are others who were in the Territorial Army."

I smiled. "My granddad used to call the T.A. weekend soldiers. He was in the regular army for a few years and didn't like people to forget it."

"I guess that's how they started," she agreed, her amazing mind, full of remembered facts, kicking into action once more, "but as the number of professional soldiers reduced through the Twentieth and Twenty-First Centuries they were deployed in more and more frontline roles and became a vital reserve for the armed forces. They've always been part-time of course, but their training and equipment rivalled most of the regular soldiers by the time things started to fall apart. Having some T.A.s here as well as professional soldiers helped get us started. I think most people were surprised at how well they could adapt things found lying around."

"I don't doubt it," I said, remembering that even I had been surprised at times with how well I adapted to my surroundings, and I was anything but a practical man.

"So, you see, you don't need to be too worried for now. Trolls or Norsemen, we're ready for them."

I forced a smile, but was not convinced. I'd seen enough to feel that it would take more than makeshift weapons to stop the horror that lay somewhere behind us.

Nevertheless, Sally gave a name to our nightmare. I'm not sure that really mattered. Not in the end.

CHAPTER 17

The exhausting monotony of our daily routine, walking, resting, walking, was enough to tax the strongest of people, and I was not that even when I was healthy. Not that I was walking all that much of course, but I could see the weariness etched deep into every face, the concentration and willpower it took to not just drop to their knees when they stopped walking, but to dig in and prepare a camp that would provide shelter for everyone. Even me.

For some time I could not look the men and women who would help build my shelter each night in the face, fearful that I would see resentment, or anger at my inability to care for myself. I needn't have worried. When I finally gathered the courage, I was greeted with smiles and the occasional frown of concern for my comfort. They were pleased to help me and I felt guilty that I had ever doubted them. The determination throughout the group to help each other was matched only by their determination to keep moving forward, to never give up.

During their journey, the group had developed a more definite plan than my vague 'heading south.' Thanks to an old A-Z someone had dug out of a snowbound car before they crossed the Mersey, Stephen and the others had outlined a route. It was little more than a straight line, most roads and landmarks were invisible beneath hard-packed snow, but it gave a focus to the daily march and provided a challenge to the map readers in the group. They shared the one and only damaged, but just about working, compass which was an invaluable tool when the needle didn't stick.

More than once I also saw evidence that I was not the only one to appreciate Sally's sometimes encyclopaedic knowledge, as she was called upon to identify a landmark or structure that poked free of the snow. When all else failed, it seemed that Stephen had an almost supernatural 'feel' for the direction we should be heading. I've no evidence for how accurate this 'feel' was, but the others trusted it and I saw no reason to disagree with them. I guess we all need a bit of blind faith sometimes.

Stephen brought the A-Z with him one evening when we camped for the night. He showed me the line, thick and ragged, drawn with the burnt end of a stick, sort of do-it-yourself charcoal.

"We dug the book out of the snow in Lancashire, so that's where it starts," he explained. "Then we kept it fairly simple running down through Merseyside, Cheshire, Shropshire, Herefordshire, Gloucestershire, and right to the border of Somerset.

"We stopped at that point because there's some disagreement about what we do next. Quite a few want to head east, across country, towards London. Others want to keep heading south, down to the coast to try to get across to the continent."

"What do you favour?"

"You know, I've spent so long listening to both sides' arguments, trying to keep things calm between them, that I not sure I know anymore? My original plan, if you can call it that, when I set out from Carlisle was to get down to London. I reckoned that if anywhere was going to be organised and prepared it would be where the government is based. They'd make sure they were safe, even if the rest of us were left to fend for ourselves."

I felt a slight twinge of pain at that remembering how Chrissy and I would disagree over whether the government had abandoned us. I took no satisfaction in Stephen agreeing with my view. I would have preferred to have Chrissy arguing with the two of us.

"And now you're thinking of heading for the continent?" I asked the question, as much as anything, to break the spell the unexpected memory was threatening to cast on me, dragging me back down into depression and despair. I was trying hard not to return there.

"I don't know. It could be just as bad as here, or they could be living a normal life just the other side of the English Channel. Sometimes it seems stupid not to go and find out."

I didn't ask any more questions. There seemed no point. It would be some time before we reached the Somerset border, giving him, and me for that matter, plenty of time to decide which way we would go. Why worry about it now? I could hear the sounds of the camp settling for the evening outside my shelter and see the glow of fires through the small doorway as the sheets overhead billowed with the strengthening wind of yet another storm. There was more than enough to concern myself with in the day-to-day living of the camp without thinking about what would happen sometime in the future.

The night was uneventful and I slept a little, better than I had for some weeks. When the morning call to pack-up came, I was already awake and ready to move, leaving only the tent itself to be collapsed and packed away.

Sally joined me as the group began another day of walking. Even wrapped in several layers of coats, a woolly hat and with a scarf wound around her head hiding everything but her eyes, she was so obviously feminine it brought a smile to my face. Perhaps it was something in the way she walked, even through knee-deep snow, or her posture, her bearing? I couldn't explain it, but I could feel it. Sally was beginning to stir something deep within me that I thought had died with Chrissy. Did the other women in the group have the same quality? I couldn't say. I didn't care.

"Good morning." She pulled down her scarf and smiled falling into step alongside my slow, lumbering gait. "We're going to make good progress today. I can feel it. How are the toes and the arm?"

"Still not there." It was an automatic, bitter response and I regretted it immediately. Sally deserved better than my self-pitying grumpiness. I quickly smiled, hoping she would think I had been joking.

"Are they giving you much pain?" She busied herself for a moment ensuring the loose sleeve of my coat was turned inwards and closed so it wouldn't let the cold air through to the stump of my right arm.

I stopped for a moment allowing her to finish the sleeve, feeling slightly awkward at needing the help but grateful all the same.

"Nothing I can't handle," I said finally as we began walking again. "Gets a little easier every day I guess. Everything okay with you?"

"Me?" She laughed before pulling her scarf back up over her nose and mouth. "You know me." Her words were muffled by the wool. "Nothing that a hot bath and a sandy beach couldn't fix."

We fell into a comfortable silence concentrating on the supposedly simple act of putting one foot in front of the other, an act fraught with the danger of buried obstacles, sudden slopes and, in the deepest snow, hidden crevices.

I felt better for being with Sally. Indeed, I looked forward to it each day, relying more and more on her naturally friendly, positive personality to get me through without too many unhappy thoughts of Chrissy. Part of me was concerned about my growing dependence, but mostly I found it preferable to the lonely, miserable alternative.

Without Sally walking alongside me each day I would have had very little idea where we were, or what the few landmarks we could see actually were. With her extensive reading and apparent interest in just about everything, she was able to act as my guide, although not even Sally could be sure of everything.

"I think we crossed into Shropshire a short while back,"

she said at one point, shouting against the daily blizzard. "Can't be certain because there's not a lot of difference between the Cheshire Plain and the North Shropshire Plain in the snow. Somewhere, either buried or broken, there are probably signs telling us, but that's not a lot of use."

I nodded, not overly concerned whether we were in Cheshire or Shropshire but always happy to listen.

In fact, it wasn't until we drew nearer to Shrewsbury that any of us could be sure where we were.

It had been a big enough town that some of its tallest buildings still broke through the snow and defiantly marked its location. Even then, it could have been anywhere if Dennis, one of the ex-soldiers at the front of the group, hadn't suddenly scrambled in the snow and tugged a twisted, metal sign from under his feet, and held it aloft.

"Shrewsbury Kebab House," he shouted. "Anyone hungry?"

Several people laughed, most smiled, less because of the joke than the fact we could now mark a point on the map showing our progress. It felt good to know for certain we weren't going around in circles.

As we walked between the jagged remains of rooftops with twisted fronds of reinforced metal poking claw-like from cracked and broken concrete walls, I slowly became aware of a sound other than the roar of the wind and the hiss of the snow. A rumble, a deep susurration of power, of *movement* that I had not heard since leaving the Mersey. A river. The thought alone made me nauseous.

The River Severn, like the Mersey, had retained enough power in its flow to avoid freezing. It kept a deep valley clear for itself through the snow and ice. Possibly it was sluggish compared to its pre-freeze speed, but it was notably faster than the Mersey had been. It could be that it was further south or it could be that, as Sally informed me, it was known to have the greatest water flow of all the rivers in England and Wales. Either way, it showed little sign of turning to slush and the slabs of ice carried on its surface looked thin and frail compared to those on the Mersey.

I felt uneasy being so close to a large river again. By finding one of the few bridges that had not collapsed under the weight of snow, we crossed without incident. We were preparing to move away from its banks when the group came to an uncharacteristically disorganised halt. The confusion seemed to centre on a group standing just off the bridge. I could see Stephen among them. As my curiosity moved me closer, temporarily overcoming my fear of the water, Mary split away from the edge of the group and hurried over.

"What's going on?" I asked, a small knot of concern tightening in my stomach as I heard raised voices.

"It's Jack Watkin," said Mary. "He was one of the men who fancied himself leader of my group before we joined Stephen. Remember me telling you?"

I nodded. "What's his problem?"

"He and some of the others think we should stop here. If not permanently, then at least for a while. Stephen thinks we should keep moving."

"Well of course we should keep moving," I said, horrified at the thought of stopping. I was aware once more of the proximity of the fast moving water. The river pushed ice floes beneath the bridge we had just crossed and on down the river. "What about the monsters? The Norsemen? What about the glacier?"

Sally placed a hand on my arm, a comforting gesture that helped me control the rising panic I was feeling.

"Chances are these people have never seen the monsters and probably only half believe in them. Only a relatively small number of us have any first-hand experience. You can't really blame them for being sceptical."

"But they believe in the glacier surely? Otherwise why did they leave in the first place?"

"The glacier's a long way off. It may have driven them from their homes up north, but here they feel safe, for a while at least."

We had continued moving forward as we spoke and I could make out the words coming from a man at the centre of the gathered group. He was a tall, broad man as ill-defined in his layers of clothing as the rest but showing a confidence of posture and gesture that singled him out. It was no surprise to me that he had once vied for leadership of his smaller group.

"We have a ready supply of water here," he shouted, his tone aggressive, confrontational. "Plenty of places to make shelter and buildings we can dig down into for supplies. Why do we keep running?"

"We agreed to keep moving south," said a second calm and quiet voice I recognised as Stephen, although I couldn't see him among the heavily bundled crowd. "At least until we're within reach of London. The glacier is still pushing down this way, and there are these creatures somewhere behind us..."

"Creatures!" Jack Watkin snorted in derision. "We've only the word of a few about these creatures, and they were probably seeing things as they panicked. It'll be months before the glacier becomes any kind of real problem here, and then we'll be ready to move on again. Until then we should set up camp, rest for a while."

I'd heard enough. What this Jack was proposing brought back too many painful memories for me to ignore.

"That's what my friend Harry and his group thought," I called out, my voice trembling slightly with the anxiety of crashing into the argument. "They made a home by the Mersey, just like you want to do here, and I watched them get slaughtered!"

"We've all heard your ravings," shouted Jack, turning his attention to me. "You've been sick. Almost died from exposure and the cold. It's no wonder you imagined things."

"The only thing I imagined was that this group had more sense than Harry's. Seems I might have been wrong." Anger had replaced anxiety now and my voice was strong and loud. "Even if you refuse to believe in the monsters that I've seen, you can't ignore the band of killers that attacked my friends at the Mersey Tunnel? I didn't imagine the butchery I saw, the noise, the *smell*. I didn't imagine wolves tearing people apart, bodies burning."

"We can take care of ourselves."

Jack still stood self-assured at the foot of the bridge, but others were shuffling with discomfort and mumbling among themselves.

"I don't doubt that you're better armed than Harry and his people. I don't doubt you're more able to fight and defend yourselves than they were. But it won't matter in the end. You can't win, not against these killers and their wolves, not against the monsters that are close behind them. All we can do is keep moving, keep ahead of them."

"Norman's right." Stephen spoke up, drawing the attention of the crowd towards him. "For now at least we must keep moving. Perhaps further south there'll be places where the government or the army are set up and we'll be safe, or maybe we really will have to go as far as the continent. Either way it's too early to stop now. It's not safe. We have to keep moving."

It was obvious, now, that the mood of the crowd had changed. They nodded at Stephen's words and began to disperse into smaller groups. A few remained around Jack but it seemed from the way he glared at me as if even he knew he had lost the argument this time.

"I don't think you've made a friend there," said Sally. "But you did the right thing speaking up. I'm proud of you Norman."

Those words made me smile and relaxed the knot of fear in my stomach. Sally was proud of me. Was it too juvenile of someone my age to feel a little euphoric at that?

"You need to be careful of Jack," said Mary, bringing my mood back down again. "He's not one to forget."

South of Shrewsbury, thankfully back on the move, we began to lose the flat of the plain and found ourselves trudging up and down hills.

"You know, this area used to be famous," said Sally as we trudged up another hill. My stick pushed into the snow, and the wood at the toes of my boots pressed hard against my feet.

"What for?" I liked to keep her talking. It distracted me from the sheer mechanical difficulty of walking.

"Loads of landmarks around here, and lots of superstition and folk tales. You've got the plateau of Long Mynd, Brown Clee Hill, Offa's Dyke, Devil's Chair. Not that you'd know it."

She was right about that. I didn't doubt her words, but it was next to impossible to make out any distinct shapes in the landscape around us. The thick shroud of snow transformed everything into monotonous, blinding whiteness.

As we came out of the Shropshire Hills, Sally announced that we were crossing into Herefordshire. The land rose again to the east, the Malvern Hills she told me, but thankfully we did not head towards them. I was grateful to be back on level ground for a while. My legs ached with the strain of pushing uphill through deep snow and my non-existent toes shot pains through my feet that were inexplicable but undeniably real. In fact, the only part of me that didn't ache, for once, was the stump of my right arm which had been able to do nothing but dangle helplessly while the rest of me struggled.

We had not travelled far into Herefordshire when we saw, in the distance, the first evidence of other people, living people, since I'd joined the group. The thought of strangers made me nervous and I said as much to Sally, feeling slightly hurt when, instead of understanding, she laughed.

"It wasn't that long ago that *we* were strangers Norman, or have you forgotten already? You need to learn to trust more."

There was some truth in what she said, but I still viewed the prospect of new people with trepidation. I wasn't alone.

As the news spread through the group, small knots of conversation formed. Many were of Sally's mindset and believed meeting other people was a good thing, an exciting development in our trek southwards. Just as many voiced doubts, concerns, and fears. I found myself leaning towards their way of thinking. While it was true that both Harry's group and my current companions had been helpful and kind, it was also true that the Norsemen were anything but. I had no way of knowing what kind of people lay before us and I could not help but remember the slaughter at the Mersey Tunnel.

With Sally's optimism and my fear reflecting the mixed emotions of the whole group, we trudged on, straining to see more detail through the snow.

It was nothing but indistinct shapes at first, shadows in the mist of the blizzard, but slowly we began to see some solidity to the shapes and realised we were looking at buildings, complete buildings *above* the snow! We also began to notice posts with coloured cloth tied to their top, markers placed in the snow. They formed a path towards the buildings, presumably marked out by those who lived there.

Keeping to the path, we were soon close enough to see that what lay before us was a large, sprawling farm with irregular plots of land. Fields, meticulously scraped clear of snow, encircled the central collection of buildings. More importantly, people tended some of the fields, planting seeds, and harvesting small crops. They were growing food.

Understandably, our arrival caused some consternation. The farmers stopped their work and gathered in an agitated crowd at the edge of their fields, seemingly as wary of us as I was of them. More people came out of the buildings to stand and stare, and I was somewhat relieved to note that, other than farming tools, none carried anything that could be used as a weapon. My initial fear of stumbling across a band similar to the Norsemen seemed unfounded. I was not sorry.

Stephen wisely brought our group to a halt some distance from the first broken fences of the farmland. After a moment's contemplation, he turned and waved me forward. Unsure why I was being called and more than a little nervous, I struggled to his side. Sally was close behind me.

"You argued well the other day," he said, smiling that relaxed, winning smile that seemed to come so effortlessly to him whatever the circumstances. "We might need some of that here, if you're willing."

"You want me to go over there with you?" I said. I looked at the farmers standing the other side of the fences. They seemed peaceful enough, but I was still unsure whether or not I trusted them. A lot of things could be hidden in those buildings. "Why me? I'm still new to the group. Shouldn't you take someone... well, someone else basically?"

Stephen lowered his voice until I could barely hear it above the constant hiss of the blizzard.

"There are generally two kinds of people in this group; those who will stand back and trust me to do everything, and those who will disagree with me just for the hell of it, like Jack. I trust you to speak out if you feel it's needed, but not to try to sabotage us. It's precisely *because* you're new I'd like you with me. Does that make sense?"

I hesitated before answering, staring into his eyes and seeing the sincerity of his words. How could I refuse? He needed me. It was not a situation I was that familiar with and what little pride I had left in my battered body grew a little in stature. It felt good to be needed.

After a little petulant resistance, Sally stayed behind as Stephen and I made our way towards the farmers. My concentration was divided equally between what lay before us and the twisting, clenching sickness of nerves in my stomach.

The original farm buildings stood thirty yards beyond the fences. The main building was, or had been, I guessed, the farmer's house. It had two storeys of weathered brick with slates missing from the roof and a half-collapsed chimney. But some of the windows still had glass in them and it looked by far the most solid of the structures.

It was from here that a delegation of three men strode. Those standing nearby moved soundlessly aside to let them through. These were leaders of this community, or at the very least spokespeople, that was obvious. When we met with them, I would need to concentrate, so I took advantage of the remaining seconds before then to study the rest of the farm as best I could.

A large barn nearby was not in much worse shape than the main house. A few sheets of corrugated iron had fallen from the roof. They'd replaced them with plywood and nails. The wooden walls were weathered but still standing. Other smaller sheds were less well-preserved. Their bricks had fallen and the wood had rotted and splintered. Perhaps these had once housed some kind of animals, cows or sheep, but the snow had overtaken them. Deep drifts filled the space between the remnants of walls that remained standing. Further back, behind these buildings, was evidence of new constructions of stone, scavenged wood and mud. My guess was that the farm had been abandoned before the current occupants moved in. That they had been here for some time was obvious by the extent of their snow clearance, farming and construction.

"We don't see many people passing through this way these days," said the man at the front of the three approaching the fence. He was tall and broad and his voice, like his physicality, was strong, assured. He wore an army surplus style grey overcoat, heavy, warm and fully buttoned up the front. On me at least, it would have reached my ankles. It barely scraped along the top of his green Wellington boots.

"To be honest," replied Stephen, his voice as loud and confident as the other, "we haven't come across many settlements like yours. Most places seem deserted."

All three had reached the fence and even though his two companions were slightly shorter and lighter than the first speaker, all were suitably imposing and grim looking.

If this was a show of confidence and strength, then I'd seen worse.

"Where are you headed?" The man spoke quieter now but with no less strength of purpose.

"South," said Stephen. "Not much more to it than that really. Possibly to London. Possibly beyond. Depends how things are down there."

The man looked over Stephen's shoulder towards our group shivering, in the driving snow.

"You've a fair number of people with you."

"Well, we don't exactly do a head count every morning, but I reckon there's about thirty or so in total?" Stephen looked to me as if for confirmation, although both he and I knew he had a much better idea of numbers than me. Nevertheless, I nodded. It was the first time I'd felt I could contribute to the meeting.

"We had over one hundred at last count."

One of the other men at the fence said this, and it brought a glare from the principal speaker. They were cautious and I couldn't blame them for that. But, to my mind, over one hundred gave them the distinct advantage.

Stephen broke the awkward silence that followed the slip-up.

"My name's Stephen and this is Norman." He turned to indicate me and I forced a smile for the three unsmiling men at the fence.

I hunched my shoulders, shivering against the unceasing drive of the blizzard. While we had been moving, I had grown used to the constant sting of ice crystals, but once still, the cold seemed to penetrate my layers of clothing, biting viciously at fingers, feet, and nose. I even felt it in the fingers of my amputated arm. That was something I doubted I'd ever get used to.

"You're heading south you say?"

Stephen nodded. Anxious seconds passed as the man turned to look at his companions. I'm certain words passed between them but, above the roar of the blizzard in my ears, it was impossible to hear what they said. When they turned their attention back to us, however, I felt there was a softening in their stare, a trace of cautious friendliness in the spokesperson's voice.

"We've been here for some months now and are well settled. There's enough food and water to share with travellers such as yourselves. You are welcome to stay awhile before journeying on. There's a gate just a bit further along. We'll unlock it while you gather your people together."

Following Stephen's lead, I smiled in response but, in truth, I was unconvinced. No doubt the news of our welcome would be greeted by a general lifting of tension and sighs of relief among our group. Perhaps they were right. Their personal experiences were generally positive with others they had met and, as I had found to my own personal benefit, they were trusting and generous in helping others. However, I could not accept that I had been totally wrong in my judgment of humanity for all those years. Luck had led me to two groups of people who were, on the whole, kind and nice, but I had also seen the other side. The Norsemen, despite their ferocious, animal-like demeanour, were nevertheless human, and they were barbaric and cruel. It seemed to me that, with each encounter with new people, we took the risk, the flip of the coin, as to which side of human nature they leaned towards.

"You do know most people are a complex mixture of good and bad, don't you Norman?" As if reading my mind, Stephen spoke as we turned and trudged down the snowy slope towards our waiting group.

I smiled. "Is my cynicism that obvious?"

"It's not hard to read once someone has gotten to know you. To be fair, you have more than enough reasons to be suspicious and wary of people. But most people in the group need a break from walking every day. This place gives us somewhere relatively safe to do that."

I had no wish to stop moving, no wish to settle and risk facing the monsters and the Norsemen again. I wanted to keep going, to stay ahead of them until... well, I had no idea how it would end, but I knew I didn't want to sit still and wait for them to catch up with me. It was obvious, however, that for the moment at least, most people wanted to rest, to eat and perhaps even get a little warm.

Although after losing Chrissy I had determined to stay on my own, I now felt part of this group of people who had saved my life and cared for me. The thought of leaving them, of facing the cold, the snow, the monsters, on my own again was frightening. I felt I had no choice but to join them as they began their slow march down towards the open gate and the farm buildings beyond. As we passed the post with the handwritten sign 'Hope Farm', my stomach churned with a fear that had almost disappeared since my rescue. I was certain that the good feeling around me would not last for long.

The farmers threw a welcome party for us. There was plenty of homegrown food, a luxury to all of us, and some homemade wine which, after seeing the grimacing faces of those who tried it, I declined. The locals had no such qualms, however, and many drank freely, no doubt accustomed to the bitter taste. With their encouragement, many of our group joined in and there can be no doubt the alcohol loosened peoples tongues, inhibitions and, in several cases, layers of clothing. I drew my pleasure voyeuristically, content to sit on the sidelines watching others drink, talk, dance and socialise in a way they had probably all but forgotten and that I had never been comfortable with even before the freeze.

At times, I caught glimpses of Sally whirling around the barn floor with different men. Some were from our group; others were farmers. I admit I felt jealous. Dancing had never been a strength of mine and now, without toes and with only one lower arm, it would never become one. I knew I had no claim on Sally, was not even sure I would want one if the opportunity arose, but I could not rationalise the feelings away. Had Chrissy been there with me, perhaps I could have hobbled around the floor with her, but no one else had that hold over me. No one could replace Chrissy. Not even Sally. I knew that, believed that, but it did not change my basic nature, a nature I was finding more and more disagreeable.

It took a lot of self-control to hold back the tears.

"You okay Norman? You seem a little distracted."

Stephen, accompanied by a tall, broad shouldered, long-bearded farmer, put his arm around my shoulders in a gesture no doubt aided by the homemade wine.

"I'm fine," I lied, but I had no wish to discuss my problems at that moment, or with people the worse for drink.

"This is Bernard, one of the elders of the farm. He wanted to meet the man who'd seen the monsters up close. Why don't you two chat while I do a bit more mingling?"

Stephen smiled and, with slightly unsteady steps, headed across the dance floor, weaving in and out of couples, apologising as he failed to avoid some.

There was an awkward silence after he left. I was slightly taken aback by the description of the farmer as an 'elder.' I guessed the title had more to do with responsibility in the farm community than actual age, or at least I hoped so as he seemed to be about my age and I wasn't ready to be called 'elder' yet! Eventually the farmer, Bernard, broke the silence.

"Stephen told me a lot about you, or as much as he knows anyway. Sounds like you had a lucky escape."

"I guess I did, yes." I forced a smile. "If not for Stephen and his people, I would probably have drowned or died of exposure."

There was a slight pause before Bernard spoke again, his voice quiet, almost a whisper.

"Do you think these monsters will come here?"

I stared at him for a moment, to ensure the seriousness of his question more than anything. Perhaps I suspected he was mocking me in some way, but his expression was grim. This question was his reason for wanting to meet me.

"Yes, I believe they will."

He nodded. "I thought so."

"They were following the Mersey." Now I had started I could not stop myself. "When they reach the sea, they'll turn, if not before. I don't know how significant their being in the river was, whether they prefer water to dry land, but my feeling is that they do. Do you have any rivers near here?"

"The Wye's not too far from us."

"If they *are* sticking to rivers, that's where they'll come from. They're running ahead of the glacier and that's definitely moving this way."

"Every day the cold bites a little deeper. I've tried to convince the other elders that we should plan to move soon, but they don't believe me. They're blind to a threat that is, to them, too distant to worry about."

I thought of Harry and his people, of how they too refused to believe the danger approaching them, and of the terrible end that befell them.

"And there are the Norsemen too," I said, trying not to think of the sights I'd seen and the even more horrible ones I'd imagined.

"The cannibals."

"Yes. They're also running from the glacier and they were already travelling across land, not following the river. They could attack at any time."

"Could we defend against them?"

"I don't know. I've no idea what kind of defences you have here."

"But you've seen *them*. You know what weapons *they* have and how many there are. You have to convince the elders of the danger."

I knew he was right, but the thought of taking on the responsibility, of people making a decision that could save or condemn them based on my memories, my words, terrified me. I remembered too well how I failed Harry with my hesitation, my doubts, my unwillingness to get involved, and knew I could not do that again.

"I'll tell you all I can, but I saw one group. There could be hundreds. We have no way of knowing."

"Tomorrow we'll talk more, see the other elders and try to come to an agreement. We'll try to come up with some sort of plan." He turned, looked out over the dance floor and waved to a middle-aged woman on the far side. "I need to get back to my wife. I'll see you tomorrow, Norman. Enjoy the rest of the night."

I watched him go. He took a much steadier and more collision free path than Stephen had earlier.

Unfortunately, any chance of my enjoying the evening went with him. I had too many memories, too many fears, not least what might come out of tomorrow's talks.

CHAPTER 18

Bernard walked me and Stephen to the meeting the following day, preparing us in hurried, hushed tones for what lay ahead.

"Hope Farm is run by committee. The Chairperson is chosen on rotation every two or three weeks. The general view on the committee these days seems more and more insular, particularly among the young. They don't really remember much before the farm."

Stephen caught my eye briefly. His look told me he felt as I did. The likelihood of any tough decisions being taken by such a committee seemed slight.

We were approaching one of the newer buildings, set just back from the old farmhouse. Its construction seemed simple, a box built from a mismatched collection of scavenged bricks and homemade blocks of mud and straw. More mud and straw had been used to cover the wooden roof, angled to prevent a build-up of snow that would eventually lead to collapse. There was no door, but a piece of tarpaulin hung across the opening and proved surprisingly heavy as we pushed it aside to enter.

Inside was as basic and functional as the outside. One open space, uncluttered by furniture save for a long table at the far end, behind which sat the committee. Homemade candles in sconces on the walls flickered some light into the gloomy interior. No doubt wax was in short supply, and I suspected they had substituted animal fat. The smell was like a barbecue gone badly wrong. And behind it rose another smell, even more sickening. I revised my earlier evaluation. It was not only *mud* and straw they had used to build this place.

As we walked further into the room, Bernard, with a final nervous smile, left us and joined his wife behind the long table. She clasped his hand briefly as he settled in his seat. Unlike her husband, she did not look nervous. She looked frightened.

The rest of the committee, now that we were close enough to see them in the candlelight, were unknown to me, other than a few faces being familiar from the previous night's party. All looked grim, unsmiling. I wished Stephen hadn't insisted I accompany him, although his reasoning was hard to argue with. I was the person with the most up-close and personal experience of the dangers we were all facing.

"How's your head?" I whispered, having already noted the grey pallor to his face and the occasional pressing of fingers to his temples.

"Pounding. I may have misjudged the homemade stuff last night."

"A little perhaps. You were entertaining at least."

"I really can't remember much after leaving you and Bernard together."

"Probably just as well, although your dance on the table was memorable."

"Oh God!"

I laughed. "Only kidding. You were fine, just got very quiet and fell asleep as far as I know."

Stephen managed a smile and I felt strangely good inside. It was probably the first real joke I'd made since before the wave hit.

We fell silent as the Chairperson of the committee, an elderly man with a nervous cough, called the meeting to order.

"I'm sure we'd all like to welcome our new friends to this session of the committee of Hope Farm." There was a murmur of agreement around the gathered elders. "They are here specifically at the request of our comrade, Bernard, who wishes to discuss, once more, his belief that we should consider moving."

The murmur this time was less agreeable and sprinkled with barely suppressed laughter from some members. I glanced towards Bernard, but he showed no reaction. I guess he was used to it. The undertone of hostility was palpable, and I wondered if it was towards us or Bernard, or both.

"Perhaps we should start," suggested the old man, "with the newcomers giving us a brief account of how they came to be here and of what they saw on their travels. It might shed some new light on Bernard's concerns."

"You're on," I whispered to Stephen.

He smiled grimly, took a step forward and began to speak.

There was nothing new in what he said, at least not to me. I had heard the story of his exodus from Carlisle, of the slow gathering of the group around him many times and, while it never grew tedious, it was no longer necessary for me to hang on every word. Instead, I studied the committee ranged before us, sitting behind a row of tables pushed together for this meeting.

The ages varied from those much older than me to those who may have been barely out of their teens, although it was hard to tell. All the men wore beards or, at the very least, several days of coarse stubble. Other than Stephen, very few men bothered with the painful routine of shaving anymore.

The genders were fairly evenly matched, perhaps a couple more men than women, and combined with the range of ages the committee seemed to be a reasonable cross-section of Hope Farm's residents.

How much they were able to think for themselves surrounded by such peer pressure, I wasn't sure. Bernard and his wife seemed to be isolated in their concerns from the reactions so far. Their own resistance to peer pressure highlighted the strength and conviction of their beliefs and worries.

I heard my name mentioned and realised Stephen was drawing to a close, introducing me as the person with the most personal experience of the oncoming danger.

Clearing my throat, trying to quiet the fluttering in my stomach, the tightness in my chest, I stepped forward alongside Stephen. For a moment I paused, caught in the glares from the committee, the hard stares, the cynical sneers, the body language of folded arms and defensive posture challenging me to convince them of something they simply did not believe.

I said my piece and told them what I had seen. I attempted to stress the vicious nature of the Norsemen, the unstoppable power of the monsters, but I could see in so many eyes around that room the naive belief that the Norsemen could be negotiated with, the monsters outwitted and either avoided or, if necessary, hunted down and killed like the undoubtedly powerful but ultimately stupid animals they were. Why did I think I had the ability to change their minds? Why did Stephen think I could do or say anything the convince them of something they just refused to accept?

A young man, probably little more than mid-twenties, leaning back in his chair, listening to me with a down-turned mouth and a glare of contempt burning out of a weather-beaten face older than his years, suddenly unfolded his arms and sat forward. The front legs of his chair slammed into the floor, making me jump. He brushed strands of limp, unwashed and untidy hair away from his eyes and scratched at the stubble on his chin.

"We're peaceful farmers willing to share our food with these Norsemen of yours. They have no reason to attack us."

A low grumble of agreement from others greeted his words.

"They don't need a reason," I said, gathering my courage

as best I could in the face of this antagonism. "The people I saw slaughtered were peaceful and would share anything they had, as they did with me. Nevertheless, they were thrown onto fires, roasted on spits, *eaten*!"

"I find it hard to believe that anyone would turn to cannibalism even in these difficult times," said a woman who looked to be the youngest person on the whole committee. Her dark hair was chopped unevenly short. Her face was hard and angular. Even so, she might have been attractive if not for the snarl of her mouth. Her statement brought agreeing nods from several other committee members.

I stared at her.

"They wouldn't eat *you,* I'm sure. They kept the women to one side. I leave it up to you what they were intending to do with them."

I had hoped for some reaction, some understanding of the danger, but she simply whispered something to the middle-aged man next to her and they both laughed quietly, no doubt at my expense. I felt humiliated by their contempt and struggled to control my anger at the insulting complacency. Perhaps I should have felt sorry for them, but that would have to wait until the anger left me.

"I presume you are in agreement with Bernard that we should think about moving on then," said the Chairperson, nodding towards the unmoving Bernard, whose face was fixed in a slight frown, his eyes betraying an awareness of yet another probable defeat.

"I am, yes. It's too dangerous to stay here."

There were murmurs of disagreement, disbelief, around the table.

"We've built a comfortable life here," said the woman who did not believe in cannibalism. "We're peaceful. We farm. We grow enough to eat well and have adjusted to nature's new climate."

"I can see you have a good life here," I said, interrupting what had sounded like the beginning of a long and well-rehearsed speech. "But, as good as it is, it won't protect you from the Norsemen, or the Trolls, or the glacier for that matter. Surely it's better to move now and settle somewhere further south, somewhere safer?"

"What Alison is saying," said the young man who had spoken earlier. His voice had an edge of sharpness, "is that it has taken us a long time to reach this point and we don't see why we should give it all up because of some scare mongering newcomer."

Scare mongering? I was about to answer, feeling the frustration and anger pumping the blood to my face. My head was filling with heat and pressure as if ready to explode in vitriol and disgust, when Alison cut in again.

"We offered you our hospitality, but it was not an invitation for you to come in and frighten our people unnecessarily."

"Unnecessarily?" I was stunned. Sheer disbelief somewhat relieved the intense angry pressure in my head. "Seeing my wife swept away by the floodwater, my friends butchered by the Norsemen and barely escaping myself from creatures that shouldn't exist was *unnecessary*! I'm a cripple because of what's heading your way, but if you're too stupid to listen then why should I bother?"

Many on the committee audibly gasped at this, no doubt insulted by my calling them stupid. Alison, who seemed to have taken on the mantle of my principle nemesis, shifted quickly backwards as though I had physically slapped her. I didn't care. They *were* stupid and it was about time someone told them.

"I just hope Bernard and his wife move on before it's too late. At least they understand the danger."

"Bernard?" Alison said, her face a grotesque mask of barely suppressed rage. "Bernard is getting senile. We indulge him because of his hard work in getting Hope Farm up and running. No one takes him seriously."

"He's our village idiot you might say," laughed the young man who had supported Alison, and several of the younger committee members, joined in his laughter. For a moment,

I thought I saw Bernard move as if to respond, but then his wife laid a hand on his arm in restraint. Obviously, this was not the first time such an insult had been thrown. The others said nothing, looking docile and, in one or two cases, ashamed. There could be no doubt where the power in this committee lay.

Bernard and his wife sat with their eyes downcast, unmoving, and I felt embarrassed for them. I glanced back at Stephen, and saw the same anger and disgust in his face that I felt in mine. Just as I was beginning to learn that people could be good and kind and selfless, They reminded me of their capacity for cruelty.

"We will, of course, take your words into consideration," said the Chairperson with a trace of embarrassment, bringing the meeting to a close. "We will no doubt discuss it further at our next meeting which is, I believe, in seven days' time."

There was no more to be said. Nothing I, or anyone, could do would sway the thoughts of people like Alison who, I suspected, represented the majority on the farm. They were comfortable here. They had plenty of food, and shelter and no doubt, some were considering starting families, beginning the repopulation of this part of Herefordshire. They had no incentive to uproot and move.

The question for me was whether Stephen and his group were willing to stay with them. And if *they* were, was I?

CHAPTER 19

Since losing Chrissy, despair and hopelessness had, at times, all but overwhelmed me. The hours after the meeting threatened to be one of those times. Had I been alone, able to wallow in the self-pity that invariably accompanied such feelings, I know I would have withdrawn, found a corner somewhere and spiralled deeper and deeper into the endless hole of depression. Thankfully that was not an option.

Word of the meeting's outcome spread quickly through Stephen's people, and many gathered around to hear the situation first-hand.

"We explained things as best we could, but they chose not to believe us," Stephen said, raising his voice above the babble of confused and concerned conversation. "There's not much more we can do. We'll rest awhile and then move on."

"Why?"

An angry voice shouted the question from the back of the crowd. I tried to see who the man was, but too many people were in the way. The voice had sounded vaguely familiar.

"Why should we move on? From what I heard there's only one person they're accusing of telling lies, trying to spread panic."

"No one was telling lies," said Stephen, focussing his eyes on someone pushing his way towards the front of the crowd. "And we certainly weren't trying to spread panic."

I could see the man as others moved out of his way to

make room for the walking mass of belligerence that was Jack Watkin. I should have known. The same man who had argued for staying back in Shrewsbury. No friend of mine, he must have shouted for joy when he heard about the outcome of the meeting.

"This isn't the first time we've heard these unsubstantiated rumours, of monsters and creatures threatening to eat us." He turned and glared at me, the cold hatred in his eyes making my heartbeat quicken, my muscles twitch, and nerves itch in anticipation of danger. I wanted to turn away, to hide, maybe even run, but I fought against it. I was surprised at my own determination to stay and face him. I was afraid, yes, but I would no longer run every time I felt threatened. Too many people had been hurt because of my running in the face of fear.

"You've got anything to say, Jack, you say it to me!" said Stephen. He seemed unable to keep the note of anger out of his voice. This was so rare that conversation in the crowd stopped, and people turned to listen. "I didn't ask to be your leader, but you chose me. Our side didn't say anything in that meeting that I don't one hundred percent agree with. So, if you have a problem with any of it, you have a problem with me. No one else."

Jack held his hate-filled glare on me for a moment longer before turning back to Stephen. Relief relaxed some of the tension in my muscles, but an atmosphere of distrust was already beginning to spread through sections of the crowd and, although none were held longer than two or three seconds, many more eyes turned my way filled with doubt, suspicion and growing resentment.

"There are those of us who never believed these fairy stories in the first place," said Jack, spitting the words out with bitterness and venom. He seemed to grow in stature as more people around him nodded, or at least mumbled their cautious agreement. "I don't know why you were so easily taken in by this nonsense, or why you've been so reluctant to stop and settle, but I wonder if you really have the best interests of the group in mind anymore."

Stephen breathed deeply, no doubt getting his temper under control. I was certain he was angry, perhaps even insulted by the accusations from Jack, but I was also certain he would strive not to show it and risk alienating more of the people. I was frightened and, for the first time since being rescued from the River Mersey, I felt less than welcome in the group of travellers.

"I can only repeat that I fully believe everything that was said in that meeting," said Stephen, his voice calm and admirably controlled. "I also believe that it is too dangerous to stop and settle yet. We need to keep moving. To stay in one place for too long is risking too much. For the sake of everyone in this group, not just for me, we need to keep moving."

It was hard to tell, in the buzz of conversation that rose following these words, how many agreed with Stephen and how many allied themselves with Jack. I suspected the majority were unsure, seeing some merit on both sides. Most people preferred not to commit themselves too early in any argument. They usually waited to see how each view would develop. I had certainly never been one to commit to anything without first trying to see which side looked like it was winning. This time was different. This time one of the sides was *mine* and those who believed my story.

"The farmers here seem to have a pretty good life," said Jack after the buzz had subsided to a gentle hum. "They're settled, and happy. The only danger they've seen is us! There's a lot of us would like to share in their happiness, to stay here and rebuild some kind of life."

"I can understand that," said Stephen, his voice soft and, I thought, tinged with a sad touch of resignation. "I think you're wrong, but I understand why you want to believe it'd be the best thing. But don't forget, you can't just decide among yourselves to stay here. The people of Hope Farm may not want you. You were right when you said they see us as a danger. They distrust us, and who can blame them? You can't force yourselves on them."

"Way I see it," said Jack, "there's only one person here who's any real threat to them."

Jack turned to glare at me once more and, as others followed his lead, fear and discomfort overwhelmed me. I wished I could melt into the shadows and disappear.

"They're frightened," said Stephen, a tone of apology in his voice. "They want it all to be over, but deep down they know it isn't. They need something, *someone* to blame."

"And I'm it!" I couldn't hide the bitterness in my voice.

Stephen, Sally and I sat in one of the newly built farm buildings. Snowflakes sprinkled onto the small fire at its centre through gaps in the roof, hissing and spitting as they melted.

"It's easier for some to believe you're crazy," said Sally, staring sadly into the fire, "or that you have some ulterior motive for spreading fear, than it is to face the fact that nowhere's safe, and that they need to keep moving."

"So I'm either insane or evil, or both."

"I'll try to calm them down and explain the reality of the situation, but I'm not sure how many will listen to me. Jack's doing a pretty good job at stirring them up." Stephen shook his head. "I was only their leader because no one else wanted to take the responsibility. Here there is a structure, a form of government, of order, and many of them want that, *need* it. It's why anarchy could never truly exist on a large scale. Too many people need stability and someone telling them what to do."

I smiled despite the grimness of the situation.

"University debating society coming through again?"

"Sorry," Stephen grinned with embarrassment. "Can't help it sometimes."

"But many of them *will* listen to you, I know they will." Desperate hopefulness filled Sally's voice. It was at once touching and sadly naive.

I wished I could believe she was right, but I still had enough of my old cynicism to doubt it.

In the early morning, the arrival of twenty or more people at the door to our building interrupted our sleep. Stephen stepped out to meet them, still wiping sleep from his eyes, while Sally and I stayed inside. She took my hand in hers and held on tightly. I thought I detected a slight trembling and looked to her face, thinking to try to calm her fears, but there were no fears only barely suppressed anger.

"There's barely been time to discuss this let alone reach a decision," she said, her voice low, her words spat between clenched teeth.

I squeezed her hand tighter.

"Like Stephen said, they're scared. Maybe they'll listen to reason."

Even as I said it, I knew it was nonsense. I had no doubt that Jack Watkin would be at the head of the group outside, and reason was the last thing he would listen to.

There was no shouting, no firebrands or pitchforks, but the tone of the conversation I could hear through the door was unpleasant and threatening and their demands, while spoken quietly, were nonetheless chilling.

"Norman has to go!"

I recognised the voice. I had been right in guessing Jack would be leading this group.

"It's not Norman's fault," said Stephen, his voice low and calm. "All he did was tell the truth."

"If you believe his fairy stories, then maybe you should leave too."

Jack acted as though he scented blood. He found a chance to promote his own position in the group, and perhaps he even wanted to topple Stephen from the top. But above all, I think he saw a chance to settle down and live something close to a normal life on Hope Farm. "I understand you don't believe what Norman says," said Stephen, still the voice of calm and reason. "That's your choice. But surely if there's even a chance that it's true, then we must keep moving. Is staying here really worth the risk?"

"There is no risk." A different voice called out and it took me a moment to place it. The woman from the committee meeting. Alison! "We're safe here, and you're welcome to join us, but not him! The scaremonger must go."

Sally let go of my hand, pushing herself quickly to her feet and through the door. I made a feeble attempt to hold her back, but she easily brushed me off.

"You can't send him out there. It'd be murder!" Her voice was pleading but shook with anger. "Have we really become that barbaric?"

"It's not barbaric to think of ourselves," said Jack. "It's just common sense. Why should the ravings of one person condemn us all?"

"He's telling us the truth. I've seen the monsters myself. Others have seen them too."

"And all of you are close to our leader, Stephen." Jack's voice held a bitterness, a hatred beyond anything he had shown before. "How convenient that your stories back up his desire to keep us moving, to never settle in any one place."

This stunned both Stephen and Sally into silence. Jack had convinced himself there was a conspiracy. I was no psychologist, but it seemed to me that he was beginning to show the signs of some kind of paranoid delusion. Stephen wanted to stop him settling to a comfortable life, and people like Sally were aiding him in this. And me? I was the weapon used to control the people through fear. Get rid of me, disarm Stephen, and the rest would fall apart.

I knew I had to join the others outside. To remain hiding was an admission of guilt, of shame, and I felt neither guilty nor ashamed. I pushed the door open staying in the slight shelter of the doorway, and glared at the crowd before me.

There were farm people there as well as people from

Stephen's group, and I noted several committee members alongside Alison. I had little doubt they had been talking to Jack, urging matters along at a quick pace. They were afraid of my possible impact on their community. They'd made that obvious during the meeting. They must have identified Jack as the person most likely to agree with their views. Jack stood at the head of the group almost face to face with Stephen. Sally took a step back towards me, protective. I was flattered and embarrassed by her show of concern.

"Your problem's with me." My voice broke as I spoke and I coughed, clearing my throat. I was scared, there was no point trying to conceal that, but I could not hide behind others my whole life. "Stephen's doing his best to help all of you survive this mess, and people like Sally here are helping him. There's no conspiracy Jack. There's only me."

"Then you should leave," said Jack, his glare boring into me, almost forcing me backwards. The hatred and contempt was like a physical assault. I doubted he was fully sane at that point, but it was clear that he had influence over the people around him. It looked as though I had little choice if I wanted to avoid starting a civil war among Stephen's people. The daily blizzard seemed to blow harder. Sudden gusts drove sleet and snow into the faces of the crowd, into our building. The fire sputtered. I felt it was not just the people, but the glacier itself bearing down on me, pushing me out, back into its winter, its fury.

"They're tired and scared," said Stephen, helping me pack clothes and as much water and food as the community was willing to let me have. "It's easier to demonise an outsider than to believe in mythic creatures and wandering hoards of cannibals. You're here, right in front of them, and you're telling them things they don't want to believe. I'm sorry Norman, really sorry. If I could change their minds..."

"I know," I said quietly, struggling to hide the shake in

my voice, a shake that was as much anger as fear. "You need to get out too, Stephen. You, Sally, Bernard and anyone else who's willing to face the truth. Don't wait for the monsters to get here. These other bastards deserve what they get, but you should escape."

"We will, but I need time to get as many on board as I can. I can't just abandon them after the journey we've taken together. Even if some of them don't see me as their leader anymore, I have to try, for my own conscience."

I hesitated, searching Stephen's face for some sign of subterfuge, of hidden agenda, but there was none. A selfless concept of duty drove his need to delay leaving and nothing more. It was something I still had a hard time understanding, but I accepted it.

Through the door, wedged open by Jack as though he feared I would sneak off denying him the satisfaction of watching me leave, I could see Sally. She was rejoining us after she stormed away in anger and disbelief when her pleas on my behalf had been ignored. She had been crying. The smudges on her cheeks, the smeared dirt where she had wiped the tears away, showed between her woolly hat and scarf as she elbowed her way through the crowd, saving one particularly sharp elbow for Jack as she pushed past him.

I watched her as she joined us around the small fire, feeling an empty, gnawing sensation in my stomach. I would miss her more than anyone. As she warmed her hands, I glanced over her shoulder to the people standing outside. They shivered in the snow as they stamped their feet and flapped their arms to keep warm. Only Jack seemed unmoved by the weather. Perhaps his burning hatred for me and for Stephen kept him warm.

"I wish you'd let me go with you Norman."

Sally's soft voice brought my attention back inside the building.

"We've been through this Sally, you know we have." And we had, painful minutes of tears, of heartfelt words that suggested but never stated the close bond that had grown between us. Perhaps if I had never known Chrissy, or if she had not been so violently dragged from me, I might have said more, wanted more, but I could not be unfaithful to Chrissy. I think I had still not quite accepted that she was truly gone forever. I clung on to some vague hope of a miracle even though I didn't believe in such things.

"It's too dangerous. You need to stay with Stephen, and be ready to leave when he does. It'll be safer in a larger group."

"If Chrissy were still alive, if she were here with you now, would you say the same to her? Or would you take her with you, and keep her close by whatever the danger?"

I felt like I'd been slapped, literally. I leaned backwards away from Sally as she spat the words at me.

Quickly the anger in her face softened to shock, to horror at what she had said.

"I'm so sorry Norman, really. I didn't mean to... that was so cruel of me. Oh God, I'm so sorry."

It took me a moment to recover, to hold back the tears, settle the dreadful empty swirling of my stomach. Chrissy. How could she ask such a thing? How could she compare? But it stirred the memory of a conversation between me and Harry, of how he was glad his wife had died before the big freeze, and I now truly understood his meaning. I would not want Chrissy to have to face this, to choose between being thrown out into the icy storms or abandoning me. Would I have taken her with me? It was an unwelcome question but a good one, and one I could not answer.

"It's okay Sally. It's okay, but it changes nothing. I need you to stay here. You'll be safer with Stephen."

She nodded, acquiescent and sorrowful. She shuffled towards me, threw her arms around my neck and hugged. Neither of us spoke and, nervously at first, I slid my one good arm around her waist, the other stump waving helplessly at her side, its lack of control still an embarrassment to me. I wondered whether I should kiss her, but then she stepped back and, with relief, I accepted the moment had passed.

She drew her hunting knife from its sheath. Holding it by the blade, she handed it to me hilt first.

"Take it. You might need it. I can make another one."

After a moment's hesitation, I took the offered knife and tucked it into my backpack, smiling a thanks to her. I couldn't imagine it would be of any use if I ran into the Trolls or the Norsemen out there, but I appreciated the gesture. It would do no harm to have some kind of weapon with me.

Shuffling and murmuring in the crowd demonstrated their displeasure at how long it was taking me to pack. Having satisfied my personal need to show anger by glaring at them, I quickly finished shoving the last of my clothes and provisions in my bag and stood up, slinging it onto my shoulder. I reached for my crutches, but changed my mind. As useful as they had been at first, they had proved cumbersome and something of a hindrance in deeper snow. They would simply slow me down.

With a final look towards Stephen and Sally, I walked out of the building, trying not to limp too heavily, to keep some semblance of pride. The waiting crowd parted. A few people were decent enough to show some embarrassment and shame. Others snarled, their faces full of hate. Most were silent, their faces blank of emotion.

"Good riddance!" Alison's voice broke through the growing roar of the wind. For a moment, I wanted to turn and unload my anger, my fear, onto her, but ultimately I knew there would be no point. It could only make matters worse for those left behind. Nevertheless, I was not completely sorry when I heard the cry of 'bitch' from behind me and the sounds of a scuffle. I turned to see Stephen pulling Sally away from Alison who sat, stunned on the cold ground with her hand held to her nose, blood dripping through her gloved fingers.

"Keep going Leonard," said Jack, taking a threatening

step towards me. If he was concerned about the fight, he showed no sign of it. His full attention was on me as if he were determined to see me leave.

The full force of the blizzard hit me as I cleared the shelter of the buildings. Fortunately, it was behind me, pushing me onward. I wanted to look back again but didn't. Seeing Sally and Stephen would be painful, and I didn't want the others to think I was hoping for some sign of compassion, some last minute change of heart.

As I trudged away, each step a battle against knee-deep snow, I told myself I was better off on my own. I didn't need anyone else. The only person I ever needed was Chrissy, and she was no longer there. On my own, master of my own destiny, I could move where and when I wanted. It was better this way. The tears in my eyes were the result of the blizzard, not any feeling of sadness or loneliness. They didn't want me on the farm. They didn't want my help, didn't want to listen to my warning. Fine with me.

Fuck them!

CHAPTER 20

Huddled uncomfortably in a snow-hole barely deep enough to protect myself from the worst of the winds and with only intermittent moonlight to relieve the darkness, I heard The Roar.

It had been some time since I last heard it, and it was distant, but there was no mistaking those overlaid, bestial bellows. As much as I could judge direction, it seemed to come from beyond the farm, towards the River Wye. It fit with their previous advance up the Mersey. They were still sticking to the rivers.

I wondered if anyone at the farm had heard it and if they would recognise it from the descriptions I'd given them. I shook my head. It was no concern of mine. Just as it was no concern of mine if they chose to stay where they were and be eaten by Trolls or cannibals. They had thrown me out. That was all I needed to remember.

I hoped Sally and Stephen would not wait too long before leaving regardless of how many others followed them. Not that I was waiting. I had no intention of staying around any longer than I had to. I was certainly not waiting for others who might not even come. I truly wanted Sally and Stephen to escape, but I was not ready to sacrifice my own safety to make sure they did.

I guess my old selfishness had been lying dormant. Being kicked out on my own had revived it. For the moment, at least, that one act of unreasonable cruelty overshadowed the many acts of kindness and generosity I had experienced. As I tried to doze in my snow-hole, that bitterness drove my determination to survive.

I lost track of how many times I woke, but when the watery light outside announced that dawn had finally come, I dug my way through the overnight drift half-filling the entrance to my snow-hole and stretched tired and aching muscles. I drank some water from a bottle that was only half iced-up and ate some hard biscuit slabs. They were largely tasteless with some flavour given by small seeds and nuts that, accidentally or otherwise, had fallen into the mixture, but they were food that had taken time and effort to prepare, perhaps by one of those same people who stood in the crowd and watched me leave. I was grateful that I had some time to adapt to being on my own again before I began foraging to stay alive, but the contradictory nature of the gift made me smile bitterly.

We're going to kick you out to almost certain death, but here's some home-cooked biscuits for your journey.

Cruelty and kindness confused and intertwined. It summed up Hope Farm quite neatly for me.

I'd walked far enough the previous day for the farm to be out of sight behind hills of snow and the skeletons of wind-bent trees dripping icicles that sparked reflections in the thin early light. It was a brutal but beautiful sight, and I was pleasantly surprised that I could see it as such. I don't think I'd appreciated the beauty of anything since Chrissy had been taken from me.

Before the sun could struggle much higher, I had re-packed my bag, hauled it with difficulty over my aching shoulder and forced my legs to begin the long drag through the snow. My toes ached with the cold, toes I no longer had. I didn't let it worry me any more than I worried about the occasional itching I felt in my amputated right arm. I saved my worrying for more important things than phantom extremities.

As long as I kept moving directly away from the farm, I believed I would be heading roughly south. That was the direction we were heading when we found the farm in the first place, and I refused to entertain any doubt in this logic. There had to be *something* to believe in. Up until now, everything else had ultimately disappointed me.

In Liverpool, the buildings had formed paths to follow, and even half-buried road signs gave a sense of direction. But out here in the country there was nothing, just miles and miles of snow drifting to depths far greater than in the city. The occasional dead tree broke the surface. Sometimes a solitary ruin, all but buried by the blizzard, would remind me that, once, people had lived here. But these interruptions to the monotony of the white desert only strengthened the sense of desolation, the feeling that life had deserted this landscape leaving behind an emptiness every bit as deep and pervasive as the one I had felt inside on losing Chrissy. No doubt there were roads of some kind far beneath the snow, but there were no signs visible and nothing to indicate which way to head. I tried to keep a straight line, but I sincerely doubted I was successful. Frustration was a constant companion. For all I knew I could be walking in circles, but I had to believe I was making some progress. If I began to doubt that, I feared I'd lose my sanity. The horizon remained featureless. It was impossible to judge distance. It could have been hundreds of miles away or I could have been about to fall off the edge of the world. There was nothing to do other than push myself on and try to trust what little sense of direction it was possible to have in this frozen countryside.

From my vague knowledge of geography, and presuming I had stayed roughly true to my starting direction, I was unsure whether I was now moving towards the South of England or South Wales. While both were south, the Welsh route would ultimately end at the sea long before the southern coast of England. It worried me, but there was nothing I could do other than struggle on and hope for some kind of sign or remnant of humanity that might provide a hint. I ate and drank sparingly, not knowing how long it would be before I could replace what I used. Dehydration was a worry. I had no method of boiling snow to produce water, and I had serious doubts about the idea of eating the snow without boiling it. I wasn't willing to try anything reckless just yet. By periodically keeping bottles of water inside my coats, I was able to stop them freezing over.

I was a long way from being a survival expert, but I was learning, putting into practice techniques and skills I had heard others talk about but never before used myself. At times, I felt able to survive anything the weather could throw at me, proud of my new-found capabilities. Other times, I felt I was simply postponing the inevitable conclusion of my exile. My death.

Several hours into the second day, I felt the ground rumble beneath my feet and heard the distant sound of an express train rushing through a tunnel. I stopped, thigh deep in snow, and stared back in what I believed was the direction of the farm. I didn't need to see to know what had just happened.

A huge wave had rushed up the River Wye, just as it had the Mersey.

I tried not to think of Chrissy being swept away in the flood, instead concentrating on the present, wondering how near *this* wave had come to the farm. Perhaps it had engulfed it, or perhaps they barely paddled at its edges? Either way, I knew what would be following close behind.

Still, it was none of my concern now. I turned back and carried on pushing through the snow, but my progress was slow and hesitant. I could not rid my thoughts of Sally and Stephen, nor of the many others at the farm who had played no active role in my expulsion. While I was angry with them for their inaction, I did not wish them harm.

Perhaps the wave would have even convinced some of the sceptics that I was telling them the truth? Some of those who were undecided, who chose to simply go with the majority, might now be having doubts, and I cannot deny a wish that I could stand before them, smiling, implying, without saying, 'I told you so.' But there were others who would not believe until a Troll bit their head off, or the Norsemen were roasting them over an open fire. Even then, they'd probably be convinced I was in some way to blame.

There was nothing I could do, nothing further I could say, to convince them of the danger they, and those who followed them, were in. Even if I chose to return to the farm and try, it would probably be too late by the time I got there. It had to be over a day's walk away at my crippled pace, even without stopping to rest. And anyway, they threw me out. I didn't choose to abandon them. They abandoned me. Even if I was to make it back in time, what could I do? The whole idea was ridiculous.

So why was I hesitating? Why had I now stopped walking again, staring back toward the unseen farm?

I thought of Sally, smiling, unconsciously picking at her hair with gloved fingers. I thought of Stephen, talking, laughing, helping me to my feet to practice walking in the wooden toed boots. I thought of Harry sharing his private thoughts about his wife, encouraging me to share mine. Most of all I thought of Chrissy, of the terrible fear she must have felt as the waters dragged her away, of my nightmares of her cursing me for not swimming after her, for not saving her.

I sat down in the snow in confusion and despair. Returning was doomed to failure. Not returning condemned me to a life of regret and self-loathing. I was a coward. I knew that. But, sometimes, even cowards feel the desire to do what's right rather than what's safest. And anyway, what was there for me further south? A dream of someplace beyond the snow where civilisation had survived and continued to thrive? Where those in charge governed sensibly and with compassion, and others obeyed the laws and lived content lives? Somewhere safe from the advance of the glacier, from Trolls and cannibals and whatever else the snow and ice brought with it?

That place did not, *could* not exist. I knew it. Perhaps I'd always known it, even before the wave and the monsters. Even before The Roar. Human civilisation in this whole hemisphere was doomed to extinction, or at best a life of scavenging, of barely existing from one day to the next, eventually following the Norsemen into cannibalism. If there was anywhere truly safe from this creeping icy death, perhaps it was somewhere in Earth's southern hemisphere, but that was pure speculation. They might have their own army of glaciers ripping upwards from the Antarctic. Where I was at the moment, or where I had been just a few days previously, could well be the best I could hope for.

I tipped my head back and screamed at the sky, unconsciously emulating The Roar in my own small way. Had I still believed in God, it would have been a scream of despair at the unfairness of it all, perhaps even of hatred. But there was nothing to hate, nothing but sky permanently heavy with clouds, pregnant with snow. I couldn't fight the daily blizzards; couldn't attack the drifts of snow; couldn't satisfy my anger on ice-covered lakes and streams, but Hope Farm was about to face something tangible, something I *could* fight, however inexpertly. And I had friends there. Among those who feared me and exiled me, I still had friends. Other people just like me.

I pushed myself resolutely to my feet and, with as much speed as I could muster on aching legs, started back towards the farm.

CHAPTER 21

Heading back, I faced into the blizzard. Snow stung the exposed areas of my face and blurred my vision. When I struggled out of the deepest snow into shallower drifts, the weight of packed snow on my trousers and boots made every step a test of endurance and determination. But I was determined, more determined than I could ever remember. In my mind, this was no longer about saving Hope Farm, nor even solely about saving Sally or Stephen. It was also about Harry and his companions at the tunnel camp. It was about all those people, pushers, users, but still people, in and around the Liver building. It was about Chrissy and trying to find a way to remember the good times we had rather than the way it had ended. But most of all it was about me feeling good about myself, feeling part of something, belonging to a group, a family, who might just need my help, whether they knew it or not.

I shouted defiance but heard nothing above the never-ending roar of the blizzard. I discovered strength that I never knew I had, strength to keep moving, to keep pushing onwards. The strength of endurance, of bloody-minded, stubborn determination.

The blizzard never eased. The wind drove it into a swirling fury. The drifts of snow began to feel more like mud dragging at my feet, pulling, reluctant to let go. I stumbled, dizzy and disoriented, gasping for air with short, shallow breaths as the blizzard hammered against my head. Someone or something pressed on my chest, although I knew I was alone. The pressure would not ease and I began to think of heart attacks and strokes. Was this how I would die? Not at the hands of Norsemen or Trolls, but by my own body failing me, leaving me to freeze and be forever buried in the snow?

I heard voices calling my name, distant but distinct. Who could be calling me? In the swirling mist of snow, I could see shapes, grey and blurred but human. As they came closer, I thought I recognised them. Sally, Stephen, Harry. But Harry was dead, I knew that. He could not be walking towards me through the blizzard. He could not be calling my name.

I shouted, screamed out my fear, my confusion, and my name became nothing more than the undulating notes of the wind. The figures became a mere thickening of the snow before it dispersed, scattered by the storm. No one was approaching me. No one called my name. Slowly the pressure on my chest eased and, despite the attempt of the wind to pull my breath from my mouth, I began to breathe a little easier, a little deeper. I was not sure whether to feel relieved or disappointed. I knew I was frustrated and frightened.

I think I had lost my mind for a while. I was driven to a kind of insanity by the relentless battering of the weather and the fear that I would be too late just as I had been for Harry. Or I'd be in time only to watch my friends die, as I had watched Chrissy die.

Not this time.

I had given no thought to how I would fight the Trolls or the Norsemen, only that I would. I couldn't allow myself to consider details in case I realised just how hopeless the situation was and my cowardice overcame my fanatical, if temporary, sense of duty.

I was so wrapped in my own thoughts and blinded by the snow that I passed several scattered, half-buried body parts without noticing before tripping on an outstretched boot. I sprawled face first in the snow, landing nose to nose with Stephen's frozen, severed head.

I lay on the ground, the surrounding storm fading into insignificant background. Time dragged slow, heavy trails through my stunned horror as I stared into that so familiar face, grey in death, its open mouth filled with snow. I didn't adhere to the belief that dead eyes showed the last thing seen by the victim, but I did, at that moment, believe they reflected the emotion that person experienced. Stephen experienced sheer terror.

Slowly, as if the camera of my mind pulled back to a wide-shot, I became aware of everything surrounding me: white snow stained red with blood, arms and legs severed, a foot still in a boot, strands of blue-grey viscera strewn on the ground. Another head.

I closed my eyes, not wanting to look but needing to know. The little I'd seen had sent a pain through my heart, a knife twisting in my belly. The woolly hat. The long brown hair fanned across the red snow. The scarf still wrapped around the stump of a neck.

I forced myself to look again, to crawl closer. I didn't care how the blood of my friends and recent companions stained my glove, my coats, my trousers. With one hand, I pulled myself along unable to push properly without toes but using my knees and the wooden blocks in my boots. It was slow and inelegant, but inch by painful inch it moved me over the snow.

A latticework of hair strands covered the face. Putting the weight on the stump of my right arm, I brushed the strands aside, gently, fearfully. The breath I had been holding exploded from me in a deep sigh.

It wasn't Sally!

I smiled involuntarily, immediately feeling guilty and ashamed. This was still a woman, a human being, horribly butchered. I didn't know her name, but even in death, the face was familiar. I knew she was one of Stephen's group. The relief I felt at it not being Sally was finally tempered with the grief of Stephen's death, of the deaths of so many who had followed him. And of course, just because the severed head was not hers did not mean that Sally was still alive.

But I still had that hope.

I should have moved on straight away, continued towards the farm, but I could not leave Stephen's remains lying in the open.

I dug into the snow with my gloved hand. When I hit harder packed snow, I took Sally's homemade knife from my pack and used it as a narrow shovel. It would not take the blizzard long to add depth to my shallow grave and to cover the blood and gore splashed around the site. In truth the blizzards would have covered the remains in less than a day had I done nothing, but digging the grave gave me some grim satisfaction. Anyway, Stephen deserved better than to be left lying on the surface.

I should have thought harder, more logically perhaps, but the violence of the scene pushed all reasoned thoughts aside. I should have thought that, just as the blizzard would cover my grave, so they would have covered the body parts had they been there for anything longer than a few hours. I should have realised from experience that the Norsemen were unlikely to leave good food lying around, that they would send someone to gather up the morsels for some future feast. Instead, I kept digging, chipping away at ice with the knife, and crying quietly to myself. I tried not to think about Sally and what she might be suffering at that moment.

I didn't realise there was anyone behind me until the low sun threw his long shadow over me.

I screamed and rolled over onto my back as the Norseman fell on me, his sharp teeth bared in a fierce growl, beard matted with blood, axe held high beginning to swing down.

I barely had time to close my eyes and wait for death as his heavy body landed on top of me, the blade of my knife sliding deep into his belly.

He grunted in surprise as his axe blow wavered missing

my head and thudding into my shoulder. Pain exploded down my good arm. He rolled off me holding his hand to his belly. He lifted it to his face and looked puzzled at the blood on his fingers.

I was stunned, gasping for breath, when my eyes focused on Stephen's severed head lying in the snow behind the Norseman. Nearby lay the head of the woman I had feared was Sally. A rage took hold of me, blinding, all consuming.

I lunged at the wounded man ignoring the pain in my legs and the burning agony from my shoulder wound as I pushed myself towards him. He put up little defence. Perhaps he was too surprised by my sudden transformation from easy victim to wild animal, or perhaps he was disoriented by loss of blood. I plunged the knife in again and again. It thudded into his body and sliced into his raised hands until I was spitting his splattered blood and the knife was almost slipping from my hand with the coating of gore.

One last thrust sliced open his cheek, severed his tongue and buried the blade in the back of his throat.

I was exhilarated, drunk on blood and rage. I jerked my head back and forth looking for more victims, but it seemed he had returned on his own to collect the food. I hung my head back and howled at the sky, but this time in triumph not despair. Let the Norsemen hear me. Let the trolls hear me! In those moments following my victory, I felt I could do anything, defeat anyone.

Less than ten minutes later, as the rage subsided and the adrenalin ceased pumping, I knelt in the snow and vomited, shaking with fear at how close I had come to death. I was appalled by what I had done, but knew now that I was capable of killing a man. No one, not cannibal, Norse warrior nor even huge man-eating Troll, was invincible.

CHAPTER 22

I didn't have time to bury the bodies.

As I calmed myself and tried to gather my thoughts, I realized just how lucky I had been. This had been a running battle. If Stephen's group had stood and fought, there would be more bodies and, for that matter, more Norsemen camped and enjoying the rewards of their victory. I could have walked into the middle of it. I wouldn't have stood a chance.

I was also lucky that only one Norseman had returned to gather the scattered food. Perhaps there were others along the bloody trail of battle, but only one had come here. Against one Norseman who fell accidentally onto my knife and was taken unawares by my sudden violent turn, I had been able to win. Had there been others, I would have been dead.

I searched the blinding white plain before me, something I should have done some time ago, and saw, on the horizon faint twisting strands of smoke. For a moment, I wondered if Norsemen had attacked the farm and it was now ablaze, but surely there would be more smoke? More likely, it was a campfire set by the Norsemen who would, even now, be cooking.

I closed my eyes, not wanting to think about it but unable to stop the flow of memories, of burning bodies on the fire at the Mersey Tunnel, of a half-eaten human thigh on a spit. Of Sally.

I had no idea whether Sally was alive or dead, but I could not forget the group of beaten, terrified women spared the fire at the Tunnel, spared to become whores and, perhaps, the unwilling mothers of a future generation of Norse cannibals. I thought it would be better if Sally were dead, but then grew uncomfortable with the feeling that those thoughts came from my own twisted jealousy and morality. That thought was both unjust and unreasonable. Did I wish her dead to save her from suffering or because, if she lived, she would somehow be *spoilt* for me? If she were forced to submit to the lusts of the Norsemen, did that make her a whore? The very word *whore* had connotations of sleaze, of degradation, in my mind. Was I really so shallow that I could not see the difference between that and survival? Would I do any less in similar circumstances?

Chrissy would be ashamed of me, of the archaic attitudes I was not even aware I possessed until that moment. I had never had that high an opinion of myself in the past, but standing among the dead bodies of recent companions, looking towards the fading smoke trails, I felt I had hit a new low.

I owed it to Sally, to everyone who had helped me, to try to reach the farm and warn them of the approaching danger. The campfire lay directly on my route, but I was sure I could swing around it as I got nearer, perhaps travel by night to avoid being spotted. It would be bitterly cold, even colder than during the day, but I could withstand that for the time necessary to help my friends.

Leaving the driving snow to conceal the evidence of battles won and lost, I trudged onwards, head down against the blizzard, tired legs dragging heavy feet.

It was a risky strategy to follow the blood trails, but it was the most direct route. Before long, a fresh layer of snow would bury the trails, but, while they were visible, they provided easy navigation.

Every few hundred yards, I found a widening of the trail, pools of congealed blood, evidence of fighting, but no more body parts. The Norsemen had gathered everything.

I wondered how organised they were. How long would it take them to realise that one of their food gatherers had not returned? And when they did, would they send out searchers, or would they simply become more wary, more careful in their march towards the farm?

I knew I should rest, save energy for the nighttime walk, but I was afraid to. It would have made sense to dig a snow hole and shelter from the wind for a while, but it would leave me an easy target should they send a search party from the Norse camp. I wouldn't see them approach, and I would not be able to escape. Fear drove me on.

When darkness fell and I continued to walk, I realised how much warmth the weak, watery sun gave. The temperature drop hit me hard even though I thought I was prepared for it. My muscles seized making every step, every movement, a painful battle of mind over body. I lost all feeling in my feet and fingers. The stump of my right arm ached, and I wished that it, too, would go numb. Unable to feel my way properly, I stumbled often. With each fall into the hard, icy crust of snow, I found it more difficult to get back up again. I was tempted just to lie there, to close my eyes and let the blackness roll over me. To die. There was so little to live for anyway. So little reason to keep going. I had lost everything I loved, everything that made living worthwhile, so why not just give up and accept death? At least I would no longer be so cold and so tired.

"Sally needs you."

Does she? If she's dead, I'm too late. If she's alive, she'll survive without me. What am I but an old cripple she took pity on?

"You're just being selfish Norm. That girl needs your help. All those people at the farm need your help."

They threw me out! Why should I help them? And why would they believe me any more now than before?

"Just because they're stupid doesn't give you the right to abandon them. You can help. You know what's coming."

But I don't know how to fight it.

"With the others, you can work it out. On their own, they don't stand a chance. Norm, you'll die out here if you don't move, and so will they."

I knew the voice was Chrissy's, and I knew it was impossible. She was gone. No. She was dead! I had to accept that, not just sometimes but always. Yet the delusion she was talking to me, was close by, was so comforting, so strengthening, that I gathered what little energy I had left and pushed myself to my knees.

I stared into the dark almost believing I could see Chrissy standing before me, so close I could reach out and touch her, but I knew that could not be. Her voice had stopped, but I still felt the strength it had given me as I fought against the weariness of my frozen limbs and muscles.

I couldn't walk any further. With great effort, I managed to dig the shallowest of snow holes and curled up into it. I didn't sleep as I feared that with sleep would come death, but the shallow depression gave me shelter from the wind. Without the wind-chill, I would survive.

Chrissy didn't speak to me anymore that night, but I thanked her.

"I love you Chrissy." The words were lost in the roar of the storm whipping the snow into a frenzy above me, but it felt important to say them out loud. "I will always love you."

CHAPTER 23

I began walking again as soon as the first weak rays of light broke the horizon. The rest and temporary boost from eating most of my remaining rations had replenished my energy enough to start moving. Once on my feet, I dragged one frozen foot then the other. I crunched through the overnight crust that would soon soften with daylight and the fall of new snow.

Smoke still curled in the distant sky, but it was weaker, lazier. The campfire had dwindled during the night but not been extinguished. No doubt, the Norsemen would break camp soon. If, as I suspected, they continued towards the farm it would be difficult for me to overtake them, having lost the advantage walking through the night would have given me. On the other hand, if they went in any other direction, I could very well run straight into them. I'd managed to kill one through luck and rage, but I had no illusions about the outcome of meeting the whole group.

In truth, however much I thought about it, worried about it and generally depressed or scared myself about it, there was little choice but to carry on. I was committed. The idea of turning back, of running away, no longer held any sway in my mind. It was not a case of what others thought of me, but what I thought of myself. By seeing this through, I could start to redeem myself in my own eyes, and one day, perhaps, even begin to forgive myself for failing to save Chrissy.

The sun was overhead by the time I entered the

abandoned Norse camp. Scraps of barely cooked meat lay stark and bloody in the snow. Gnawed bones gave no indication whether the Norsemen or their wolves had been the last to rip the flesh from them. Shallow depressions ranged in a roughly circular pattern about the central fire where they had set up shelters or dug into the ground just as I had. They'd left no tools, weapons or clothing behind. There was only the barest evidence that anyone had ever been there. All of which would soon be buried by another layer of snow.

The wind had strengthened over the last hour and the daily blizzard was now in full flow, stinging my eyes, making my face too numb to feel. The last embers glowed in the remains of the campfire. If they had broken camp late morning, they were probably not too far ahead of me. I risked coming across stragglers. I needed to be ready.

With Sally's knife gripped in my hand, I hurried through the camp. I didn't look towards the remains of last night's meal scattered about the snow, didn't allow myself to think about it. I concentrated on moving forward towards Hope Farm.

The Norsemen were running ahead of the glacier that was steadily descending on us from the north. With Stephen's group, I had been heading south when we came across the farm. When they kicked me out, I continued to head south. The Norsemen were now between the farm and me. Had they circled around, perhaps planning a raid from an unexpected direction, or had they marched straight through? There was no way of knowing. The farm could be in imminent danger, or I could already be too late. All I could do was keep moving.

When I reached the first cultivated fields on the outskirts of the farm, I found drifts of snow gathering in the ploughed furrows, crops broken and bent by the blizzard. Why hadn't they cleared the snow, tended the crops?

As I reached the main buildings, the farmhouse, the

barn where we had danced on our arrival, not even the layers of snow covering the blood and however few bodies had been left behind could mask the atmosphere of violent death, of fear and agony that hung almost palpable in the air. The Norsemen had not circled around the farm. They had attacked. Perhaps Stephen and others had escaped before they arrived and been caught as they headed south, or perhaps they ran during the attack and had been hunted down. It didn't matter.

Slowly, despondently, I shuffled towards the farmhouse thinking I could shelter for a while from the incessant snow and wind. I tried not to imagine the people who had died within. It may have crossed my mind briefly to wonder at how many buildings still stood, relatively unscathed, unburned, but it didn't seem of any importance. I couldn't understand the minds of those Norse butchers.

I should have tried.

They were as surprised to see me as I was them. A Norseman pulled open the farmhouse door. Two men exited laughing and talking, wrapped in their usual furs with layers of farm-woven cloth around their shoulders. In a moment of stunned silence, I noted one wore a string of human teeth as a necklace, and the other gripped a bone, still heavy with chunks of dripping meat, in his fist.

I tried to run, but they reacted more quickly. Their years of battle experience gave them the advantage.

I was clubbed round the head. The blow staggered me, dropping me to my knees.

Dizzy, disoriented, watching my blood drip onto the snow with almost lyrical slowness, I tried to crawl away. My vision swam with each small movement. The pounding in my head made anything but the most basic thoughts impossible. Even so, before the second blow landed, I was able to realise how obvious it was that they would use the buildings as shelter, just as I was going to do. The club, the snow and blackness hit me in that order.

CHAPTER 24

The first surprise was that I wasn't dead. The second? I wasn't the only one still alive.

Sounds of mumbled conversations, of sobbing, of bodies shuffling on a hard floor entered my consciousness. An icy draught snaked over me. The smell of unwashed bodies and clothes, of sweat, urine and faeces was overpowering. Slowly, from blackness to blurred darkness to dim light, shadows around me, people, wavered into view. One face hovered close by, concerned and familiar.

"I was beginning to wonder whether you were ever coming round."

"Bernard?" The voice was unmistakable. Although having been so recently convinced I'd heard Chrissy's voice, I was not quite sure I believed it.

"Yes Norman, it's me. Bernard."

I tried to lift my head, crying out at the sharp pain that spiked in my brain. I touched ungloved fingers to sticky half-congealed blood matted in my hair.

"How did you rescue me?"

There was an uncomfortable silence and I noted the slump of his broad shoulders, the unkempt tangle of his long beard. When he answered it was in low, sombre tones.

"We didn't. We're all prisoners here, locked up in our own barn. They threw you in here about two hours ago."

"Prisoners?" I struggled to fully comprehend what Bernard was telling me. I'd seen the Norsemen take women prisoners, but from the voices around me, and from Bernard's presence, there were obviously men here as well.

"Believe me, Norman, we were just as surprised as you. When they attacked, I think everyone finally realised the truth in what you'd been telling us, and with that came the certainty that we would die." He paused, sighed. "Most did. Certainly a lot of the younger men and women who grabbed anything they could use as weapons were cut ruthlessly to the ground. The old and sick too, murdered where they stood."

I looked around the barn at the barely distinguishable shapes of other people, dark masses of humanity, slumped, dejected, defeated.

"But not all of you."

"No, not all of us. Mostly women, some middle-aged and slightly younger men who did not resist and who, like me, accepted the inevitability of death."

"But you didn't die."

He hesitated before continuing and, although I could not clearly see his face in the gloom, I had the impression tears were trickling down his cheeks.

"We were beaten, stripped of most of our clothes, and humiliated. They raped many of the women and some of the men while we were forced to watch. Any who resisted or turned away were beaten again, often until they died. Miriam, my wife, fought back against the monster who dragged her to the ground..."

He was sobbing. I reached up a hand to his arm ignoring the sharp stab of pain from the axe wound in my shoulder and tried to show I understood his pain, his sorrow.

"He killed her." He sobbed heavier. His body shook. "I tried to help her but they dragged me back, beat me. I should have died too!"

I could think of nothing to say. I knew the terrible grief he must be feeling, the agony of his perceived failure to save his wife, but nothing I could have said would have done anything to help. I simply squeezed his arm to show my support and felt his hand cover mine. In that moment,

I think I became closer to Bernard than I had to any man my whole life. My kinship with Harry was strong, would always be so, but Bernard's sorrow was so recent, so powerful, I could not help but compare it to the grief and guilt I still felt so keenly.

Slowly he regained control, an admirable show of self-discipline, more than I had ever managed. He sniffed, released my hand and wiped at the streaks on his face left by tears. Even with my eyes gradually adjusting to the low light, I couldn't see his expression clearly, but I think he forced a smile. This gave me the go-ahead to ask the question I'm sure everyone there had asked at some point.

"So, what happens now?"

"It's only been a few days, I think. Difficult to tell locked in here. We get a few scraps of food: withered vegetables from our own fields, small lumps of raw meat that no one has yet had the courage to eat, and just about enough water to live on. We're cold. They took everyone's extra clothing leaving us with the bare minimum."

I nodded, trying to ignore the pain in my head and shoulder, noticing for the first time how cold I was, and how naked I felt without my glove, extra coats, and special boots.

"How many prisoners?"

"Maybe twenty, twenty-five. I've not counted. But the numbers are falling."

"Falling?"

"They come and take people without warning. Some, usually the women, come back, bruised and terrified. No one asks them what happened. Their suffering is obvious. Others we never see again." He paused lowering his voice to a deep, raspy whisper. "I don't think these bastards go hungry."

That thought terrified me more than any other. To be taken and butchered for food. I'd have preferred a quick, clean death and my body left to rot, buried by the snow.

"I'm sorry you came back Norman. You should have

kept going. You wouldn't have ended up here with us as a prisoner."

"No, we're not prisoners." The word had leapt into my mind as unexpected as it was grimly fitting. "We're cattle."

I was finally able to sit up. My shoulder, while stiff, was beginning to scab over and heal. The axe-blow was fortunately not too deep. Bernard, or one of the others, had done their best to patch it up while I lay unconscious.

I decided to keep the story of my brief time away from the farm short ignoring the dilemma I had felt, the struggle to decide whether to return or not, and concentrating on the purely physical aspects.

"I think the snow's even deeper going south. It certainly felt like it. Every step was an effort. Maybe I've just forgotten what it's like to struggle by on your own, but if I'm right then, while I still think heading south is the best option, it's certainly not going to be an easy one."

Bernard nodded and said nothing. He could have pointed out that none of us were going anywhere unless we found a way to escape the Norsemen.

"Even when I was heading back, it was all I could do to keep moving through the blizzard. That's why I didn't see the bodies until I was right among them." I paused, knowing the next part of my story would likely be distressing to Bernard, as it still was to me. But I could think of no way other than being blunt. "Then I tripped and there he was. Stephen. Decapitated."

Bernard gasped, quickly covering his mouth with his hand as if afraid the noise would draw attention to us.

"Stephen and a few others, mostly from his original group but with some from the farm, were almost ready to leave when the attack began," said Bernard. "They were quick and prepared enough to run southwards through the fields and into the wasteland beyond. They were sensible enough not to try to stand and fight. I saw them go. I really hoped they'd gotten away." He shook his head sadly.

"It would have been better for all of you if you'd never come across Hope Farm."

"Was Sally with Stephen's group? Did you see her with them?" I dreaded asking the question, but I needed to know.

"She was at his side when I saw them running." He paused and squeezed my hand with his. "I'm sorry Norman."

I felt as though I'd been punched in the stomach. All the air left my lungs in one enormous gasp, and my head dropped as tears filled my eyes.

"She could have escaped," said Bernard, his tone clearly conveying the doubt in his own words. "After all, you never found her body."

I nodded without conviction. I knew Bernard was trying to ease my pain a little, but I also knew that we both understood the reality. Body or no body, in all likelihood Sally was killed in the running battle between Stephen's people and the Norsemen. She was dead. Her body was cut up and eaten by the people who held me captive.

I felt nauseous so I lay back down and tried, without success, to block the gruesome images that filled my head.

"Mr. Leonard."

At some point, I had fallen asleep and was woken by the sound of my name spoken softly and with grave formality.

"Mr. Leonard, I need to speak to you for my own peace of mind."

I opened my eyes, wincing at the sudden stab of pain in my head, and looked at the woman who knelt next to me. It took a moment for recognition to filter through my tiredness and the many aches of my body. The hard angular face was drawn and aged by fear. The snarling mouth trembled, lips dry and split, but there could be no mistaking the uneven short-cropped hair nor the memory of humiliation and rejection that was still fresh in my mind.

"What do *you* want?" I snapped the words, sneered them, put every ounce of my disgust into them.

The committee member named Alison, who had not believed in cannibalism, who had stood among the crowd kicking me out of the farm, straightened her shoulders and tried to maintain the aloof, superior expression she had so successfully mastered in farm meetings. But I could sense her nervousness and see the underlying shame she felt at facing me. Her eyes flicked back and forth never resting on me for more than a moment. She clasped the fingers of her right hand in her left, running her thumb agitatedly over the knuckles.

"Mr. Leonard, I am not afraid to acknowledge my mistakes and, obviously, my not believing what you told us was a mistake."

"It wasn't just disbelief though, was it? You ridiculed me, belittled Bernard, and then stood there and watched me get thrown out. You were probably one of those stirring the whole thing up."

The brief downward shift of her eyes told me that she had, indeed, been one of those responsible. My anger intensified.

"I made a mistake. I know that. And yes, I was cruel to both you and Bernard, and I was foolish and naive and any other criticism you want to throw at me. I can't do anything to change that, but I couldn't have us both in this terrible situation without offering an apology and hoping that we can forget all that unpleasantness."

Unpleasantness! The word was in no way strong enough to describe what had transpired in that committee meeting and afterwards but, just as I was about to launch into a tirade of abuse against this women, I noticed her trembling, the paleness of her skin, the wringing of hands held in her lap. She was scared, and I realised that, whatever had happened in the past, she was now a prisoner just like me, like everyone in that barn, and every bit as terrified.

"Forget it," I said wishing I could. "The only enemy is outside this barn not inside it. I don't promise I can forgive you, but I can try to forget."

She nodded, unsmiling.

"Thank you Mr. Leonard. I do appreciate it. I couldn't stop thinking about what I'd done. What I'd said..."

Bernard appeared at her shoulder and, reaching down, helped her to her feet.

"It's okay Alison. You did the right thing coming over here and talking. Now go and rest for a while."

I watched as she forced a slight smile at Bernard and moved away to the far side of the barn where she curled into a foetal ball. I could have been mistaken in the general low noise of prisoners whispering, snoring, and coughing, but I thought I heard her sobbing quietly.

"It took a lot of courage for her to come here and say that," said Bernard, sitting himself beside me.

"Given the things she said about you, I'm surprised you can feel sorry for her."

"She's young. I watched Alison change from a nervous teenager to a confident, perhaps over-confident, young woman. She got involved with the reformers, the ones who felt we were all too old to be running things. She became one of the youngest committee members we ever had. In the end, though, the responsibility went to her head and she thought she had a right to say what she thought when she thought it, regardless of anyone else's feelings. She's not a bad person, Norman, just inexperienced."

"It doesn't excuse her behaviour."

"Perhaps not, but it explains it a little. She lacks the experience to debate and argue effectively, so she turns to attack and personal insult even. It's childish when you think about it. Straight out of the schoolyard."

I understood what Bernard was saying, and I even think it softened my feelings towards Alison a little, but I could not be as forgiving as he was.

CHAPTER 25

The smell of unwashed clothes and bodies, of urine and faeces, faded into the background surprisingly quickly. I could never quite ignore it, but I grew used to it. Similarly the never-ending moans and sobs, the mumbled prayers of those few who still clung to their faith, even the occasional sudden cries of pain and despair, became no more notable than the constant roar of the wind outside, or its scream as it found another narrow opening in the wall.

Time was difficult to judge. At first I tried to keep track by following day and night through the gaps left by warped timbers in the walls, but I soon lost count. The light inside the barn barely altered, regardless of the time of day. The shortening and lengthening of shadows around the edges of the floor provided some variation, but few people bothered to look at them. Everyone slept when they were tired, nothing more.

I can't be certain, therefore, but I feel it was about my third day in the barn that I saw my captors for the first time since they had imprisoned me.

The rattling of the barn door sent an audible ripple of fear through the prisoners. There was a mass shuffling of bodies turning away from the door. Everyone lowered their heads and tried to be as inconspicuous as possible. I didn't follow suit. Curiosity kept my head high, my eyes on the events unfolding.

"Norman, look away," hissed Bernard. "If they see you looking at them you might be chosen!"

I lowered my head a little. Fear of what might happen

dampened my curiosity, but I kept my eyes open and watched.

The barn door crashed open. Snow puffed into the air from the impact. Flakes fell from the roof. Three Norsemen marched in. Their expressions were grim, and their weapons were ready. They wore furs augmented by clothing stolen from the farmers, as had the two who captured me. It was difficult to judge age beneath the layers of grime, the smears of blood on their faces, but everything about their lithe movement, the almost hyperactive speed of their gestures, suggested youth. Whatever their age might be, they were organised and well-practiced. One stayed at the opening while the other two strode among the cowering prisoners. Without warning, and through some instinct that required no visible sign between them, they reached down and pulled a tall, middle-aged man to his feet. He was not familiar to me; the few scraps of clothing he wore suggested he was of Hope Farm rather than Stephen's group. I knew it should not matter whether he was familiar or not, but I couldn't suppress a moment of relief.

"No!" he cried, struggling ineffectively in the tight grip of their fists. His broad shoulders and thick arms, strengthened through hard work in the fields, were of little use against them. "No, not me! Take someone else, not me!" The pitch of his voice rose higher as he was dragged towards the door. "Please God, not me!"

I watched, horrified, as he struggled harder and was clubbed viciously to the ground. People who had sat near him, some of whom must have known him, kept their eyes turned away, their heads down, too terrified even to look, let alone help. The Norsemen lifted the man's limp body. Blood ran from his head dripping from the tangled mesh of his long beard. It left a ragged line of dots through the barn door as they dragged him out. They quickly closed and locked the door behind them.

The casual brutality shocked me. Bernard had told me they took prisoners away, but I had not been ready for the reality. Seeing a man that terrified, struggling for his life, and knowing he was probably going to his death, horrified me. I'd watched the Norsemen hold life and death in their hands. They chose a particular victim for no other reason than they wanted to. It was random and brutal, and my feelings of horror were mixed with the guilt I felt at the relief that it was not my turn to be chosen.

There seemed to be no rule or regularity. The door just opened and another victim dragged out, screaming. None of the men were seen again, but they returned some of the women, battered and bruised, their clothing ripped, their eyes filled with fear and shame.

I soon joined the others in turning away from the door, looking down at the ground and hoping they would choose anyone but me. Does that make me a terrible person? I've heard it said that to see an atrocity committed and do nothing to stop it makes you as guilty as the person carrying it out. Perhaps. But I was scared, terrified. All I could think about was surviving for a little longer. I wasn't the only one. No one in that barn tried to help those dragged away by the Norsemen. Bernard told me that, early on, some had tried, but they were either beaten down or taken as well. It wasn't long before the prisoners started looking the other way. Just as I did.

Around the fifth day, the door to the barn opened once more but, instead of the Norsemen dragging another captive out, they threw a handful of items inside.

"Food and drink," explained Bernard at my side.

I was dry and starving and made to move but Bernard held me back.

"No need to hurry Norman. You'll get your share."

There was no panicked scrambling or fighting among the prisoners to reach the small amount of food and water provided. Five or maybe six men and women shuffled forward and gathered the items together. They carefully avoided the stare of the Norseman still standing in the open doorway. In the gloom, it was not easy to judge his expression from that distance, but it seemed to me it was one of disappointment. Perhaps he had hoped to see a battle for food among the captives? He stepped back and slammed the door closed as if he were angry. I was impressed with the way the prisoners shared the scraps. Although, as Bernard had said, no one touched the lumps of raw, bleeding meat that lay among the more palatable root vegetables, seeds and nuts. The water, too, was shared around. If anyone questioned what the pouches were made of, they never said so out loud. I was certain I saw the corner of a tattoo along the seam of one, but, I too, said nothing.

Perhaps six days, maybe more, into my captivity I heard The Roar. It pulled me back from the edge of sleep, and I knew by the restless shuffling and frightened whispering around me I was not the only one who had heard it. Bernard sat nearby looking towards me and I could see the fear in his eyes. I knew it was reflected in my own. It sounded close.

On the seventh or eighth day as a prisoner, the voice of the chosen was horribly familiar. No longer an unidentifiable screaming and shouting, this was a voice I knew. Alison. Perhaps I should have felt a sense of ironic justice at that moment, but not even I was that heartless.

I looked up, risking being noticed by our captors, and saw them dragging her towards the door, kicking and screaming. Her wide staring eyes jerked from side to side, pleading for help.

She saw me.

I felt my stomach twist, my heart pound with fear as her eyes fixed on mine.

"Mr. Leonard. Help me. Please! I'm sorry."

One of the Norsemen looked straight at me. I turned my eyes to the floor, rejecting Alison's call for help. I was no hero. I was a prisoner like the others in that barn. I told myself it was the only realistic choice to make. I had to wait, to survive, however hopeless it might seem at times. Perhaps eventually, I would get the opportunity to prove that I was not the same bitter, self-obsessed coward I used to be. All I could do was hope.

Alison's cries faded as the barn door closed. I breathed a sigh of relief that the Norseman who had looked at me hadn't grabbed me and taken me out too.

"There was nothing you could have done, Norman," said Bernard, appearing at my side and laying a hand on my shoulder. "Nothing any of us could have done."

I knew he was right, but she had called out *my* name.

The Norsemen returned several hours later bundling Alison through the door and throwing her to the ground. She was battered and sobbing. Her clothes were ripped and tattered. I didn't have the courage to go and see how she was. I just hid in my corner and hoped she didn't notice me.

That night we heard The Roar again. It was even closer. The sound was deafening, shaking the timbers of the barn.

As The Roar died away, I could hear the Norsemen outside. Their voices were agitated, shouting and responding to unintelligible orders. Normally, we would not hear them at all. They had obviously heard The Roar. I just wasn't sure whether they welcomed or feared it.

As the shadows at the edge shifted and the faint light of dawn peered through the wall, a large group of Norsemen, maybe fifteen or so, crashed through the door of the barn. They gestured wildly, poking prisoners with sticks, pulling some to their feet. No one understood what was happening, what they were meant to do, only that this was different from the previous times. The Norsemen shouted orders in a harsh, guttural language none of us understood, but slowly it became obvious they were moving us out of the barn. All of us.

The barn had been cold, but as I stepped out into the almost forgotten force of the blizzard, I faltered. A sharp push in the back from one of the Norsemen had me stumbling into the full power of the never-ending winter. Without my extra coats and with no glove or boots, I shivered uncontrollably. In seconds my socks were soaked through and my feet frozen. My fingers, too, ached with the cold and for once I was grateful I only had one hand to suffer with. I had no idea how far the Norsemen were planning to walk before finding shelter again, but it wouldn't take long for some of my fellow prisoners to die from hypothermia. Many of them had less clothing than me, and I wasn't very confident of my own ability to survive for long.

Another push in the back, another stumble, and for a moment I lost my temper and my sense. I turned, angry, glaring at the Norseman behind me who immediately raised his club to strike me down. Bernard stepped in, almost certainly saving my life, placing a restraining hand on my shoulder and smiling at the Norseman.

"Please excuse my friend here," said Bernard in his best diplomatic voice, calm and soothing. "He's not quite right in the head, I'm afraid."

I doubt the Norseman understood the words, but the tone of voice was clear. The Norseman slowly lowered his club and then, without warning, pushed Bernard in the chest with his other hand.

Bernard fell awkwardly landing hard on his right hip. He let out a grunt of pain but almost immediately called out to me, "I'm all right Norman. It's okay."

His words were enough, just barely, to control my temper and for the second time in as many minutes, I knew Bernard had saved my life.

Other Norsemen had moved closer, fighting to restrain wolves eager to join the argument, and either would have torn me apart before I reached my grinning tormentor. Moving slowly, I helped Bernard to his feet, and together, Bernard now limping slightly, we turned to resume our walk. The Norseman at my back prodded me once or twice more but I refused to react.

We were herded into the farmyard in front of the

main house where the rest of the Norsemen stood, ready to march, unconcerned with our discomfort. From their point of view, I suppose, any of us who died on the way were just more food for round the campfire later. Frozen food. I almost laughed, despite the pain and fear. I was more than a little manic in my thoughts at that time.

In an unexpected show of kindness, or more likely a desire not to see the food supply die off too quickly, the Norsemen threw a collection of shoes and boots at us. Everyone found something, however ill fitting. I was unable to find my specially adapted boots and settled for an old pair of shoes a size too big for me. With no toes and my heels sliding out with every step they were far from comfortable, but they were comparatively warm once I took my soaking, fast freezing socks off. It may seem counter-intuitive but I felt the wet socks were of more immediate danger to my feet than the dry cold felt through the shoes. I've no idea whether it was the correct thing to do, but it seemed so at the time.

I was not surprised when the march began heading southwards. As I've said before, I had always felt the Norsemen were running ahead of the glacier.

The main group moved ahead of us led by the wolf handlers. A small number hung back and moved us along, prodding us with sticks, threatening us with spears and knives, and mercilessly clubbing anyone who strayed or stumbled. I have no idea whether they lifted those people back to their feet or left them to die in the snow. I was too scared to look.

Bernard was beside me, still limping from his fall, and, although we said nothing, it felt good to have a friend close by. Not far in front of me, I could see Alison, shuffling. Her hands were already blue with the cold. She tried to hold her ripped clothing closed about her. It was a heart-breaking sight and any vestige of ill-feeling I had towards her was banished at that moment. I didn't have to like the woman to feel compassion and, yes, pity for her.

Without allowing myself further thought about my actions, I pulled my heavy overcoat off, the only one the Norsemen had left me with, and pushed forward. She turned to look at me as I placed it round her shoulders, her eyes red and puffed with crying. I managed a weak smile as I helped her arms into the sleeves and fastened the buttons at the front. It was far too big for her, but it gave her some warmth and covered a body that I had seen blotted with bruises and ripped with raw wounds before I closed the coat over it. If it was possible, my hatred of the Norsemen deepened at that moment.

She looked forward once again concentrating on shuffling through the deep snow, and I returned to my place next to Bernard, already shivering as the cold bled through my thick woollen sweater. He nodded his appreciation of my actions, and I felt that at least some of my guilt and shame had been appeased.

We were barely clear of the last farm buildings when, above the constant drone of the wind and the threatening, unintelligible shouting of those driving us forward, we heard The Roar. It sounded even closer than it had just a few hours earlier, and for the first time I saw fear, or at least concern, in the eyes of those Norsemen closest to us. I had not, until that point, assumed the relationship between the Norsemen and the Trolls was anything other than friendly, supportive, even symbiotic given their likely similar origins. But at that moment, as our captors grew more restless and urged us to move faster, I realised I had been wrong. The Norsemen were every bit as frightened of the Trolls as I was.

Layer upon layer of bellowing cries rolled through the storm, deafening in their volume, terrifying in their closeness.

The farmers around me, despite being numb from cold, broke out of the shambling, ragged line we had been marching in as if they feared The Roar more than the Norsemen. They shouted and screamed in panic as they stumbled over each other, treading on friends and comrades in their attempt to escape.

The ground shook and a great booming, thudding noise made me turn my eyes northwards.

Out of the mist of the blizzard, like giant ghosts against the pale sky, came the Trolls, powering forward with long strides. They moved faster than I had seen them move in Liverpool. Three of the creatures ran into battle with an awe-inspiring muscular grace. It may seem a fanciful thought, but as the Norsemen spread out into a defensive line, no longer interested in whether we stayed or ran, it was obvious to me that this was not the first time these two had faced each other.

Not wanting to join the panicked flight of the farmers, and certainly having no intention of joining the fight, I dragged myself away from the coming confrontation, cursing the depth of the snow, the loose fitting of the shoes, and the sheer impracticality of running without toes. I lay down in the snow and forced myself to stay still remembering how, in the flood water of the Mersey, I had seemed invisible to the Troll standing above me as long as I did not move. It was a risky strategy but, as long as they didn't tread on me by accident, I felt it was safer than trying to run away from creatures that could outdistance me with one stride.

Bernard must have trusted my experience as, following my lead, he joined me in the snow. We did not speak, but it was comforting to have a friend at my side.

Through the blizzard and the scattering prisoners, I saw a figure standing alone, unmoving, as though frozen. Alison.

I called to her, but my voice was lost in the wind and the shouts of the Norsemen. I made to push myself up, but Bernard grabbed me and dragged me back down again.

"You'll get yourself killed," he shouted. "She'll move in a moment."

The first Troll to reach the defensive line stamped down,

crushing several Norsemen beneath its foot. It reached low and scooped up more in its hand, shovelling them ungraciously into its open, salivating mouth. As the other Trolls joined the fight, I expected the Norsemen to scatter, run for their lives, but they attacked with a strategy that told of many such battles in the past.

Clubs swiped at grasping fingers. A defensive circle gathered around those with blades. They charged towards the feet of the Trolls. Dodging angry stamps and ignoring the cries of their comrades as sharp teeth ripped them apart, they attacked the ankles of the giant creatures. They chopped with axes, stabbed with spears, and sliced with knives. I knew enough human biology to know we had an Achilles tendon that was relatively unprotected by muscle and bone. I could only assume the Trolls had something similar. The Norsemen's blades cut through matted hair and tough skin to draw blood and tear great bellows of pain and rage from the injured Trolls.

With an angry sweep of its foot, one Troll scattered the attackers crushing at least two beneath its heel, breaking the bones of others as they tumbled through the snow. More took their place. Some grabbed up the weapons of their fallen comrades.

The roaring of the Trolls, the battle cries and death screams of Norsemen, the snapping of bones, the thumping of sticks and clubs, the slicing and chopping of blades was so loud it distorted in my head. Blood stained the snow crimson faster than the fierce blizzard could cover it.

Two of the Trolls shuffled backwards burying Norsemen in the snow as they did. One, its ankle torn and bloody, skin curling away from the wound, could not move. With a snap that echoed across the snowy wastes, its leg gave way and it fell. For one terrible moment, as the great body toppled slowly over, I thought it would crush Bernard and me. Luckily, its angle shifted. My relief turned quickly to horror as it fell towards Alison.

She remained frozen, silent and apparently unaware.

An explosion of snow burst into the air as the huge beast hit the ground crushing Alison beneath its back. It was impossible to say whether the spray of blood was human or Troll.

The Norsemen swarmed onto the fallen creature, attacking its head, its belly, its genitals. The Troll thrashed and roared killing many but not enough to stop the attack. A Norseman thrust a spear into a huge eye. Jelly and fluid burst forth. Axes ripped open the distended belly. I turned away as knives slashed into enormous hanging testicles.

The wolf handlers, who had kept their animals back from the action up to that point, let them loose. The graceful but deadly animals swarmed onto the fallen Troll joining the Norsemen in the gruesome tearing and ripping of the creature.

To my surprise, the other two Trolls did not attempt to aid their fallen comrade, but took the chance to back away. The few Norsemen who were not occupied with butchering, watched them go.

In a last defiant gesture, the retreating Trolls turned their heads to the sky and emitted a Roar louder and more sorrowful than any I had heard before. Then they turned and loped away into the blizzard.

A cry of triumph went up from the Norsemen as if they didn't care that over half their number lay dead or dying around them, or had simply disappeared into the cavernous stomachs of the Trolls. They concentrated on slicing up their enemy. Its great muscles still spasmodically twitched although it was dead. I was about to turn to Bernard and suggest escaping when a hand dropped onto my shoulder and I froze, certain that I had been caught and would once again be a prisoner.

"Norman?"

I recognised the voice and turned. Sally! Alive and wrapped in her usual coats, hat and woolly scarves. There were others with her. Someone helped Bernard to his feet. I had so many questions but could not speak. I simply smiled despite the dangerous cold gripping my body after lying in the snow so long without a coat.

"We have to go."

With those words, she helped pull me to my feet and, with me limping along at the best speed I could manage, we headed away from the carnage.

CHAPTER 26

"Stephen hung back with the majority of the group while a few of us went ahead to scout. While we were away, the Norsemen caught up with them. We heard it. We knew what was happening, but there was nothing we could do to help." Sally looked away from me as though she were ashamed and unwilling to hold eye contact.

Her face was grey, drawn. Her cheeks were a little more hollow than before. The loss of Stephen, of other friends and companions, seemed to have taken a heavy toll on her. The brightness, the humour, was gone from her eyes.

"We ran."

I placed my hand, now once again safely in a glove, on her arm.

"You did the right thing Sally. If you'd gone back, you would have been killed as well. At least you're alive."

She looked up, eyes shining with tears, a weak smile on her face.

"I'm glad you're alive too, Norman."

My heart skipped a little at this. My stomach knotted. I knew I could be reading too much into what she said, but she *had* missed me. Uncertain as I was about my own feelings towards her, or perhaps unwilling to face the truth through fear of further hurt or guilt at recent memories, it nevertheless felt good to know she cared enough to miss me.

I was still trying to formulate a response that was neither embarrassing nor dismissive when the moment was lost. One of the five rescuers with Sally pointed ahead at a black outcrop, stark against the white of the surroundings. An army truck, wheel-arches lost in deep drifts, the canvas covering bowing under the weight of snowfall, but otherwise intact. A rosy glow painted the packed snow on the backboard and lit the interior with a welcome warmth.

"We found it a day or so ago," explained Sally as she helped me climb into the back. Inside were another six or so people huddled around a small fire burning at the truck-bed's centre. Someone handed me an old overcoat and, with Sally's help, I wrapped it around my shoulders trying not to think of my other one lost with Alison.

"How did you...?" I didn't even finish the question before Sally correctly guessed what I was about to say.

"We've been keeping an eye on the farm, trying to make sure they didn't sneak up on us."

"Why were you even still around here?"

Sally glanced at the others, and I sensed the issue had caused some tension among the small group.

"We couldn't agree on what to do next. Some wanted to get as far away as possible; others hoped that loved ones might still be alive at the farm and didn't want to leave. In the end, we decided to stay for a short while. We'd planned to move when we were ready or when the Norsemen came looking for us."

With the help of the fire and the coat, some warmth was gradually easing back into my body. Numb fingers began to tingle, almost painfully, but any feeling was a good sign.

"So you saw us leaving the farm?"

"Yes, and some of us felt vindicated when we saw faces we knew and cared about among the prisoners." She may have blushed. It was hard to tell in the dim light and with so many layers of clothes, but I like to think she did. "We had no idea how we could rescue any of you though."

"And then the Trolls and the Norsemen decided to go head-to-head."

She smiled. "Yes. Whatever the outcome, it gave us an opportunity to move in closer and get as many of you away as we could."

It had not been many. Looking around the truck-bed, I recognised four of my fellow prisoners including Bernard. We were all wrapped up as best we could be thanks to the generosity of Sally and the others. It was hard to believe that out of the combined numbers of Hope Farm and Stephen's group this dozen or so cold, bedraggled but un-beaten few were all that remained alive and free.

"I was surprised to see you with the prisoners," said Sally. She spoke slowly, as if wary of offending me in some way. "I thought you'd be out ahead of us, on your own af-ter they kicked you out."

"I decided to go back. Got lonely."

She smiled. "You went back to help."

It was not a question, and I felt faintly embarrassed by the certainty with which she said it. More certainty than I had felt when I made the decision in the first place.

"We all make mistakes."

It was a pathetically weak attempt at a joke but Sally laughed anyway and I felt better for that.

"So, what do we do now?" I asked, uneasy talking about my decision to return to the farm. I was still not sure I fully understood it myself.

"We head south like Stephen wanted us to. It's the only logical thing to do."

The man who spoke was sitting a few feet to my right. He was familiar. His square jaw and high cheekbones were prominent even through the dirty-brown thickness of his unkempt beard. I remembered him as one of Stephen's original group, but I had no idea of his name. For the first time, I felt embarrassed that I had never bothered to learn the names of more of the people who had helped me.

Sally seemed to sense my hesitation, my embarrassment.

"Dennis was in charge of our scouting group," she said. "Stephen trusted his experience. He used to be in the army."

I remembered. I'd seen him in huddled conversations with Stephen. Tall, straight-backed, broad shouldered. I could have guessed he was a military man, if I'd bothered to take enough notice.

"Nothing fancy," he said. "Just the regular infantry. But I saw action in China, before the Beijing Agreement, so Stephen felt my experience might be of some help."

Dennis. It was time I started remembering some names, particularly of those nominally in charge.

"The Norsemen will be heading south too," I said, not wishing to challenge Dennis's authority, but my recent memories were too vivid and terrible to wish an early re-match with the cannibals.

"It'll take them time to finish feasting on that monster and celebrate their victory. Then they'll need to prepare what remains for taking with them now that they've lost most of their mobile larder."

Dennis smiled at me when he said this and I couldn't help but smile back. After all, 'mobile larder' sounded slightly better than 'cattle.'

"As soon as the sun's up we can get moving," said Sally. "That should give us quite a head start on them even if they're quicker than we expect."

"Okay." I smiled at Sally. I said nothing of my, now firm, belief that there was nothing more south of us than there was north. Being a victim of my own pessimism did not mean I had to bring everyone else down with me. Anyway, I might be wrong. Either way, I'd be travelling with Sally once more. I don't think the direction mattered to me at that moment.

We settled as best we could and tried to sleep, all of us huddled close together to share body warmth. There were several people pressed against me, but I only truly remember Sally's warmth and closeness, even through several layers of clothing. I fell asleep more content than I had been since the Mersey broke its banks and took my Chrissy from me.

CHAPTER 27

I was woken by others moving around me. I'd slept until nearly dawn, my first unbroken sleep in what seemed like forever.

Sally smiled and said, "good morning." I should have been rested, untroubled, but I could not shake the feeling that something was wrong. While my body slept, my brain had been working, leaving the seed of a concern behind.

I have never been the quickest of people, mentally. I'll get there eventually, plodding along, persistent until I solve the problem, but I have always lacked the intuitive leap, the sudden realisation that proves key to the solution. As we gathered our sparse belongings and climbed out of the back of the truck into the fresh snow, the final piece finally clicked into place and I knew what my subconscious had been trying to tell me all night.

The army truck.

The army truck we had slept in, that Sally and my other rescuers had found, was only half-buried, even after the overnight snowfall. Back in Liverpool, great mounds of snow on the streets had been the only indication that there were cars underneath Yet this army truck, out in the country where the snowfall was heavier than back home, had been clear enough that we were able to climb into the back and rest.

As Sally helped settle my pack over my shoulders, I spoke quietly, not wanting to draw anyone else's attention until I was certain.

"Did you have to dig this truck out of the snow?"

Sally shook her head. "We found it like this. I mean, it gets a bit more buried every day and we probably wouldn't be able to sleep in it for many more nights if we were staying, but we were lucky."

"So, given the depth of the snow when you found it, how long would you say it had been sitting here?"

Sally paused in her answer and I could see the implications of my question playing in her eyes. She understood much quicker than I would have in her situation.

"We're stupid! Why didn't anyone think about it? This truck could only have been here a few days before we found it."

"There's been no motorised traffic that I've seen since the exodus from the cities. The government commandeered everything that could still move to get its people out."

"So," said Sally, her thoughts moving faster than mine, "did this get here on its own, or were there others? Are we talking one person or the army? But why leave it here?"

I shrugged. "It got stuck? Or ran out of petrol? Doesn't really matter. The point is someone was driving it recently which means there could be other people close by."

"Must be the army, Norman. Don't you think? They've come back to rescue us. We're going to be okay."

The certainty behind her optimism brought so much brightness and life back to her that I just smiled, keeping my doubts to myself. She was so sure that whoever might be out there would be friendly, so happy and excited at the prospect of a rescue, that I couldn't deflate her dreams. And my cynicism and distrust *had* been proved wrong before. So, while Sally moved off to tell Dennis and the others, I simply watched her. I could not, *would* not, destroy that hope, that optimism. Perhaps some time ago, or perhaps with other people, but not now and not with Sally.

As we moved off, conversations were underway on all sides. They were full of the possibility of the army, authority, order and, ultimately, safety.

Sally slowed her step to match mine, staying alongside me. I'm sure she wanted to talk about what the truck could mean, but I kept silent, deliberately not looking towards her. If we spoke, I was afraid I would voice my fears, my negativity, and I didn't want to do that to her.

We made good speed at first. The snow was deep, as always, but the overnight drop in temperature gave the drifts a temporary hardness that helped walking. The wind and snowfall remained light for several hours. However, by the time the hazy sun had climbed high, the usual blizzard had begun, driving at our backs. The heat of the day, while imperceptible to us, was enough to soften the snow until we were wading thigh deep in places. Progress slowed and both the talking and morale dropped. We dragged ourselves on, heads down, fighting both physical exhaustion and mental weariness.

When our muscles weakened to the point of needing the help of others to extricate ourselves from the deeper drifts, we decided to stop and rest. Despite the heaviness of our arms and legs, we dug into the snow, deep enough to huddle down out of the wind. Without the wind chill, it was bearable if not exactly comfortable. These windbreaks would be no good to us overnight, but for a short rest in daylight they were fine.

I thought I heard The Roar so distant it was almost indistinguishable from the wind that drove horizontal snow over our shallow shelters. Perhaps it *was* the wind. Sally stayed huddled close to me, giving no indication that she had heard anything unusual, and I decided I had imagined it, allowed my fear to misinterpret the deafening noise that surrounded us as the blizzard strengthened.

A few minutes later when I heard it again, I knew it was no misinterpretation, no imagination. This time The Roar continued. One faded as another rose to take its place. More and more distant voices joined the call until I could hear it clearly over the blizzard, echoing off hills too distant to see, making the ground tremble beneath us.

Sally looked at me, the fear in her eyes a reflection of my own. Others stirred, rising out of their shelters, braving the blizzard to squint towards the snow-blurred horizon. I saw Bernard among them, and he caught my eye briefly. He was scared. We all were.

At that moment I realised that, when the Norsemen killed the Troll and its companions turned away, they were not running. They were retreating to rejoin others of their kind, to gather, to prepare. As the cacophonous Roaring finally died, fading behind the wind, I knew that all we had encountered up to now had been small scouting parties.

The full might of the Troll army was finally on the move.

CHAPTER 28

All thoughts of resting any longer were gone. We were scared, and we wanted to be moving away from that sound as quickly as we could. No one spoke. The resulting silence was eerie, I would have almost preferred it if people had been crying or shouting or just voicing their fears.

Sally took hold of my hand in a firm grip as we joined the others in the slow, ponderous march through ever-deepening snow. I was grateful for the physical contact, for the feel of another human being. She was probably every bit as scared as I was but her touch was undeniably a source of comfort and strength.

Up ahead, Bernard had stopped and was looking back with his hand shielding his eyes. "There's something fol-lowing us," he said as I stopped alongside him. "Look, back there."

I turned and at first saw nothing. Then, slowly fading out of the snow-mist, shadows, blurred but unmistakably human and moving faster than we had been able to do.

Norsemen!

Others had seen them too. For a moment, people were stunned into immobility. Their faces dropped into expres-sions of fear and disbelief.

I understood, felt it myself. Why couldn't they leave us alone?

The initial shock lasted barely a second, then people panicked, myself and Sally included. We tried to speed our tortuous movement through the snow. Because of my disabilities, we were near the back of the group and I was frightened that, because of her concern for me, Sally would be caught, raped, butchered. Guilt and fear drove me on. I ignored the burning cold of toes that were not there and used my good hand and my stump to dig into the snow, drag myself forward. I reached back to pull Sally after me.

I tried to push her in front. "You need to go ahead. I'm just slowing you down." I tried again to push her, to make her leave me behind. "I won't be responsible for you being captured by those bastards. You've got more chance to escape without me!"

"You're not responsible for me Norman. I make my own decisions," she shouted above the noise of the blizzard and the frightened people around us. "I'm not leaving you behind."

I could see there was no point in arguing further. She was strong, and she could be stubborn that was evident. Arguing would simply waste time we did not have.

People were shouting, screaming, sobbing. Several simply sat down and waited as if they were physically unable to move any further, mentally unable to run anymore. I was shocked to see Bernard among them.

I stopped, tried to pull him to his feet with my good arm, but he shrugged me off, refusing to move.

"Come on Bernard. You need to get up," I shouted, desperation edging my voice with a harshness I did not intend. "You have to come with us."

He turned his face to me, tears rolling down his cheeks.

"I'm sorry Norman. I just can't do it anymore. I can't run. Miriam's gone. I've nothing left."

"We're all frightened, Bernard, but you're not alone. You have us!" I pleaded as I kept my eyes on the fast approaching killers.

"It doesn't matter. We can't escape." Bernard took my hand in his. "They'll never give up and eventually they'll kill us all. I can't keep running for that. You go, spend some time with Sally before it's too late."

He let go of my hand. I stared at him, unable to think of

anything more to say. He was a broken man, completely at the end of his reserves. He no longer wanted to live.

He was not the only one. Not far from me, Dennis tried to lift others to their feet, using the full strength of his broad shoulders and strong hands to grip them under their arms and pull, but he could no more persuade them to move than I could Bernard. He shouted, cajoled, ordered, and used everything his military training had taught him, but they had given up. The incessant weather and the unstoppable Norsemen had broken and beaten them.

At Sally's urging, I ran on. Both of us cried for our comrades; both of us determined to escape.

I didn't have to look back to know the Norsemen were closing the distance between us. Faster and fitter, better equipped to run through the snow, it would not take them long to reach those who had surrendered. I could hear their enraged shouts, their battle cries, the barking and howling of the wolves above the blizzard. It spurred me on, adrenalin pumping through me as I cursed the frostbite that had made me a burden on Sally.

I heard no screams, but I did hear the unmistakable sound of blades cutting through flesh, muscle and bone. The wind at our backs pushed the sound unmercifully into my ears. The Norsemen had reached those who had sat down and surrendered to their fate.

Bernard!

I made the mistake of glancing back over my shoulder. I stumbled, sprawling face first into the snow. I tried to push myself up, had almost succeeded, when a heavy-booted foot smashed into my shoulder blades and forced me back into the snow. Hot pain shot through the recently healed axe-wound in my shoulder. I struggled, but the foot held firm. My heartbeat was racing, palpitations of panic shortening my breathing, tightening my chest. I turned my head enough to see the blood-spattered, grinning face of the Norseman who stood above me with his spear raised ready to drive into the back of my skull. I cried out, unable to face death as anything other than a miserable, terrified wreck.

As he was about to thrust, something thudded into him. A screaming, punching, clawing ball of fury knocked him clear of me.

Sally.

I rolled onto my back and began to push myself upright, staring in horrified fascination as Sally and the Norseman tumbled in the snow. I saw a rough-hewn knife in her hand, a replacement for the one she had given me. With it she stabbed downwards once, twice. She rose up spitting blood into the blizzard. The Norseman would not die so easily, however. His fist struck upwards, catching Sally on the side of the head, knocking her onto her side. The bloodied, growling man rolled on top of her, sitting astride her small body, pinning her to the ground as he pummelled her with huge fists.

I pulled myself towards them, finally getting up to my knees, barely aware of similar struggles going on around me as the Norsemen overtook us. I knew I was moving too slowly, cursed my stump and my lack of toes for the delay they caused, a delay that could mean Sally's death.

My hand nudged something hard, a stick, no, the shaft of the Norseman's spear. A weapon! A slim chance to save Sally. I grabbed it in my fist, screamed unintelligible obscenities, spat phlegm and vitriol with uncontrolled rage, and lunged forward.

The man attacking Sally snapped his head around. Initial anger at the interruption changed abruptly to stunned surprise. The tip of the spear caught him under the chin more by luck than design. It drove up into his jaw and sliced through the roof of his mouth. His tongue hung on his lip, barely attached. The spearhead was clearly visible behind it in his forced-open mouth. He fell into the snow spewing blood, twitching in his death throes.

I reached the battered, blood covered, barely conscious Sally and cradled her in my good arm. Looking up, I saw another Norsemen running towards us, a sword held high above his head, ready to strike.

I was done, beaten, spent. I had no more to give and could do nothing but vainly try to shield Sally from the blow I knew was coming.

Firecrackers burst into life around us. The forehead of the man with the sword exploded in a puff of red. He fell, hitting the snow before the blood began to pump out of him. Other Norsemen were falling, dying. I realised I was hearing gunshots.

Fifty yards ahead of us, soldiers rose from their hiding places in the snow, rifles spitting bullets into the Norsemen in short, controlled bursts. They didn't spare the wolves either. The soldiers killed them as they buried their muzzles in the blood and meat of my dead companions.

In brief seconds the gunfire stopped and an eerie silence settled around us like the moments after a loud noise leaves your ears ringing and dull. Even the continuous roar of the blizzard seemed subdued. Looking around, I could see why. No Norsemen were left standing. Their bodies were scattered in crimson-stained snow. Their primitive weapons had been ineffective against a modern army. Among them was the bloody fur of the wolves they had tamed and trained to kill. Every one was shot down. Perhaps I should have felt some remorse, some sadness at the bloodshed before me, but the only sadness I felt was for my fallen companions. For the Norsemen and their wolves, I felt nothing.

I held Sally closer, hearing her ragged breathing through a bloody nose, and managed a weak smile.

She had been right. We were saved.

CHAPTER 29

Captain Price introduced himself and his men as a scouting patrol. They were two days out of Camp Enterprise, so named, he told us, because the Commanding Officer was a great fan of the archaic TV series Star Trek. I guessed the Captain was several years younger than me, but experience had hardened his eyes and the weather had gouged creases in the tough leathery skin of his face giving the illusion of greater age. He seemed, beneath the heavy arctic military uniform, to be of slight build and was little taller than me, but I did not doubt his fitness or ability to do the job. He radiated confidence and leadership in his every action and word.

"Camp Enterprise is our most northerly base," he said as his patrol's medic performed field first aid on Sally's injuries. "We're outside our perimeter here. Behind enemy lines as it were. If our truck hadn't died a couple of days ago, we'd have been long gone by now. Lucky we spotted you."

I was about to comment about how his words made it sound like we were at war when, looking at the blood-stained snow all around me, the dead bodies still sprawled where they fell, the walking wounded, the soldiers scanning the horizon through their rifles' scopes, I realised we were. This was war, a war for our survival. Thinking of it in those terms knotted my stomach and made me nauseous.

The medic nodded to his Captain. "She'll need more medical attention back at Camp, but she can travel."

"Right." The Captain held out a hand to help me to my feet. "We need to get everyone together and get moving."

It felt good to be following someone decisive and in control again. That surprised me. I had not realised, until they kicked me out of the farm, how much having Stephen take over the basic responsibilities of day-to-day life had eased the pressure I put on myself. For so long I had been in charge of my own existence that I had believed that was what I wanted, what was best for me. It took tragedy and heartbreak to show me that, sometimes, there were others who were better suited to make decisions than I was, and that following them did not strip me of my individuality or independence.

I took Sally's arm as the medic helped her to her unsteady feet and smiled weakly at her bruised and bloodied face.

She tried to smile back, wincing at the pain.

"I'm sorry I can't call for a heli to evac your friend but resources are tight."

"I can manage," whispered Sally as, with my help, she took a few tentative steps.

Still thankfully distant, The Roar rose again, layer on layer, lacking the earth trembling intensity of that first call to arms but chilling nonetheless.

Captain Price glanced briefly towards the horizon with no trace of emotion on his harsh, weather-beaten face.

"We'd better get moving."

As he marched off calling orders to his men, I turned to Sally.

"You saved my life. Thank you."

I kissed her ever so gently on her swollen lips.

We headed off at as brisk a pace as we could manage. Soldiers in snowshoes stepped easily across the snow at our sides and back, weapons held ready. At the head, Captain Price and four other soldiers, wearing skis, tested the depth of the snow with their ski poles. They selected, wherever possible, the shallowest route for the rest of us, with nothing but our boots and shoes, to follow. I didn't do an accurate count, but I would say there were at least fifteen soldiers in the patrol. Of the dozen or so of us who had headed off from the old military truck at dawn, only six survived. Six! Among the dead, of course, was Bernard. I tried not to think too much about that. It hurt too much. Like Harry, Bernard had quickly become a friend, and I felt the loss of them both greatly. Concentrating on the now, the current, helped me avoid too much wallowing in the past. There were things I was grateful for. I was alive. Sally was alive. But it was hard to ignore the memories.

Sally walked as fast as she could, wincing with each step, occasionally moaning in pain. I wished there was some way I could relieve her suffering, help her as she had helped me when Stephen's group first rescued me from the Mersey, but I could think of nothing. I forgot about my own disabilities, although I'll admit that the speed of her walking, while slow to others, was comfortable for me. What were a few phantom pains in non-existent toes and the occasional irritating itch on a forearm that wasn't there compared to her brutal injuries? The guilt I felt knowing those injuries were the direct result of her saving me was palpable, as was the feeling of helplessness, uselessness, over my inability to ease her pain. If I could have swapped places with her, I would have willingly. Had I believed in God, I would have hated him. Instead, I hated the world in general, the glacier, the Trolls, and most of all the Norsemen.

Time and again, I relived the moment I had thrust that spear into the man attacking her. Each time I became more desensitised to the taking of a life. Each time I experienced grim pleasure at killing the bastard. I had never considered myself a violent man, uncaring yes, cynical and selfish certainly, but not violent. Now I had killed two men and was worried that I was beginning to feel good about it.

Several times during the rest of that day, we heard The Roar behind us. It was always distant, always in multiples, sometimes barely an echo, other times shaking the ground beneath our feet.

I was scared, all of the survivors were, but the soldiers seemed unmoved, unconcerned, and their professional stoicism helped calm us and keep us moving at a steady pace.

Before the sun fell below the horizon and the freezing night set in, we stopped. The soldiers dug good-sized snow holes with their fold-away shovels for all of us. They shared their rations and boiled a hot but largely tasteless stew over a small fire. We knew the blizzard would soon extinguish the flames, but they, and the stew, gave us some much-needed warmth before we settled in our snow holes for the night.

Dennis joined Sally and me in our snow hole and, before we all tried to get to sleep, he whispered to me, "Take it from an old soldier, these boys are SAS. If anyone can get us to this camp of theirs, they can."

I've never been particularly knowledgeable about military matters, but even I had heard of the SAS. I felt a little safer as I gently held Sally in my arms and listened to her laboured, exhausted breathing.

I slept badly, woken often by The Roar, still distant but getting closer, by the movement of soldiers on guard duty, by Sally shifting and moaning in her sleep. Each time I woke, I remembered a different nightmare: Chrissy, Sally, Harry, Stephen, Bernard, Alison, Trolls, Norsemen. My mind jumbled great waves with lumbering ice, drowning with turning slowly on a spit, being killed with killing.

Often as I jerked, frightened, from sleep, I would see Dennis, equally awake, looking at me. He would nod and I knew his nightmares were every bit as bad as mine. I was not the only one to experience terror, death, the loss of loved ones. Every one of those few of us who remained had suffered and, no doubt, slept as badly as Dennis and me. I was not unique. I was not alone.

Before dawn, the soldiers were awake and preparing to move out. They let us rest until the last possible moment, a courtesy that was well-meant but, by the dark bags underneath everyone's eyes and the tired, exhausted, and drawn faces, was unnecessary. None of us looked like we'd slept much.

With Dennis's help, I got Sally up. There had been fresh bleeding from cuts on her face during the night and, as she forced a weak smile, dried blood cracked on her cheeks. I wanted to cry, the feeling of helplessness, of wanting so much to ease her pain but being unable to, twisted my stomach in knots. Nevertheless, I smiled back. I needed to be strong for her, to give whatever help and support I could, to forget about my own difficulties, my own self-pitying memories. It was the very least she deserved.

Captain Price skied down the flank of the gathered column. He briefly inspected his men. The line of soldiers, straight and orderly, gave me a feeling of security that I had not felt for a long time. I was looking forward to setting off, to finding the military base and being safe behind its walls. For the first time in a long time, there was some kind of sanctuary waiting for me.

"We should reach Camp Enterprise before sunset as long as we keep moving." The captain glanced back over his shoulder as a low Roar rumbled through the dawn. "We have very little intelligence on those creatures, so the C.O. will want to talk to all of you when we get there."

A true Roar rose at that moment forcing all conversation to stop. It grew louder, deafening, with each second as more and more voices joined. Cracks appeared in the ice-crusted surface of the snow around us, and the ground shook violently.

As the sound gradually receded, Captain Price pulled his snow goggles down over his eyes. He hesitated.

"You deserve to know as much as I do, given what you've all gone through. I sent a couple of lads back there during the night. They got back just over half an hour ago. Fortunately, it seems those creatures rest at night as we do. Otherwise, we would have been overrun. There's a lot of them. The lads did a rough estimate of about seventy, and they're coming our way. I've radioed the camp so they can start preparing, but we need to reach it before the creatures reach us."

Seventy! One had been enough at close quarters by the Mersey. The three who attacked the Norsemen had seemed an overwhelming mass of brutish force. Seventy was unimaginable. Too terrifying to fully comprehend. What could any of us do against so many? The hoped for sanctuary of Camp Enterprise no longer seemed so secure.

Before the Captain moved off to join his men at the head of the column, one of his words suddenly raised a question in my mind. Unsure whether I truly wanted the answer, I nevertheless knew I had to ask.

"You said 'prepare.' What is the camp preparing for? Are we pulling back? Joining with others further south?"

The Captain's eyes narrowed behind the goggles. His face visibly stiffened with determination and pride.

"Mr. Leonard, there are almost two thousand soldiers in Camp Enterprise, not to mention the equipment, the weaponry, the vehicles, and the aircraft. It would be a logistical nightmare to try to move so much in so short a time, even if we wanted to."

My heart sank and I felt nauseous with fear. I had known the probable answer to my question, but I had hoped I was wrong.

"What's left of the government is barely surviving in the ruins of London. They're in desperate talks with our allies abroad," continued the Captain. "Until some sort of agreement is reached, *if* it can be reached, we are the last line of defence."

He smiled grimly. The deep creases in his face seeming to strain against the movement, and his back straightened almost imperceptibly. He was all but standing to attention, and I could not help but feel he was looking forward to what was to come.

"Camp Enterprise is where it ends."

CHAPTER 30

Fading out of the blizzard with great walls of stone and ice rising out of deep drifts of snow, Camp Enterprise was an impressive sight. A wide path led to huge metal doors that stood like the gateway to an ancient Chinese palace. The approaching sunset burnished them bronze, casting a ruddy reflected glow over the surrounding snow.

We had walked all day without resting and barely eating and drinking. No one complained. The increased frequency of The Roar made it clear to everyone that the army of Trolls was gaining on us. If we had rested, or if the camp had been half a day further on, we would have been overtaken and, SAS or not, we wouldn't have stood a chance.

Our pace quickened as we drew nearer our goal. The now almost constant tremors running beneath us urged us on.

Sally slipped several times from my one-handed grip and I cursed the useless stump that prevented me holding her tighter. Not so long ago, even with two arms, I had been unable to hold onto Chrissy. What use was I with only one arm? Dennis, his square jaw set with grim determination, broad shoulders rounded with exhaustion, helped, but even with one-and-a-half men we were slowing dangerously. One of the soldiers bringing up the rear shouldered his weapon and took my place, throwing Sally's slight form over his shoulder in a fireman's lift and pushing on ahead of us. I was grateful but felt shamed at my own inability to give her the help she needed. Dennis placed a hand on my arm as though sensing my discomfort.

"Don't worry about it Norman," he said, breathing heavily. "They train hard to get that fit. It's a long time since I did more than a bit of jogging and a few push-ups, so there's no shame in handing over to these guys."

I nodded, understanding that he was right but unable to completely suppress my guilt.

The doors to the camp swung inwards. Soldiers ran out, forming an honour guard on either side, their weapons raised and trained on the snow-blurred horizon behind us. Unlike the patrol that found us, these soldiers wore various uniforms and carried a variety of weapons. My knowledge of our armed forces was limited to the little I'd picked up from TV and films over the years before the freeze, but I saw Army, Navy, RAF and Paratroopers as well as others unknown to me. We hurried inside followed by our guard, and the doors swung shut with a heavy *clang*.

Dennis, still at my side, looked around with a keen interest.

"This is a collection of allsorts," he said quietly. "Not that many professional soldiers either."

I knew that what he was saying was important, but my mind was obsessed with one thing only. Finding Sally.

I breathed a sigh of relief as I saw the soldier who had carried her putting her gently down not far from me.

A medical team hurried towards us, some military, some civilian, and they quickly assessed our condition.

"We could re-sew and re-dress that for you," said a military doctor, examining the stump of my right arm.

I shook my head barely paying any attention to him. "It's fine, really."

He shrugged and moved on to the next person.

I watched one of the civilian doctors as he crouched beside Sally. He checked her heart, her breathing. Was she okay? I hadn't seen her move since the soldier had brought her inside the camp. I couldn't lose her. Not Sally!

The doctor waved to a couple of soldiers standing nearby, and they unfolded a stretcher alongside Sally's motionless body. I dared not move or speak. She had to be alive. She *had* to be!

As the soldiers lifted her onto the stretcher, her arm rose just for a moment before falling by her side once more. It wasn't much, but it was movement. She was alive! I let go the breath I had been holding, almost collapsing from the relief washing through my body, and watched as she was carried on the stretcher to one of several stone buildings within the camp walls. A red cross hurriedly painted on the side, indicated it was the camp hospital. I made to follow, but Captain Price stepped in front of me.

"The C.O. needs to see any of you who are able to talk right away. We haven't got long to gather extra intelligence before these things hit us."

I didn't move. I had just watched Sally rushed to the hospital, probably in critical condition. She had been alive, but I had no idea if she would be okay or was, at that very moment, hanging desperately on to what little of her life remained. I could not leave her. I knew there were important things I could tell the C.O. of this camp, but I needed to be with Sally.

"Mr. Leonard?" Captain Price seemed to sense my indecision and had stepped closer. "That means you too."

I stared at him, seeing the hard determination to carry out his orders etched in that weather-beaten face, those steady, unblinking eyes. Perhaps for the first time in my life, I was not afraid of someone who could, undoubtedly, kill me in a second if they wished.

"I need to know she's all right," I said, my voice surprisingly steady, despite the adrenalin rushing through me. My muscles tensed, and my one good hand rolled into a fist. I would do what was necessary. It was a stunning revelation, but I knew at that moment that there were things I would fight for, even die for. Some things just were that important.

Other soldiers from Captain Price's unit had moved in. They lifted their weapons ready to fire. Captain Price

himself did not move. If other people in the camp continued about their work, I was not aware of it. I was aware
only of myself, Captain Price, his soldiers and Sally in the
hospital. They were all that mattered.

"Captain Price? Norman? Surely we can work something out?"

Dennis's voice broke some of the tension and, although
neither Captain Price or I looked away, we relaxed our
stances just slightly.

"Captain Price," continued Dennis, standing a little way
off but close enough for us to hear without him raising his
voice. "Couldn't one of your men check on Sally? Get a report from the doctor so that Norman here isn't so worried?
It must be terrible for him not to know."

Price barely moved his head, but one of his soldiers immediately turned and sprinted for the hospital.

"Norman, once you know she's fine then you should really come with us and talk to the C.O.," said Dennis, his
voice calm, level. "After all, you more than any of us can
give him plenty of information about these creatures."

I knew he was right. I knew that my knowledge could
be of potentially great worth, but Sally was more important. I never stopped staring at the Captain, but I'm sure
he noticed that I shuffled from foot to foot as doubts about
my stubborn disobedience wormed their way into my
thoughts.

The soldier was back in under a minute. He approached
us but stopped before he found himself part of the stand-off.

"The doctor says the lady's in a serious condition but
stable, Sir."

Serious. Stable. It wasn't good, but she wasn't about
to die either. Didn't 'stable' mean that? Bad but not
life-threatening?

"You see Norman?" said Dennis. "She'll be fine. She just
needs time. You can visit her as soon as we've seen the
C.O., isn't that right Captain?"

For the first time since the tense situation had arisen,

Captain Price's eyes shifted slightly to look towards Dennis.

"Yes, of course," he said. "As soon as you've passed on your information, you can do whatever you like."

I hesitated. Did I need to actually see Sally, or was the report from the doctor enough to satisfy me? Perhaps I was being stubborn just for the sake of it if I continued to refuse Captain Price's demand, and, anyway, the adrenalin rush was leaving me. I could feel my muscles reacting, starting to shake, my stomach turning and twisting. The soldiers would have shot me down at one word of command from their Captain. As the truth of that statement became apparent to me, I felt nauseous. Now I was scared, but strangely proud of myself. I had not only stood up to an authority figure I had gained a concession. I knew Sally was okay. I could afford to be gracious.

I forced a smile onto my face as I said to Captain Price, "Shall we go?" I saw a faint flicker of a return smile before he turned and marched away across the compound.

Dennis joined me as we followed. We hurried to match the Captain's pace. I half limped half skipped to overcome the unsuitability of my shoes for a man with no toes. As we walked, I heard a low laugh from Dennis and he patted me gently on the back.

"I would never have thought you had it in you Norman," he said as he smiled. "Well done."

I smiled too, but it was mostly to hide how scared I still was.

As well as the mix of uniforms hurrying around, preparing for battle, there was a mix of buildings. Simple squat stone structures stood next to army tents. Igloos seemed clean and neat next to corrugated iron shacks. While Camp Enterprise was enormous, spreading out as far as I could see through the blizzard, it was obvious that the most time and care had been taken with its outer walls and a few important buildings such as the hospital and the command centre. The rest looked like they had been built from whatever resources were at hand by people who didn't have the skills required. Not that I was any better, of course. We all had to turn our hands to unfamiliar and uncomfortable tasks these days, and I had no doubt the work done here was of a better standard than I could have managed. Nevertheless, I had expected something more from the principal military camp in the region. More permanent. More professional.

The mismatch of personnel and the haphazard construction of many of the buildings raised my fears that despite the early move south, the government and its resources had been severely weakened, damaged, perhaps beyond repair. Just how secure was I here? More importantly, how safe was Sally in their makeshift hospital? Captain Price had said the government was negotiating with our allies. Implicit in that was that our allies had not been immediately forthcoming with offers of help. Were they as badly off as us? Was the whole world falling apart in the face of encroaching ice and the creatures it pushed before it?

Had it really been such a smart move to continually head south?

As Captain Price showed us into a stone building, a hand-written sign announcing *Commanding Officer* hanging on the wall by the door, I couldn't ignore one final thought. It sent a chill through me.

When Captain Price had said this was the last line of defence, did he really mean the *only* line of defence?

General Thornton was a big man, tall and broad with a slight paunch at his beltline. Close-cropped grey hair and a weather-beaten and heavily lined face told of his advancing years, but his eyes were alive and alert as he appraised the two of us standing before his desk. Despite the mismatched and patchwork troops outside, his uniform was perfectly pressed and spotless.

"I'm told you've had some close experiences with these creatures." His voice was every bit as deep as I had expected given his size.

"Twice in my case," I said, not waiting to see if Dennis spoke up.

His eyes focused on me, and he leaned forward.

"Tell me everything you know."

I swallowed nervously. I'd no plan but, faced with the situation, I decided there were some things I needed to straighten out before I told everything. My only bargaining chip was knowledge. I had to use it.

"First there are things I need assurances on, and some information I need from you."

The General did not move for a moment. He stood frozen as though time itself had stopped. Only the nervous shuffling of my feet proved otherwise. Slowly he stood straight, glancing towards Captain Price. Captain Price gave a resigned shrug.

"I think you're pushing it now Norman," whispered Dennis.

I knew he was probably right, but I had to try.

"And what is it you need from me, exactly, before you divulge information that could be crucial to our survival?" The General's voice was calm, level, but a flicker in the eyes suggested he was close to losing his well-controlled temper. Nevertheless, having started down this track, I could not give up.

"First, there's a friend of mine in your hospital. I need to know she will get the best care you can offer and that you'll let me know, at each step, how she's doing."

"Of course. You didn't need to ask that. It would have happened anyway. We are not barbarians you know."

I thought I saw the faintest flicker of annoyance twitch the corner of his mouth, but otherwise he remained impassive.

"Secondly, I was heading south. We all were. What's actually happening there? Were we doing the right thing?" It should have gotten easier as I continued speaking, but with each word my mouth grew drier, the nervous fear twisted my stomach tighter.

"Are you being serious?" The General's command over his face finally broke as an expression of incredulity spread across it. "I would have given you all this information without you having to resort to such dramatic measures. Did you really think all this was necessary?"

"In my experience," I answered, aware that I was floundering a little, "people don't like to tell me the truth unless they have no choice." In reality, I had little experience of this, but nevertheless, my long-held antagonism and distrust of authority was enough to convince me.

The General sighed. "South is as good a direction as any, I guess. The weather's no better. It's like this countrywide. Probably across the whole of Europe and further afield. Listen," he glanced down at a piece of paper on his desk, "Mr. Leonard is it? Can I continue this after you give me your story? I'm concerned we could run out of time, and I really would like to hear what you have to say."

I knew at that point there was no sense in holding back any longer. My concerns over any lack of clarity, of truthfulness, from the General seemed unfounded, and, I had to admit, he had won me over with his self-control and apparent open manner. No doubt he could be as duplicitous as the next authority figure, but there seemed no sign of that at present. As I had earlier trusted Captain Price, so I had to now trust General Thornton. Not to do so left me no hope at all.

I nodded my agreement and, hearing a loud sigh of relief from Dennis, even smiled.

I have no idea whether my story was of any real benefit to the General, but he nodded, asked a few questions and took particular interest in our naming of the creatures.

"Trolls," he said, as if rolling the word around in his mouth, tasting it.

"Yes," I said. "Sally saw similarities between them and Icelandic trolls she had seen in various books on mythology. It's unbelievable of course, but no more than the creatures themselves."

He thought for a moment and then nodded. "I like it. Trolls it is."

I finished my story with the battle between the Norsemen and the three Trolls. Both the General and Captain Price seemed pleased to hear that one of the Trolls had been brought down by men armed only with clubs, spears and knives.

"It proves they can die, just like any other animal," explained the General. "There have been rumours going around the camp. The men have been talking of supernatural creatures, demons and other superstitious bullshit. Once *this* news is spread around it will put a stop to most of that, and the fact that we're so much better armed than those barbarians makes it look like we have the advantage."

"But there are seventy-odd out there General," I cut in. "I can't help thinking that evens up the odds whatever weapons you have."

"I'm not stupid Mr. Leonard. I said it makes it *look* like we have the advantage, not that we *do*. It's about morale. It's about perception. As long as most of the soldiers out there *believe* we are in a strong position, the truth doesn't really matter."

"So what do you *really* think?"

The General hesitated. I believe that was the moment he decided to take me and the others in the room, into his confidence. I'm not sure why he made this decision. Perhaps the General needed to share the burden, and we were less of a risk as confidants than the men under his command? I'm no psychologist, but for whatever reason, he began to speak quietly and with grim seriousness.

"They brought me out of retirement for this. No one else left, you see, except one or two bigwigs and they needed to stay with the government as advisors. So, they bring me out of retirement and tell me to get together every available fighting man I can and build this camp. I had been planning to spend my time in front of the TV watching every episode of Star Trek ever made, my personal weakness, but that wasn't to be. Naming this camp was my revenge on them for ruining my plans."

He smiled slightly at that and I smiled with him. It was not a programme I had ever seen, but I knew of it, everyone did. The General looked old enough to have seen some of the earlier series first time round, and I could imagine him spending his retirement immersed in his fantasies.

The smile slipped from his face as he jabbed a finger towards the outer wall of his office.

"Most of the people out there aren't even full time soldiers. I've got Territorials, cadets, kids barely out of school for Christ's sake! We were lucky we found a helicopter and a few jets, along with the pilots to fly them, and our artillery is manned by professionals, but for a lot of those people this will be the first combat they've ever seen."

"What happened to the regular army?"

"We'd been heavily committed overseas for decades Mr. Leonard, and the politicians in charge didn't see the freezing of Great Britain as cause to bring them home. As the full extent of the crisis became apparent, they tried to backtrack, but, by then, it was impossible. The few troops we were still in communication with were stranded in whatever country they had been sent to. This freeze is worldwide, Mr. Leonard. About the only place free, as far as I know, is a small band around the equator, and the last I heard *that* was shrinking rapidly. The big planes can't fly because they freeze and fall out the sky. Where the oceans are not actually frozen there are huge icebergs in the hundreds, making any travel by sea an almost certain disaster."

"And the armed forces we still had here?" I was almost afraid to ask but I needed to know.

"A lot of people deserted to be with their families. Can't say I fully blame them."

"But there were plenty when they came and evacuated the chosen from Liverpool," I said. "What happened to them?"

"They died, Mr. Leonard. All those trucks full of people, all those soldiers escorting them... hardly any made it to London."

There was nothing I could say. The bald statement of fact stunned me. Not made it to London? All those people! I'd been envious of them, bitterly resenting that they had been chosen and not me and Chrissy. It no longer seemed to matter.

"I used to think they just froze," continued the General. "But now I wonder how many ran into your Norsemen or Trolls. You see, a lot of people have made the same mistake you were making, thinking you would be safer in the south. Let me tell you, Mr. Leonard, far from being safer, things are very much worse the closer you get to London."

"But the glacier," I said, trying to recover something of my self belief as it was stripped methodically away. "The glacier coming down from Scotland. I had to move away from that."

"Glaciers hit us from the south even harder than they are doing from the north. The Thames flooded and froze, burying most of London's streets in ice twenty feet or more deep. What's left of the government is trying to run things from underground bunkers, no longer through choice but because they are trapped there. They have supplies for maybe another twelve months. That's why they're desperately talking to our allies. But guess what? Our allies are in as much shit as we are."

The bitterness in his voice was clear and, for a moment, the volume rose, but he quickly regained his composure.

"We had a few problems with roving bands of nutcases, bit like your Norsemen though not as organised. What we didn't have from the south were these Trolls. They are exclusively yours. That's why we're here. We'd seen enough from a distance to know they were dangerous. We now know a lot more about them thanks to you."

I was aware of the compliment but felt nothing. My mind was too occupied trying to assimilate the dismantling of so much I had believed in. Without the goal of heading south, what was I to do?

"We've got to stop them from taking the whole country," said the General, slapping his hand down on the desk for emphasis. "We're all that's left Mr. Leonard. Us and a buried remnant of government who are more concerned with their own predicament than they are with ours."

"So, I guess retreat is out of the question then?" It was a flippant remark born out of fear and I regretted it the moment I said it.

The General's lips pressed together and I waited for the shout of indignation. Instead, a laugh exploded from him that made all of us, even Captain Price, jump.

"Quite right Mr. Leonard. Retreat is not an option. I've heard rumours that you can walk across the English Channel if you're careful, but you'd only end up in France. They're no better off than us. Sooner or later the Trolls will follow us across, and then what? I think I'd rather make my stand here."

I was considering how to respond when the first shouts went up from outside, and the radio on the General's desk crackled to life.

"Our forward Observation Posts have eyes-on the creatures sir. At their current speed they'll reach us by nightfall."

Nightfall. Not long, and with Sally still hospitalised I could not run even if I had wanted to. I wasn't leaving her behind. This time I had to stand and fight.

CHAPTER 31

Sally was sitting up in one of a row of hospital beds, most of them empty, although I feared that would change soon. She was hooked up to a drip. It didn't look like she'd be able to eat with her battered and swollen mouth for a while. The right side of her face was purple, shiny, the skin stretching over the swelling that began just below her badly injured eye and finished at the corner of her mouth. Both eyes had heavy, black bags beneath them, the right one encrusted with dried blood. Stitches on her forehead and her chin and at the corner of her left eye were big and looked hurried, but at least they closed the wounds.

I sat on the edge of her bed, forcing a smile, and covered her hand gently with mine.

"I'm so sorry Sally. This is my fault. If you hadn't..."

She shook her head slowly, carefully, and spoke through barely moving lips.

"You're alive. I'm alive. That's all that matters."

Those few words made me happier than I could ever have imagined I'd be after losing Chrissy. Even with possible death lumbering its way towards the camp, I felt a fluttering excitement in my stomach and, for a moment, fear and gloom and despondency were forgotten. All because Sally cared that I was alive. That we were alive.

I could see the pain talking caused her so bit down on any further remarks. They would no doubt have been my usual self-pitying bullshit anyway: How could she care about a cripple like me? What could I offer a young girl like her? I was too old. I was too cynical. I was a cripple for god's sake, both physically and emotionally, and certainly not worthy of the bravery and selflessness she had demonstrated in saving my life. Is it really any wonder I spend so much time despising myself?

"What's happening out there? I'm guessing we made the camp?"

I smiled.

Despite the pain, it seemed Sally wanted to talk a little longer.

"Yes, we made the camp. Everything's going to be fine. They'll get you back on your feet soon."

I saw no reason to tell her about the approaching Trolls at that point. There was nothing she could do about the situation, and it would only worry her.

"Is Dennis okay?"

I felt a momentary, and foolish, flash of jealousy that she asked about someone else but quickly shoved it aside. Why shouldn't she ask? I had no exclusive right to her thoughts, her caring. She was a caring person. It was one of the many things I found so delightful about her.

"Yes, Dennis is fine. I was with him just a short time ago, talking to the General of this camp, filling him in on our adventures."

"And all the others?"

I hesitated, but I couldn't deny her every truth, just the one heading straight for us at that moment.

"Not many of us made it. I'm sorry Sally. We lost a lot of people."

A tear formed in the corner of her left eye, spilling over and trickling down her cheek. I wiped it away with the back of my finger. No tears came from her right eye; it was too dry, swollen and crusted with blood.

"I'm glad we didn't all die," she said, her voice growing weaker. "I'm glad *you* didn't die."

Again that fluttering in the stomach, that unexpected and unfamiliar rush of happiness as she expressed some special thought for me. It raised questions about my own feelings for her. I knew she was special to me, that I cared greatly for her, but did I love her? Was I capable of love after Chrissy? Would my personal feelings of guilt allow that? Trying to answer those questions made my head spin and I knew I would have to abandon any hope of working out my complicated, screwed up feelings for now. Plenty of time later if we survived the next few hours.

Sally's eyes fluttered closed, and I saw no reason to disturb her further. Sleep would do her more good than talking to me. A civilian doctor came through the end door and, leaving Sally to rest, I pushed myself up and approached him.

"She looks worse than when she was brought in Doctor." It was not, perhaps, the most polite opening, but the extent of Sally's bruising and the heavy stitches worried me. Could she possibly be okay after such a savage beating? It seemed unlikely that she could recover fully.

"A lot of the swelling has increased, certainly, but it will go down before long. It actually looks much worse than it is. It's nearly all soft tissue damage, some chipped bone, broken teeth and so on, but thankfully no internal injuries as far as we can tell. Very painful but not, ultimately, life threatening. There'll be scars and, unfortunately, we don't have the equipment here to remove them. But don't worry too much. She'll be fine given time."

"If any of us have time," I said, unable to repress my pessimism.

"Yes, well." His bedside manner slipped a little and the true worry of the approaching situation etched itself in stress lines on his face. "I need to be getting on and preparing."

The Roar rose in the background, shaking dust and plaster from the walls of the hospital ward. It was close.

CHAPTER 32

The ground shuddered as I exited the hospital. Captain Price, coming out of the C.O.'s building, raised a hand in brief greeting. He seemed unperturbed by the tremor. I had no idea how far from the camp the Trolls were, but by the urgency with which people were grabbing weapons and hurrying to their defensive posts around the walls, I guessed they weren't too far.

The General emerged behind Captain Price, tall and straight, showing no signs of nerves or concern. His was a steadying presence. Several of the younger soldiers calmed themselves as they saw him striding among them. Retired or not, and even with a rag-tag army, there could be no doubting the respect those under his command held for him. I admit I was impressed.

A soldier dressed in similar combat fatigues as Captain Price ran to the General.

"We've lost contact with the O.P.'s, Sir."

The General showed no reaction other than a brief nod that he had heard.

The soldier hurried away.

I turned to Captain Price who, it was obvious, had also heard the report.

"Could their radios have failed?"

Price looked at me with steady, unemotive eyes.

"We have to presume the Trolls have overrun their positions and that they're dead."

"Couldn't they...?"

"No," insisted Price, his expression halting any further

questions. "They were my men. If they were still alive, they'd have been in contact. They're dead. Shit happens."

He hurried off to join his men at the walls. I limped after him, shaken but not surprised at his brutal assessment of the situation. His attitude to death was not unique among battle-hardened men and women. Feelings of grief were, of necessity, buried beneath a hard, professional surface until a more appropriate time and place. I had felt the adrenalin rush of fighting, of killing, but I could never take the death of friends as stoically. I'm not sure I would want to even if I could.

I reached Captain Price up on one of the front walls of the camp. His men surrounded him. All of them calm while barely organised chaos reigned around them. They seemed impervious to the rushing back and forth of less experienced soldiers, and had expressions of excitement and fear etched on their faces. The constant, metallic rattle of guns being readied, loaded, hefted into firing position made me wince, but Price and his men seemed as though they had heard and seen it all, and more, before.

"How's your friend?" asked Price, without taking his eyes off the near white-out conditions outside the camp.

"The Doctor says she'll be fine. Mostly soft tissue damage."

"I saw her take on that savage. She saved your life."

"I know."

"You saved hers too. You shouldn't feel guilty that she was hurt saving you, or that you took a life to save her. That's what friends do."

I nodded, wondering at just how obvious my feelings were to others, particularly to Sally.

"You understand I had to wait until all targets were guaranteed kills before I ordered my men to open fire."

It wasn't a question, but nevertheless, there was a trace of concern, perhaps even of guilt, that I didn't expect from so hard and professional a man.

"I honestly hadn't considered it," I said, feeling he

expected something of me. "I'm just grateful you were there."

"I had the one who attacked the two of you in my sights, but if I'd fired it might have scared the others away. I wanted to eliminate the threat completely."

"I understand, Captain." This show of humanity unnerved me. It had the worrying touch of a deathbed confession, the final baring of the soul. "There's really no need to explain. You saved a lot of lives out there. That's the only thing worth remembering."

Captain Price said nothing. He simply nodded.

The noise of the approaching Trolls was no longer an indistinct rumble but heavy, thunderous footsteps. Had the weather been clearer I'm certain we would have been able to see them, but the daily blizzard had unleashed its full fury and visibility was down to a few feet.

"What's the plan?" I asked, hoping that they did actually have one.

Captain Price glanced up at the sky but seemed disinclined to answer.

"Come on Captain," I said, scared and frustrated, hoping that knowledge would somehow provide calm and confidence. "I've been through this already with the General. He saw fit to be open and honest with me. Surely, you can do the same? After all, I am the closest thing you have to an expert on the Trolls."

Price studied the sky as though considering my words. Finally he spoke.

"The C.O. had hoped to hit them with an air strike before they got too close, but in this weather the pilots would be shooting blind. We can't afford to waste ordnance like that."

"So, what then? We wait until they're right on top of us and open fire? No offence, but your guns aren't going to do that much damage to those things."

I could feel the panic rising in me and tried to force it back. So much for knowledge bringing confidence!

I should be running. Escaping. But what about Sally? Was I still such a selfish coward that I could leave her behind? She cared about me. Perhaps more, I didn't dare hope. And even if Sally were not there, could I really go back to being that person who left it too late to save Harry and his friends? The person who always ran, who always thought of saving himself first? No! I didn't want to be that person any more. I *wasn't* that person. I had changed. I was better!

"We can hurt them," said Price, unaware I'd been wrestling with my personal demons. "All we need to do is push them far enough back so the General can get his target fixed and call in the heavy stuff. Don't worry Mr. Leonard."

I had to trust them. I did trust them. The General, all of them. I knew not all the men and women in the camp were professional soldiers, but those leading them were. Nevertheless, it wasn't easy for me to place so much trust in others. All that time with Chrissy in our below-pavement nest, I had never put my trust in another human being. Not even Chrissy, now I thought about it, not fully. That I felt guilty for. My distrust of others had been so strong I had converted Chrissy to the same sad view of mankind. I trusted no one to help us because I knew, if the situation was reversed, I would not help them. It was safer to assume that everyone else was as selfish and cynical as I was.

It had taken other people's sacrifices to slowly reveal how wrong I was. Chrissy, Harry, Stephen, Bernard, and too many others whose names I had never bothered to learn. So many people had died before I finally realised the truth— not everyone was as selfish as I was. I could and should have trusted them, believed in them. I wasn't about to make the same mistake again. I trusted the people around me and, what's more, I knew they could trust me. I would do the best I could for them, and for Sally, and, ultimately, for me. But it felt good not to put myself at the head of the list for once.

A shout somewhere off to the left was the first warning

that the time for worrying had gone. The words were unintelligible, but the hoarseness of the voice, the slight tremble of fear in it, was enough to understand its meaning. I felt nauseous. My stomach cramped. My heart pounded. Despite the cold, there was sweat on my forehead, my top lip, my hand. This was it. The Trolls were here.

Great shapes loomed out of the blizzard, huge and snarling. They were so close they could almost reach out and grab the defenders. Ten or twelve Trolls, in the first line of attack, blocked what little sun forced its way through the snow. Even knowing what to expect, the sight of so many together, and so close, terrified and sickened me. These were more than animals facing us, they were animate nightmares. I heard mumbled exclamations from the men around me, someone praying off to my right. Several people further down the wall took a step back as if their instinct to flee took over.

"Hold your places!"

The order came from Captain Price. To their credit, every man held his ground, even those who were not truly soldiers. Those who had let their weapons drop in horror lifted them again. More than one barrel shook, but all were aimed at the enemy.

The defenders of Camp Enterprise opened fire.

Rocket launchers, grenades, small arms, all spat venom at the attacking creatures. Tracer rounds blazed glowing lines of fire through the blizzard. Bullet hits puffed plumes of filth from thick, matted hair. Explosions spouted flame, dragging forth roars of pain and anger. The Trolls staggered, hesitated. The smell of hot copper was pervasive. It was challenged only by the rising stench of burning damp hair. I gagged but would not step away from the wall. There was little I could do to help, unarmed and crippled, but I would not leave the front line. While others fought, I would not run.

A great arm swung down to my right, crashing into the camp wall. Stone and ice shattered under the heavy blow.

Flying shards sliced through flesh in a fantail of blood and bodies spreading from the breech. Huge hands scooped up the wounded and the dead. Fingers crushed the remaining life from already dying men and women. Bloody, twisted remains dropped like garbage into the snow below.

Another Troll reached the wall and rained down wild blows. People screamed as they tried to run. They were pulped under the giant fists, bodies bursting like rotten fruit. Trolls lifted others, still alive, still screaming, and smashed against the stone. Through the smoke and people and chaos, I could see the faces of those plucked from the wall. They wore frozen expressions of utter terror, as if they had the brutal knowledge of their own impending death. I could do nothing to help. I felt nauseous and useless, a crippled voyeur.

Under incessant fire that drew pinpricks of blood but did not kill, the Trolls retreated. They pulled back with surprising uniformity. I could not shift the impression of an organised army in tactical retreat. It was not the panicked fleeing of wild animals. We might have hurt them, but we certainly hadn't defeated them. The blizzard swallowed the Trolls, their matted white hair merging into the driving snow, uncomfortably like ghosts fading out of existence.

"Cease firing!"

The shout came from Captain Price and was echoed around the walls by other officers. Spasmodically, the gunfire stopped, and weapons were lowered. People seemed to be too stunned, too horrified by their experiences, to do anything but stand and stare out into the blizzard.

Almost immediately, the deafening sound of jet fighters roared overhead, unseen in the storm. Surely, they risked their lives in such visibility.

"They've got their speed and heading," said Captain Price. "They know where the things are now."

Huge explosions ripped through the storm, melting snow and blasting the blizzard temporarily aside. The shock waves shook the walls of the camp. Rubble clattered loose from the already damaged areas.

I could see the shapes of Trolls falling, scattering under the bombardment.

A direct hit ripped a Troll apart. Its internal organs shredded, a bloody mess of offal and shattered bone staining both ground and air. Near misses maimed. A blast completely severed an arm. It spun away, fingers still clenching and unclenching. A leg swung loose on ragged tendons. It seemed the Trolls had little defence against our air strike.

The soldiers cheered along the camp walls as the destruction revived them from their stupor. I began to believe that if only we could keep this up long enough; we had a real chance of winning. But all too quickly, the bombs and rockets stopped, and the jets flew back overhead, returning to their landing strips at the rear of the camp. The blizzard closed in again and, after a moment of near silence, The Roar rose in rage and hatred, shaking the walls with its ferocity.

I turned to Captain Price, no longer trying to hide the fear in my eyes.

"Are they re-arming? Heading back out?"

He shook his head grimly.

"They've nothing to re-arm with. Everything we had was on board. I just hope we took enough of them out to even the odds a little."

I said nothing. I was too stunned and horrified to speak. For a moment, it had seemed we would survive, that we could beat the Trolls. Now, however many we had killed, the others would be coming for us again. And this time they knew what to expect.

CHAPTER 33

We lost twenty-two people in the two areas where the Trolls breached the walls. At least another thirty were injured. I tried my best to help, searching through the rubble and bodies, calling for the medics when I found someone still breathing. I tried not to look too closely at the expressions of fear and agony frozen on the faces of the dead. The smell of blood and raw meat, of urine and faeces evacuated at the moment of death gagged me. If I had ever doubted it before, I knew then that there was no graceful or easy way to die. Death was just fear and pain and uncontrolled bodily functions. There is no spirituality in violent death just pure corporeal unpleasantness.

Once we carried the injured to the hospital, the same hospital where Sally lay in recovery, we could begin to remove the dead. I knew my help was minimal, but no one complained. I could not move much on my own, but I could join others, adding my one arm to their two as we dragged the heavy, grotesquely loose-limbed bodies across the rubble. Blood still seeped from wounds trailing bloody streaks over ice and stone. We pulled the bodies to the back edge of the wall and pushed them unceremoniously over. I didn't watch them fall. The heavy, wet sound of them hitting the ground below was nauseating enough without seeing it. It was not a respectful or honourable way to treat the dead, but it was practical. And practicality was all we had time for. Others had hacked a shallow pit out of the frozen ground. Others dragged the bodies we dumped into it. Perhaps there would be time for some kind of ceremony later. I did not, personally, think it mattered. Grief had always been a private thing to me. I had never seen the need to share it with others at funerals or wakes. Such public outpourings made me uncomfortable. There was no longer any need to pretend otherwise.

Once we had cleared the area of the dead, teams of military and civilian engineers moved in to survey the damage.

"How does it look?" I asked a tall, weary looking man dressed in battle fatigues.

He shrugged. "Bad, but not beyond repair. We can build it back up, as long as we have the time."

I stared out into the darkness, wondering just how much time we did have.

"You okay Norman?"

Captain Price brought me out of my daze. He joined me in staring out at the night. His uniform was bloody from helping with the wounded and the dead and I realised that I too was grubby and stained from the tasks. It was the first time he had called me by my first name, I think. The previously formal relations between the two of us seemed to be relaxing. It just seemed natural after what we had been through.

"I'm still alive, which is better than some."

Price nodded and for a short time we fell silent, both absorbed with our own thoughts, mine filled with relief that I lived mixed with my ever-present guilt at not doing more. Before long, another disturbing thought insinuated its way into my mind.

"So, how much firepower do we have left? If they've used pretty much everything already, what do we do next time?"

The Captain glanced around, but the only people close by where engineers. They were too busy in heavy rebuilding work to take any notice of us.

"We have five planes," he said. "Three Typhoons and two Tornados no longer in active use by the RAF but good solid machines nonetheless. Like I said, the heavy ordnance they use has gone and the ammunition for the Mauser 27mm

Cannons they carry is severely depleted. They'll only be of limited use in any further battles."

I nodded, trying to look calm while inside I panicked. The planes had been effective. With more of them, or more ammunition, we could have destroyed the Trolls. Without them...

"What else have we got?" I hoped there was something else, some major weapon that the Captain and the General were keeping quiet about, but I didn't truly have much confidence in that.

"The only other aircraft we have is an army Apache helicopter. When the General found her, all the armaments had been deactivated. She was stationed at a funfair in Devon providing rides to tourists. He was lucky to find most of her technicians still with her, and they were able to reactivate the 30mm Cannon but could do nothing about the lack of rockets and missiles. Like with everything else, ammunition is scarce."

It wasn't sounding too good, but I clung on to what little hope I still had.

"The General mentioned something about artillery?"

"Four L118 Light Guns used primarily, before the freeze for training exercises by the army. They're fully functional but, again, ammunition is limited."

Captain Price, no doubt sensing my growing despondency by the slump in my shoulders if nothing else, nudged me and gave one of his rare, if slight, smiles.

"It's not all bad, Norman. We've plenty of small arms, assault rifles, sub-machine guns, and sidearms. The General gathered them from all over. A lot are military. Some were privately owned and others police issue. The professionals had first choice of weapons and tended to choose those they were most familiar with. After that, it was first come first served. Me and my team have our own weapons. We were on active duty when the General managed to contact us, so we've still got all our kit."

I almost asked but, at the last moment, decided it was

probably not a wise thing to do. That Captain Price and his team were SAS seemed to be an accepted fact throughout the camp, but, as far as I was aware, it wasn't something that the General, Captain Price or any of his men had ever confirmed. If he wanted to tell me, he would. It didn't feel right to ask.

"We've still got plenty of ammunition for the smaller weapons," continued Price. "Although a lot was used in that first attack, which reminds me of something I need to do. Get back to you later."

With that, he stepped away from me and headed back along the wall. He called out as he went, his voice clear even above the sounds of improvised construction going on next to me.

"Next time people, aim your shots and fire in short bursts. We wasted a lot of bullets last time 'round and I'd like to keep that to a minimum. So, aim and don't keep your finger on the trigger!"

I don't think any of the professionals needed to be told, but I'm sure many of the others did. As he continued around the wall, he repeated the order to be certain everyone heard it.

All the military terminology and technical detail he had gone into was beyond me. I could repeat what he said, but it made no real sense. I had never fired a gun, let alone flown a jet or helicopter. Before the camp, my knowledge of the military was limited to whatever I picked up from TV shows and films. I still couldn't tell the difference between a 27mm Cannon and a 30mm, but at least I now knew they existed.

After that first Roar following the battle, the Trolls had been eerily silent and invisible in the driving blizzard. The wind and the faint hiss of snow were the only sounds outside the camp and the defenders, facing that dark silence, must have been unnerved. They shuffled their feet, talked in whispers, bit their lips and rubbed their hands together showing all the classic signs of nervousness, of uncertainty. In the camp itself, as well as on the walls, conversation was muted as many listened for the warning sounds of another attack and others rested, exhausted as the adrenalin rush left them.

After a short while, I followed Captain Price's earlier direction and found him sitting at the base of the wall. He stripped down his gun, wiping it clean of debris, checked for any obstructions in the barrel, and reassembled it with stunning speed and dexterity. I watched in silence while he checked the ammunition in his pack and the fully loaded clip of the gun. This was a man ready for battle and, apparently, unafraid of the enemy. I, on the other hand, felt virtually useless. I was constantly afraid and of little help in defending the camp. Even if I knew how to handle an assault rifle, it would have been difficult with only one arm. Nevertheless, I wanted to be at the frontline, in the middle of it, and no one was more surprised by that than me.

I told myself it was simply that I preferred to know what was happening rather than being somewhere further back waiting for the outcome. But in truth, I think I'd finally found a little of that courage and even what some of the soldiers called a 'gung-ho' attitude that kept all the others around me fighting. With that in mind, I made a decision and finally broke the silence.

"Show me how to use a pistol."

Captain Price looked up from his weapon with curiosity rather than surprise in his eyes.

"I can fire a pistol with one hand, even if it is my left. Show me how to use one."

Without a word, he reached into the pack and pulled out a weapon. He handed it to me. It felt solid, heavy and, despite my initial qualms, satisfying.

"That's a Browning Double-Action 9mm automatic. It's pretty ancient to be honest, almost a museum piece, but I like it because it's proven and reliable. Plus the magazine release can be reversed for your left hand. I've got clips in the pack and more ammunition to load them with when they run out. It's a relatively easy gun to aim, although it'll take you a few shots to get used to the kick. Basically, you point and pull the trigger. Just make sure of what you're pointing at. I don't want any accidents."

I was nervous and my hand trembled as he took me through all I needed to know: how to aim, how to fire, how to reload. He made me practice releasing the clip, pushing the gun upside down between my knees and locking a new clip into place until I got it right. I found I could use the stump of my right arm to help steady the gun for better aim. The one thing he would not let me do was practice firing it.

"We need every bullet and, anyway, you start firing and people are likely to think the attack's underway. You'll soon get used to it when you have to."

Making sure the safety was on, he let me keep the Browning. Even though I knew the feeling was false and, to be honest, slightly pathetic, I admit to feeling a stronger man with it in my hand.

Towards evening, the blizzard eased slightly, no longer blowing horizontal snow but pushing it sideways into drifts. The silence from the Trolls was complete and I began to wonder whether they were still there at all. Perhaps we had shown ourselves dangerous enough to be avoided. When I suggested this to Captain Price, however, he shook his head grimly.

"Where would they go? These Trolls may be a different enemy, one unlike any I've faced before, but I doubt their instincts or their needs are that much different from other opponents. I saw enough in that one battle to believe they have some kind of intelligence, even if it's more animal than human, and they work together like any other army. It's reasonable to presume they'll behave in an identifiable way."

It seemed a reasoned argument. The retreat alone had proved to me that they were organised to some degree at least.

"But you still haven't explained to me why you're so sure they'll attack again."

"Simple," said Price. "The glacier is more or less at their back, so they have to come south. The quickest way is through us. Your Norsemen killing one of them was what brought them out in force to start with, and now we've killed more of them. I doubt very much that they see any difference between those barbarians and us."

I forced a smile. "Thanks for depressing the shit out of me."

Price smiled in return. "My pleasure."

It was at that point that I felt the bond between us strengthen even more. I shouldn't think a man like Captain Price could ever forge strong relationships outside of the military, but I think we were as close to friends as we could be given our completely disparate backgrounds.

As we watched the last light of the sun drain from the sky, Sally joined us. She was aided by a young soldier who saluted Captain Price, passed him a folded piece of paper, and left. She looked slightly better than when I had last seen her lying in the hospital bed. The massive bruise on the right side of her face had reduced slightly and her eyes seemed a little more open, but she still looked battered, in pain and in no condition to be out.

"What are you doing out of the hospital?" I took her arm, led her gently to a spot where she could sit. "You're not fit to be up."

"I've been up for a while," she said, in obvious discomfort from speaking. "They needed the beds for people worse off than me, so I've been helping with the wounded. Well, as much as I was able anyway."

I wanted to hug her but was afraid of the pain it would cause. How typical of her to be helping others when she herself was injured.

"You need to be more careful," I said, gently taking her hand.

She smiled and, although it still obviously hurt, it seemed a little easier than before.

From the darkness beyond the wall, we heard a strange keening sound rising behind the blowing of the blizzard.

This was no Roar, rather a melancholy, haunting rise and fall. It was surprisingly subtle when you knew the creatures it emanated from. More voices joined and, although it never reached the deafening volume of The Roar, it nevertheless hurt the ears with its high-pitched whine.

"What the hell are they doing?" I said, blinking into the blizzard, looking for any movement.

"They're mourning their dead," said Sally sadly. I believe she truly felt some empathy with those creatures at that moment.

"What do you mean, mourning their dead?" asked Captain Price as he joined us, having read his note and slipped it into his pocket.

"That singing…"

"Singing?" I almost laughed.

"Yes, singing," said Sally. "It's very reminiscent of some of the more obscure ancient tribes of the far north I've heard recordings of. Part of their rituals of death. Sunset is the ideal time."

"But the Trolls?"

"They're animals certainly, but then so are we, Norman. I believe they're intelligent, so why shouldn't they also have an understanding of death and rituals to go with it? I'm certain that's a song of mourning. They've buried their dead, done whatever needs to be done and now they're remembering them."

The 'singing' reached a crescendo and was suddenly gone. It left a whistling, humming silence that even the blizzard struggled to overcome.

"Now what?" asked Captain Price.

"Now I think they'll rest for the night and in the morning…"

She didn't need to finish. Both Captain Price and I knew what she was about to say. In the morning, the Trolls would want revenge.

Price broke the tense silence.

"That note was from the General. He wants a bit of a job

doing. Shouldn't take long."

"What kind of job?" I asked as the Captain signalled to his team on the walls around us drawing them close.

"I could tell you, but I'd have to kill you." Captain Price stared steadily at me and it was a nervous few seconds before I saw the laughter soften his eyes and that slight but welcome smile twitch the corners of his mouth.

"You know," I said, "I wish I could be sure you were only joking when you said things like that."

Price's smile broadened as he turned and headed for the steps down from the wall. His men followed him in silence. He shared a quick word with one who then headed back towards us and stopped in front of Sally.

"The Captain would like to know if you've ever fired a gun, Marm?"

"I had a couple of years in the T.A. a while back, but I'm a bit rusty."

I smiled and wondered if I'd ever get to know Sally well enough not to be constantly surprised by her.

"Assault rifles?"

"One or two."

The soldier nodded, unshouldered his assault rifle and handed it to Sally.

"Compliments of the Captain, Marm. It's just like riding a bike. It'll soon come back to you."

Sally took the weapon, weighing it in her hands. She studied it and nodding with recognition.

"Thank you soldier. And thank the Captain for me."

He saluted, made ready to leave then hesitated in front of me.

"You know Sir, the Captain is very particular about the people he shares a joke with. It's a rare thing." He took my hand in his and shook it firmly. "Welcome to the team."

It was one of the nicest things anyone had ever said to me, and I was too stunned to reply as the soldier hurried after his comrades down from the wall.

"Congratulations, Norman," said Sally, smiling despite

bruised lips. "That's quite an honour from such an elite team."

I held up the Browning automatic and tried to look brave.

"We're armed and ready to fight."

But, I wanted to add, *not ready to die.*

Sally stayed with me on that stretch of wall. It was strangely eerie without Captain Price and his men alongside us. Conversation was sparse, but we kept close together, gaining comfort from the other's presence. Beyond the wall was stygian black. The moon and stars were nonexistent. Anything could approach us unseen. I wondered how certain we could be that the Trolls rested at night. If Sally had not been with me, I might have retreated to one of the small campfires spotted about the compound behind us.

Perhaps forty-five minutes after Captain Price had left us, I heard the unmistakable sound of the metal doors to the camp opening. Peering carefully over the edge of the wall, I could make out the vague, ghostly shapes of a small number of men, barely visible in the flickering of firelight, filing out from the camp into the night storm. I had no doubt it was Captain Price and his team heading out on whatever job the General had given them.

"Price?" asked Sally.

I pushed back from the edge and nodded.

"Thought it would be."

I stared at her for a moment, thinking how her time in the Territorial Army had obviously given her a greater understanding of the military mind than I would ever have. She looked comfortable cradling the assault rifle in her arms and in some strange way it suited her more than I would ever have imagined. It would not have sat right with Chrissy, that I was sure of. The thought of Chrissy with a weapon of any kind was nonsense. She was, *had been*, one of the gentlest souls I'd ever met.

I felt guilty for thinking of Chrissy while looking at Sally, and guilty for suggesting, even if only in my own mind, that Sally was in any way not gentle or feminine. Sometimes, it was just easier to know I felt guilty and not worry about the why.

We said nothing for the next hour, just stared out over the wall into the night. The droning of the storm was no more than background noise by that time. The whole camp was quiet. Perhaps not silent but quiet. Some slept, others sat, like us, watching and waiting. A few moved about either on jobs or just stretching their legs. I saw the General pacing once or twice. Perhaps he was waiting for Captain Price's men to return from whatever job he had sent them on. Perhaps he was just thinking about the whole situation. I hoped he was busy formulating a plan to get us out of this, but I had my doubts.

"I guess it's a calculated risk that whatever Captain Price is up to won't make the Trolls decide to attack us now," said Sally, leaning towards me to whisper. "They're probably right. Whatever the provocation, I don't think the Trolls are nocturnal animals. Certainly not to the extent of fighting. I've not heard any mythology give them the benefits of night vision."

"Did you know," I whispered back to her, "that you're amazing? I'm glad you're here."

She smiled, leaned further in and kissed me on the cheek.

"I'm glad I'm here too."

Not much later, we heard the camp doors opening. Captain Price had returned. There had been no gunfire, no sounds of battle, so I guessed the purpose of his mission was reconnaissance. I hoped he had discovered something of use to our survival.

The Trolls' song of mourning drifted once more across the snowy wastes, but this time I felt there was an almost indefinable, harder edge to it. I saw how Sally shuddered as she listened.

"Do you feel it too?" I asked.

"Yes," she whispered, so quiet I could barely hear her over the song. "It's different from last time. It's still sad. They're still mourning their dead, but there's something else. Something more strident. More aggressive."

"A challenge," I said, the thought coming unasked for and unwelcome in my mind. "They're challenging us to a fight. Telling us that they're coming to kill us."

When Sally looked up at me and didn't smile, I knew she thought I was right, and that frightened me more than the song did.

All of us inside Camp Enterprise's walls greeted the normally welcome sight of the sun pushing above the horizon with nervous silence and worry. Everyone knew that the dawn brought with it the prospect of a second attack from the Trolls.

Our night spent on the wall had been, not unexpectedly, freezing, but we had huddled together and enjoyed the hot drinks that soldiers not currently on duty regularly distributed. The drinks themselves were tasteless and unidentifiable, but they were warm and that was all that mattered. The song of the Trolls had continued intermittently but, after a while, even that became commonplace, a background noise along with the wind and the low babble of conversation within the camp.

As dawn broke, Captain Price and his team rejoined us.

"Find much out?" I asked as he took his place alongside Sally and me.

"Nothing too surprising, but it's good to be sure of the situation."

"I'm guessing there are still plenty of them out there then." It was an attempt at humour, but the underlying fear was too evident in the shake of my voice.

"Plenty," he said without a smile. "And more joining

them. It looks like we've the whole Troll nation gathering out there, if there is such a thing."

Nothing I could have said would have seemed other than trivial in the face of such a statement, so I fell silent.

"Were you able to observe their mourning ritual at all?"

Sally's question surprised me, and my expression must have shown it. She looked at me and smiled.

"Sorry, but I'm interested. Still a librarian at heart."

"You're much more than that," said Captain Price.

Sally might have blushed, but in the dim light and beneath her bruises and cuts it was difficult to be certain.

"So, did you see it?" she asked again.

"Some," said Price. "I can tell you that they don't so much bury their dead as simply cover them with rocks, blocks of ice and snow."

Sally nodded. "It's not uncommon. Could be that they have always done that, or it could be that there simply isn't time in this situation to do anything more elaborate."

"You make them sound almost human." I moved to scratch an itch in my right hand, stopping in embarrassment when I remembered I didn't have one. If anyone else noticed, they were kind enough to ignore it.

"That could be closer to the truth than we think," said Sally. "It's very easy to put human emotions and motives onto a lot of their actions. Much more than I would have expected. There are certainly times when they seem more human than the Norsemen."

I saw the brief flash of fear and then hatred in her eyes as she said it. Once her physical scars had healed, the mental ones would remain for some time.

"I wish they were as easy to kill."

Captain Price's simple statement made all three of us laugh. It wasn't funny, as such, but it broke the tension that had been building, undetected, in the conversation.

"It would certainly make things easier," I said. "Got any surprises planned for the day?"

The Captain grew serious again.

"Unfortunately, with the aircraft out of ammo and most of our explosives and rockets used during yesterday's fight, we haven't got much left to surprise them with."

Before I was able to think of a suitable response to this bad news, The Roar, rolling across the snow, layer after layer, voice after voice interrupted our conversation. It hit a resonance with the camp walls and throbbed under our feet. It was deafening, painful somewhere deep inside the ear, inside the head. Then it was gone, leaving my ears buzzing, my head pounding.

"I think they're awake and raring to go." Sally shifted forward. She looked over the wall towards where the Trolls were and positioned the assault rifle firmly on her shoulder as she put her eye to the sight. I saw her wince at the pain the movement had caused her, but she did not complain.

Captain Price took a position alongside her. "Won't be long now."

Feeling inadequate and something of a fake, I nevertheless positioned myself the other side of Sally with the automatic pistol gripped shakily in my hand.

"Is this it then? We just face them head-on?"

I couldn't see how we could do anything but lose in such a straight confrontation. Last time we had been lucky and the Trolls had not expected our firepower. This time they would be ready.

"There's not a million other things we can do," said Price. As if he noticed the look of utter defeat flow across my face, he added, "but the General does have a plan."

"Are we allowed to know it?" asked Sally.

"Under normal circumstances, no. But you're hardly likely to pass the information to the enemy, so I guess it's okay. Know anything about the Pincer Ambush?"

The term had a vague ring of familiarity about it, but I wasn't sure of its meaning.

"It's pretty simple really," continued Captain Price. "We're going to let the Trolls come and attack us head-on.

When they're all here in the middle, bashing the hell out of us, the men the General is already moving into position will ambush them from both sides. They'll be hidden, hopefully, from the Trolls as they charge us. Ideally it would have been nice to have enough men to get right behind them and attack the flanks and trap them with a full Pincer Manoeuvre, but the Ambush is better than nothing."

"And you think that will work?" I asked incredulously. "What's to stop the Trolls just turning and stepping on our men out there?"

"What would *you* suggest, Norman? A Tactical Withdrawal? We'd be slaughtered. And we do have one other trick, thanks to you."

"Me?"

"Yes, you. The information you gave us about the Norsemen's battle with the Trolls showed that there is a way for men to attack and defeat a Troll, by attacking their heels. Just like toppling a huge building from the bottom up. When we spring the trap, all firepower will be concentrated on bringing the Trolls down. Once they're on the ground, we can finish them off more efficiently than the Norsemen with their spears and knives."

I was stunned, horrified at the perceived responsibility I now took on. If it failed, if we were overrun, the strategy based on my testimony would be at fault. *I* would be at fault, and everyone would know it.

As if she could read my mind, Sally laid a comforting hand on my arm.

"Don't worry Norman. No one's going to blame you if it doesn't work. And anyway, I'm sure it *will* work, don't you think so Captain?"

"It's our best shot," said Price. "We'll find out soon enough whether it's a good one."

"Thought I'd come and keep you company."

The voice behind startled me and I jerked my head around, breaking into a smile.

"Dennis! Where the hell have you been?"

Dennis settled in alongside me.

"When they found out about my military background they had me doing some weapons training. But I reckon it's too late to teach anyone anything now. Thought I'd find my old friends to face this with."

I suspected he meant 'face death,' but I said nothing trying, for once, to ignore my morbid nature.

He lifted his own assault rifle and settled it into his shoulder adjusting the sights.

"It's a little like shooting elephants with a pea-shooter, but I didn't want to be left out."

It was a joke, of course, but I heard the truth beneath the humour. Did we really believe that, with small arms fire and little else, we stood a chance against the Trolls?

Sally, once again, seemed to read my mind.

"We'll hold them until the General's plan kicks in. Anyway, Norman, you and me have got some serious talking to do later on, and no ugly, mythological creature lacking even basic hygiene is going to get in the way of that, however big they are!"

Captain Price and Dennis laughed and, after a moment of stunned hesitation, I laughed too. I had no idea what the 'serious talking' would be about, but my stomach fluttered and a chill of anticipation ran up my spine at the possibilities. It made a pleasant change from fear. I felt I should reply with some suitably witty comment, not that such things were ever my strong point, but before I could even begin to think of one, the nightmare we had all been waiting for began.

I felt the thunder of charging feet before I heard it. It shook the camp walls and toppled loose equipment off tables. When the first indistinct shapes solidified out of the increasing blizzard, huge and terrible with a lumbering gait that belied their speed, there could be no doubt left in anyone's mind.

The Trolls were coming.

CHAPTER 35

"Hold your fire," called Captain Price. His order was relayed quickly around the wall by other officers. We all waited, and I'm certain I wasn't the only one so afraid he could barely stop his legs from simply folding up beneath him.

I stared at the solid mass of muscle, hair and fury pounding towards us. We had to be insane. What hope did we have against that? Just one Troll could decimate the camp, and we were facing, even after yesterday's battle, at least forty. It was suicide to stay and fight, but I was not going to be the first to run. I'd been running for as long as I could remember. This time, I would stay with my friends whatever the outcome.

The Trolls' roars of anger buffeted us. Great heaving breaths drowned the blizzard. The wet, fetid, rotting smell was stronger than before, overpowering. A wall of terrible sensations slammed into me: abject terror, nausea, revulsion. Several younger cadets abandoned their posts and ran further back into the camp. No one tried to stop them. Fear and panic were not things to be ashamed of when facing this onslaught.

"Open fire!"

The camp walls crackled into life. The muzzles of older guns flashed. Gunfire popped and banged. Machine guns blasted a low repetitive thud. The weapons' power seemed lost in the desert of snow.

Sally, Price and Dennis fired with impressive composure. After some hesitation, I raised my arm and pulled the trigger on the Browning Automatic.

It kicked and bucked in my hand more than I had expected, and I'm certain most of my first shots flew high above even the Trolls' heads. But once I knew what to expect, I managed to gain some control and join the others in firing into the midst of the advancing army.

To my surprise, the charge of the Trolls did stutter. Those in the front slowed under the strikes of what would in regular warfare be withering fire. Great hands swatted irritably at the bullets. Matted hair bristled with each hit.

"Not so much pea-shooters," I heard Sally say to Dennis as she dropped an empty clip from her rifle and slammed another into place. "More like bee stings I should think."

My own reloading was not as smooth and quick as Sally's, but with a little fumbling and cursing I managed to release the empty clips and get full ones in. I don't believe for one moment that my bullets caused the Trolls any problems, and most of them probably missed anyway, but standing there with the others, firing the gun, made me feel an integral part of the whole camp. I was no longer just an onlooker, a loner thinking only of himself. I accepted that I might die, but for the first time ever in my life I thought my death might actually be worth something.

The great creatures charged across the open snowfield and closed in on the camp. What the hell was the General waiting for?

The whine and thud of RPGs, personal rocket launchers, grenades and heavy calibre machine guns burst in from both sides of the Trolls. The attack nearly drowned out the sound of our own small arms fire. Great gouts of snow and flame spurted into the air from the feet of the creatures. Miraculously, some of them fell. Clouds of snow and ice rolled into the air as they hit the ground.

As a Troll fell, fire bombarded its head. The skull cracked and splintered. Blood spurted and splattered across the snow. Bone fragments scattered like stones in the crimson flow. It made me nauseous but elated. Perhaps we had a chance after all.

Despite the casualties being inflicted on them, most of the Trolls pushed forward, albeit at a slower pace. Confirming our belief in their intelligence, others had turned towards the hidden soldiers and advanced on their positions. Even stepping over their own dead only slowed them a little.

A crash followed by screams from my left drew my attention. Our men had targeted a Troll as it reached the camp walls. It fell towards rather than away from the wall. Its bulk hit the concrete crushing wood and splintering ice. It killed everyone beneath. The creature lay half inside the camp, twitching. A wooden pillar jutted from the back of its neck.

We were holding our own against the terrible assault. I had not believed it before the attack began, but it looked as though we had a chance. Trolls were dying. The increasing number of fallen bodies under their feet and the firepower from three sides was forcing their advance to slow. It had not stopped, but it had slowed.

I looked towards Captain Price expecting to see him smiling, or at least wearing a satisfied expression. Instead, his brow was furrowed with worry. He turned his head from side to side as he scanned the killing field below.

"What's wrong?" I called over the incessant gunfire.

"We should be closing the gap behind them and fencing them in," he said, never taking his eyes of the battle before him. "And where are the others?"

"The others? What others?"

"I told you. On our recce last night I saw other Trolls arriving, boosting the numbers."

I hesitated, remembering the conversation.

"You said it looked like the whole Troll nation was gathering."

"So, where are they?"

He turned his head away from the fight long enough to lock eyes with me. I could see genuine worry there. It was the first time I'd seen Captain Price look anything other than calm, professional and in control. It scared me.

"They're retreating!"

The shout came from my right.

I turned away from Captain Price towards the Trolls. It was true. They had turned and were running back through the gap in our ambush. A ragged cheer rose up. It was a little unsure. Most people were probably as surprised and cautious as I felt. There was no reason for the Trolls to retreat. We were doing damage, but not enough to make them run.

Captain Price, who had not joined the cheer, looked equally disbelieving.

"Keep your positions," he shouted. "Keep your weapons ready!"

Below, in the bloodied snow, stepping round fallen Trolls, the men from the ambush appeared. They aimed their weapons at the backs of the retreating creatures and fired a few token shots.

"Idiots!" snarled Price. He leaned over the wall and shouted above sporadic gunfire and another slightly more assured cheer.

"Get back under cover! Get back to your positions!"

Roars erupted from right and left out in the blizzard. The thundering of great feet rumbled through the scream of the storm. From the mist of snow behind our ambush lumbered the rest of the Troll army. A wall of rage and death. I didn't have time to count, but there must have been at least thirty on each side, more than doubling the number we faced.

The Trolls that had tricked us with their retreat turned around to rejoin the fight, their job of drawing out the ambush done. They ploughed through the snow heading once more towards the camp.

Cheers changed to screams, to shouts of horror and despair, as hopes of victory turned to fears of almost certain defeat. It was all I could do to stay on my feet. My desire to crawl into a corner and cower was strong, but I fought it.

Sally glanced at me and smiled. It should have been re-assuring. It felt like a goodbye.

The soldiers from the ambush tried to scatter in the face of the three-sided Troll attack. They had no chance. Trolls pounded them. The clouds of snow and ice thrown into the air all but obliterated the view of the ground, but unfortunately it was not hard to imagine. Gunfire did little more than irritate the Trolls. They turned and stormed the walls. As the snow settled, I saw the bloody streaks left behind. There was no time to mourn the loss of our comrades. The Trolls ignored our feeble weaponry. The first to reach the walls swept dozens of people to their deaths. They smashed our defences with their fists. Our plans had failed.

More Trolls reached the walls. Too many to stop.

"Fall back!" yelled Price.

I scrambled down from the walls along with Sally, Dennis, Captain Price and others, all the time expecting one of the monsters at my back to sweep me up.

The camp walls, broad enough and tall enough to withstand many months of siege from a human enemy, were no barrier to the Trolls. They waded through them scattering debris into the camp. Huge boulders, rolling like bowling balls, smashed the bones of people as they tried to escape. Blocks of ice crushed those too slow or infirm to move out of the way.

A spinning splinter of ice, sharp and heavy, crashed into the back of my skull. A sudden blackness fell over my eyes and pain stabbed through my head. I fell, sprawling awkwardly on the ground. My body crushed the stump of my arm underneath me. The pain was agonising.

As a spinning, hazy vision returned, I could see Sally, coming back for me.

"Keep going!" I shouted. "Don't stop for me!"

She ignored me and, although I was frightened for her safety, I was also grateful for her helping hands as I struggled to my feet. I pulled my hand away from the back of my head. It was covered in blood, but there was no time to worry about it. I was slowing Sally down too much, and her injuries were still fresh enough that every exertion pulled grimaces of pain from her. They'd kill us both if she didn't leave me and save herself.

I was about to pull free and tell her to go when other hands joined hers and lifted me.

"You seemed to be struggling a little," said Dennis, grimacing with the extra effort of carrying me.

General Thornton stood outside the door to his office with a small, snub-nosed machine gun in his fist.

"General," shouted Dennis. "We've got to get out of here, now!"

"Be with you soon," shouted the General, barely glancing at us. "Got to make sure as many people escape as possible."

As I was about to join Dennis in trying to persuade the General to come right away, he ran towards a small group of young soldiers cowering beneath the looming figure of a solitary Troll. The General opened fire, his bullets hitting the creature. Its hair ruffled with each strike, but the gunfire didn't stop its advance. As the General reached the soldiers, the Troll swept its great arm down, scooped them all up and pulled them into its open jaws. I shouted. Sally screamed, but I could not look away from the General. He dropped his gun and pulled something from his pockets. Grenades. One in each hand. They exploded as the Troll stuffed the screaming people into its mouth. The double blast ripped a great slab of its upper lip free to flap in the blizzard. It knocked several teeth loose and severed its tongue. The Troll fell clumsily, first to its knees then onto its face Blood pouring from its mouth. Nothing remained of the soldiers or the General.

"This is crazy," I muttered, numb with shock.

"War always is," said Dennis. I knew by the look in his eyes that he had witnessed terrible things during his time as a soldier, and that was why he seldom spoke of it.

Sally and Dennis renewed their efforts and half dragged, half carried me away from the carnage.

Somewhere beneath the screams and shouts, beneath the roars, the sounds of panic and death, I heard a strange whirring, chopping sound.

Sally and Dennis looked up.

The Apache Helicopter flew low. It was heading in the Trolls' direction with 30mm cannon pounding shells into the creatures, gouging huge furrows out of their flesh, smashing bones, blinding eyes.

Five, maybe six Trolls fell under the onslaught before a Troll flung its arm and clipped the rotors. The helicopter spun out of control. It didn't stop firing. Shells ripped through humans as well as Trolls before the helicopter crashed into a snow drift in a scream of twisting metal.

Before we could fully react to the sudden death of the helicopter crew, the unmistakable roar of jet engines sounded overhead. The Typhoons and Tornados opened fire with their cannons. More Trolls fell. Blood, bone and hair flew, mixing with the increasing fury of the blizzard. In seconds, however, the cannon fire fell silent, and the jets peeled away.

"No more ammunition," explained Captain Price as he joined us. His arm was around the waist of a young soldier I did not recognise. The captain helped him struggle along on one good leg.

Together we headed towards the back of the camp. Sally and Dennis still carried me. I'd be embarrassed about being such a burden later. At that moment, I was grateful for the help.

The jets sounded as though they were diving back in for another run.

"If they've no ammo, what are they doing?" I shouted, now looking upwards and seeing the rapidly approaching planes.

Captain Price gritted his teeth, his jaw locking with the effort of suppressing the emotions he felt.

"Giving us a chance to get away."

Five jets roared towards the Trolls. A terrible under-standing came to me, draining all energy from my aching body. By the stillness and silence of those around me, I knew I was not alone.

The jets fanned out at the last moment and ploughed into the ground among the giant creatures. Great balls of flame rolled into the sky enveloping everyone and every-thing around them. Trolls fell. The flames from the avia-tion fuel were too strong for the snow to extinguish. Trolls burned. The smell of charred flesh and hair blown to us by the blizzard stuck in my throat and made me dry heave.

The selfless sacrifice of such an act stunned me. I had believed I was becoming a less selfish, more caring person, but I had a long way to go before I could truly understand the courage and desire to help others displayed by those pilots.

I couldn't be sure, but I think I saw a solitary tear slide down Captain Price's cheek.

CHAPTER 36

In the confusion we had managed to escape out the back of the camp and head once more into the ice and snow.

"How many Trolls do you think are still alive in there?" I asked Dennis as he and Sally took a brief rest from carrying me.

"I heard someone say they were down to single figures, or at least no more than twelve or fifteen. No one really knows, but one thing's for sure. They may have overrun the camp, but they paid a high price for it."

"So did we," said Sally softly. "There must have been about two thousand people in that camp and it looks like the people in this group are the only survivors. And what are we, a little over a hundred?"

"Others might have escaped," I said,

"Maybe," said Sally. "But any way you look at it over fifteen hundred people lost their lives in that battle."

The conversation could not continue after such a stark and undeniably accurate statement. Without another word, Sally and Dennis stood up and lifted me once more. We could not afford to stop for long.

Our ragged line of bloodied, beaten and shocked survivors pushed through the unceasing weather southwards.

"The General tried to contact the remains of the Government in London when we realised how hopeless our situation was becoming. He never got a reply," said Captain Price during one of our brief stops. Most people were sitting in the snow, their heads hanging with exhaustion, and paid little attention to him, but Sally, Dennis and

I listened, as did a small group of others, gathered in a circle about him.

"Could have been radio failure," said Dennis.

"Possibly," agreed Price. "Or atmospheric interference or any number of other natural phenomena. However, it could also be that the politicians and their advisors trapped underground are dead. To be honest, it doesn't really matter. All it proves is what we suspected for some time. We can't rely on our government for any help."

"So, if there's no help to be had in London," I said. "Where do we go?"

"The General talked about walking across the Channel to France," said Price. "I know the continent has it just as bad as us, or so we hear, but I'm not planning to stop. It's up to everyone here to decide what they want to do, but I'm heading for the equator. The ice might be closing in there, but it hasn't taken over yet."

"The thought of even a few months of snow-free weather is very tempting," I said. "It's a long way to go, though."

"Where there's water we'll get a boat," said Sally. "Where there's ice we'll walk."

"Sounds like a plan to me," agreed Dennis. "And we may as well stick together after all we've been through."

Captain Price smiled one of his rare, genuine smiles.

"Glad to hear it. I'll pass the word around and the others can make their own decision whether to come with us or go their own way."

With that, Captain Price moved off, pushing through the snow, showing no sign of the weariness the rest of us felt.

CHAPTER 37

Remember that talk Sally said we needed? Well, we still haven't had it yet. Things have been too busy, too hectic. But we're only a couple of days travel away from what used to be the Republic of Congo, and already the weather's getting warmer. We've even seen patches of bare rock, small islands of hope among the snow. Once we're settled on the equator and enjoying life without constant blizzards, we might just have the time to sit and talk. If it goes the way I hope, then I'm sure Chrissy would understand.

I'll never forget Chrissy, and she'll always be my wife, my first true love, but the time has come for me to start a new life. At least until the glaciers get closer and bring the snow, the ice, the daily blizzards.

I still lie awake some nights, marvelling at the clear sky, the moon and the stars, but I doubt I'll ever fully relax. You see, I'm waiting. Waiting until the night when I hear The Roar in the distance. Until then, I can at least pretend the nightmare has ended.

If I'm lucky, it may be true.

ABOUT THE AUTHOR

Neil Davies was born in 1959 and has found everything else to be an uphill struggle. He currently lives in the North West of England with his wife and two children. Any spare time he can find he spends writing. His previous publishing credits include the short story collection The Midnight Hour, the serial killer ebook Welcome Home and the supernatural horror ebook Raised In Evil. For more information please visit his official website, http://www.nwdavies. co.uk. You can also contact him through Facebook (http:// www.facebook.com/nwdavies) and twitter (http://www. twitter.com/nwdavies).

ACKNOWLEDGEMENTS

Thanks to Kate Jonez for her support and hard work editing this book.

My thanks to Eternal Press for accepting the original short story for publication. Without that there would be no novel.

3170374R00131

Printed in Great Britain
by Amazon.co.uk, Ltd.,
Marston Gate.